BLACK ROSES

BLACK ROSES

BY

FRANCIS BRETT YOUNG

2049

LONDON
WILLIAM HEINEMANN LTD

First published September 1929
New Impression October 1929

Printed in Great Britain
at The Windmill Press, Kingswood
Surrey

To
Edwin Cerio
who nows what really happened.

CONTENTS

❖

BOOK ONE
POGEROLA. *Page Three*

BOOK TWO
VITA NUOVA. *Page Sixty-one*

BOOK THREE
PURGATORIO. *Page One-thirty-seven*

BOOK FOUR
PARADISO. *Page One-ninety-seven*

Lento.
pp

For sorrow has black petal'd ro - - ses,

pp

Ped.   *

JOSEPHSON-SIBELIUS,
Op. 36, No. 1.

Book One

POGEROLA

POGEROLA

I

WHEN the cruising liner swayed to her moorings alongside the quay at Naples a moonless summer night had fallen. For ten days turbines had driven her throbbing hull, with the short respite of calls at Gibraltar and Algiers, out of the Atlantic swell into a paler, glassier sea ; and already her three hundred passengers, each certified first-class, compelled, like castaways on some uninhabited atoll, to accept the isolations and congregations of sea-life, had arranged themselves in a microcosmic society divided into strata that marked their social and financial differences, their tastes and their distastes.

Throughout the voyage Paul Ritchie had passed for a lonely, undistinguished figure. Grey-bearded, dapper, correct, carrying in his neat severity the air of a minor diplomat rather than that of an artist, he had steered his way silently, courteously, through the steamer's crowded decks and her Gargantuan bills-of-fare. The agents at Southampton had allotted to him a seat at the captain's table ; but this unenviable distinction was clearly the result of an accident, since none of the table's other occupants had ever heard of him, and feverish consultations of " Who's Who " in the smoke-room left his past and present still shrouded. He was, it appeared, a painter. So much his neighbour at table, the cousin, as he soon learned, of a Lancashire baronet, extracted from him. But since, as it also appeared, he had never exhibited at the Royal Academy, he couldn't amount to much. However, an artist—particularly an artist who doesn't dress like one and who has reached middle-age without starving, an artist, above all, who can travel first-class—is still, in the eyes of a tourist ship's company, a romantic figure. Perhaps though he didn't exhibit at the Royal Academy, he was a leisured amateur, which was even more respectable. For a time, indeed, Mr. Ritchie's reputation enjoyed the full benefit of mystery; until Jacob Levine, the famous dealer, who had been trailing the scent of a possible Goya for the American market in Estremadura, joined the ship at Gibraltar, and blew that bubble away with one puff of his full sardonic lips.

"Paul Ritchie?" he told the lady from Lancashire, "Paul Ritchie? Of course I've heard of him. On board the ship, is he?" Mr. Levine's heavy eyes brightened momentarily at the mere suggestion of paint. "Well, what do you want to know about him?"

"We were wondering about his position, his standing," said Ritchie's neighbour anxiously.

"As a commercial proposition he stands just nowhere. If you were thinking of buying anything . . ."

"Of course, in a matter of that kind, I'd take your advice."

Mr. Levine smiled grimly. Would she? People couldn't, as a rule, take his advice without paying for it. Still, this was a holiday, so, in a holida spirit, and in a matter where, as far as he could see, there wasn't any money, he found it difficult to resist the temptation of talking shop.

"This man, Ritchie," he said, "is a curious phenomenon—but very, very curious! He's known—if that's the right word—as an inexpensive portrait-painter: the kind of fellow, who can be relied upon to please the average alderman's wife— draw out the linked sweetness of a mayoral chain; make his worship wear his robes as if they meant no more to him than a dressing-gown, and reproduce, at a moderate figure, figures that are anything but moderate. You see what I mean? You'll find his portraits scattered all over England in municipal council-chambers. I remember one of a client of mine, Astill, the brewer, in the gallery at North Bromwich—negligible as a composition, but, really, quite strikingly ' like.' Of course there are dozens of fellows painting portraits at the moment who can do that. The queer thing about Ritchie's stuff is his technique. It isn't in the least like that of a modern painter. An under-painting of *tempera* with oil on top—like some of the early Venetians, the transitional Bellini for example—which wouldn't be remarkable, mind you, if it weren't applied to such subjects, hung in such places, and perpetrated by a man who, roughly speaking, must be just about a contemporary of Matisse. I suppose he's sixty, or thereabouts, isn't he?"

"It's difficult to judge. Mr. Ritchie looks so un-English. Until he speaks you'd almost think him a foreigner."

"Ah, there you've got it!" the dealer cried

triumphantly. Un-English. That's just what I'm
driving at. He doesn't paint like an Englishman,
or a Frenchman, for that matter. That's what's so
curious in a man who's devoted his life to painting
British beef and beer. He paints like a Latin, and a
Latin of four hundred years ago at that. And now
that I come to think of it," he went on, raptly
unconscious of the boredom in his companion's
intent and bewildered eyes, " now that I come to
think of it, I remember a show of his. Interiors
mostly. Great high, baroque interiors, with dark,
red hangings. Incredibly gloomy. Plague, pestilence,
and famine. Battle, murder and sudden death.
That's what they made you think of. Emblems of
mortality hidden in out of the way corners. Ha !
I've got it at last ! Ribera. Giuseppe Ribera. You
probably know him better under the name of
Spagnoletto ? "

She didn't ; but her denial was swamped under
the wave of Mr. Levine's surging triumph in his
own acumen.

" Spagnoletto. You'll see his *Pietà* in a few
days in the sacristy of San Martino at Naples.
Strange, gloomy, terrible stuff. But how in the
name of wonder, I ask you, does a middle-aged
twentieth century Britisher with a good Scotch
name to him ever come to imitating the work of
Giuseppe Ribera ? "

" So he is only an imitator ? " The word was
clutched like a life-line. " His work isn't really
interesting ? "

" As a problem in psychology, terrifically. As
art, no. That's my opinion, at any rate."

"*Your* opinion ? Oh, Mr. Levine ! As a matter of fact, " she confided, " you've only confirmed what I was thinking myself." And the Lancashire baronet's cousin retreated hastily from Mr. Levine's splutterings, partly because she had got what she wanted, partly because she wasn't sure that her informant was quite rich enough to be one of the Jews whom a lady can know, with the result that, from that day forward, Paul Ritchie found himself more than ever alone.

Not that he wished to be otherwise. Through all his life he had been solitary and self-sufficient, and this winter cruise to Egypt, imposed on him by a stern physician as the after-cure for an influenzal convalescence, had been shadowed all through by a dread of the gregarious. Mr. Ritchie was not, in the current phrase, a ' good mixer.' He did not play bridge. His regimen impartially forbade cocktails and deck-tennis. The sweepstake on the day's run left him, frankly, unmoved. *Farouche* was the word which the baronet's cousin (who had been educated in a convent) applied to him. Among this crowd of cheerful, sun-intoxicated Philistines, deprived, for the time, of the protective illusions of his art in which he habitually swathed himself, he shivered, almost physically, at the exposure of a naked, sensitive personality. He belonged, as his table companion had intuitively divined, to another race; he was an alien, bound, like some blundering Gulliver, by the threads of a myriad unimaginable conventions.

During the last few days of the ship's approach toward Naples, this social terror had been reinforced

B

by deeper spiritual qualms. Those leisurely turbines throbbed in his ears like the noise of a river
whose flood is broken upon the verge of thunderous
rapids. Each hour, each second as it passed drew
him nearer with the unrelenting force of that
tremendous machine, to the moment when his
eyes, so long and so deliberately blinded to reality,
must gaze into an abyss from which his shuddering
shaken spirit had recoiled more than forty years
ago ; the moment at which his mind, so carefully
schooled and lulled by reassuring suggestions,
must pass, once more, through the furnace of
emotions whose gigantic flame and shadows had
given to all his work—apart from that by which he
earned his living—that lurid, nightmare quality
which shrewd Jacob Levine had likened to that of
Spagnoletto. The Naples that his eyes would see
must be the Naples of forty years ago, and the soul
that would feel what those eyes saw, must be the
soul of a boy whom people called " Paolo " and
' Ricci," all young and passionate, not the soul of
the man Paul Ritchie, whose dark dreams Mr.
Levine had so patronisingly dismissed.

Yet, when the gangways went down at Naples that
night, and crowds of passengers, unsuitably dressed,
began to swarm ashore, calling to each other in
high-pitched bewildered voices, above the stuttering
exhausts of taxi-cabs that waited, like famished
saurians, to gorge them whole and transfer them as
ruinously and swiftly as possible to Cook's Funicular
which trailed like a broken necklace down the
volcano's cone, Paul Ritchie, in his dark cloak—the
only concession which this precise man of sixty

made to the obviously artistic—stood possessed by a chill, hallucinated calm.

Under the swinging arc-lamps the live mass of tourists pullulated, their whitened faces turned backward toward the ship's bejewelled carcase. Ritchie stood by the rail, watching them disappear into the mass of darkness that marked the customs-house ; he saw their cars swirl desperately down the sombre length of roadway that faced the dock where long trams went crawling and clanking past the unimaginable squalor of sailors' drinking-dens.

Long after they had gone, Ritchie still stood staring landward, like a man fixed in some strange catalepsy. On the maindeck only a few elderly ladies, too staid for nocturnal adventure, were left. They sat in their deck-chairs with rugs tucked round their modest feet, drinking in the romantic qualities of the Italian night without reserve. Among them vendors of tortoiseshell circled greedily, settling on their possible victims again and again with the persistence of teasing flies. One of them, scenting the obvious Englishman, waylaid Paul Ritchie in the accents of Italian New England : " Wanabuy a mandolin, all hand-made ? Say, mister, beautiful cameos, very chip."

He refused, with an instinctive tilt of the head, a flicker of the left hand, more expressive than words. The gesture was Neapolitan. The hawker fell behind him, and Ritchie passed moodily to the companion that led to the boat-deck. He climbed it. The deck was empty. For'ard, the block of the officers' quarters showed squares of curtained light beneath the white ghost of the bridge. Above, in a velvety darkness, the cylinders of the ship's raked funnels loomed enormously. Nothing but the spidery tracery of her still wireless aerials hung between him and the stars. Soft, southern starlight ; lonely, mysterious. Too lonely, too mysterious for me, Paul Ritchie thought. Mysterious, too, were the lights of Naples, a swarm of fireflies flickering among her invisible hills, a flight of fireflies, blown Eastward along the volcanic shore to Torre del Greco, Torre Annunziata, Pompeii, Castellamare : names lovely in themselves waking tempestuous memories.

Memories, alas, too tempestuous ! Memories of youth : he feared them. His soul was carried away with them, further than he dared to release it.

Resolutely he turned his back upon all this beauty. His eyes, brought westward, probed the unlighted mass of ancient houses that clustered around the port. Above these, a single cupola, sheathed in green glazed tiles, imprisoned some vagrant gleams, of starlight maybe, within its lustre.

" La Carmine," he heard himself murmur.

The church of the Madonna del Carmine, old and scabrous as ever ; his eyes had not rested on it for more than forty years. Beneath that cupola, somewhere in the darkness, he remembered, there lay a square : a great square littered with market refuse, scattered with stalls, booths, puppet-shows. Out of that square, between houses so old and steep and rotten that they seemed tottering towards each other for support, ran a narrow lane; the *Vicolo degli Angeli*. " Angel lane . . . Angels in Hell," he thought. Young Paolo Ricci would never have

thought like that ! Wait. . . . Half way down the
Vicolo on the left an arched aperture in the house-
walls, iron-gated, admitted one to a court-yard that
was like a well. So deep, so dark, so dank ! He
could smell it even now. And though he turned
away his body, walking along the deck, his thoughts
still ran on, escaped him, as though they were
determined to function of themselves. Within the
courtyard, on the right, a wide door opened on to
marble stairs. Long echoing marble. Marble was
cheap enough in those days. Wide, echoing
marble that narrowed as one ascended. *Sixty-two,
sixty-three, sixty-four*. . . . The sixty-fifth was a
landing, and opposite, stood a closed door. He
might knock at it and wait there for ever ; that door
would never open. Forty-five years. . . .

Paul Ritchie sat down heavily on a bench made
gritty by the smuts from the steamer's funnels. He
pressed his hands to his eyes. But still he could see
the locked door that would never, never open.
And the thoughts which knocked upon the door in
vain flew back into his mind, filling it, as with a
confusion of beating wings. He remembered. . . .

II

HE remembered the days of his childhood, fifty,
more than fifty years ago. Of late he had noticed
that his memory was more acutely vigorous on
long flights than on short ones. This vivid re-
capture of a past from which sheer time had
smoothed away asperities was, he supposed, one of

the few privileges of age : a sinister privilege,
maybe ; symptom of the crystallised brain that
cannot be expanded to embrace new content, so
turns back wearily to ransack dusty corners, where
long-forgotten rubble lies hidden. Yet, to-night
on the deserted boat-deck, his closed eyes saw with
a fey clarity which, however sinister its implications,
was startling and impressive. He saw himself, a
brown, mop-headed boy, in the village that had
bred him, Pogerola, ledged like a raven's nest in a
dip of the Sorrentine uplands. A sad, savage
place, the people of the shining sea-board thought
it. You might judge how wild it was by the oaken
bolts, thick as a man's thigh, that closed the house-
doors, the flayed skins of grey wolves nailed flat
inside them. Four times a week a muddy or
dusted carrier's-cart strained upward over stony
tracks or through torrents of grey snow-water to the
little *piazza* edged with mutilated plane-trees.
On one side the square lay open, commanding an
immensity of tumbled foothills, the haunt of cloud-
shadows that moved slowly like giant flocks at
pasture. On the three others stood the dilapidated
town-hall, from whose lintel the Bourbon arms had
never been obliterated, the inn, with its shiny
benches of chestnut warped by bitter sleet and sun,
and the pharmacy, kept by Andrea his mother's
brother, with whom the mad Englishman, John
Ritchie, Paul's father, lodged.

It is just possible that John Ritchie was not so
mad as the people of Pogerola, his Italian relatives
included, imagined him. Even if he were mad, he
was, in a manner, typical. To this day those

smiling lands remain the haunt of strayed, ex-
patriated Northerners, English, Americans, Ger-
mans, whom the lure of a kindly climate (or one that
is reputed to be kindly) the prospect of freedom
from civilised conventions and the cheapness of
living has drawn Southward. Some few are
artists, striving, in the solitude prescribed by
Goethe, to perfect their talent among surroundings
of a unique, intoxicating beauty. Upon these
sunny slopes they alight, like lonely, dishevelled
migrants, until a warmer wind blows from the
North, carrying with it some scent of approaching
prosperity, and they pack their shabby easels and
canvases and preen themselves and are gone—and
nobody remembers them, except perhaps some
girls to whom they have made love in a dusk
thrilled by the high song of cicalas. There are
others, again, of origin more mysterious : men of
all ages, with pasts of all degrees of shadiness and no
visible excuse for their existence or visible ties
uniting them to the world which they have volun-
tarily or involuntarily left. A sad company these ;
most lonely, suspicious even of each other ; fleeing
from any intimacy in which a chance word may
pierce their own dark secrets. Mysteriously restless, like shy pariahs, they drag their shabby vices
from village to village. None knows how they
live ; they possess nothing ; perhaps not even their
names are their own ; yet, even beneath the contempt with which the shrewd peasant eye regards
them lurks a consciousness that in the veins of
many flows good blood turned rotten ; and sometimes, from tongues freed in liquor, one may hear

words of an arrogance that is more sinister than silent humility. *Disperati*, the countryfolk call them. *All hope abandon.* . . . The word is a sad and a just one.

John Ritchie, Paul's father, however, belonged to neither of these categories. At the time when he arrived in Pogerola from Capri, in the eighteen-sixties, he was nothing more remarkable, to all appearances, than an ordinary English tourist. His luggage, which came up by pack-mule, was impressive in its bulk, and included, as evidence of some purpose in life, the paraphernalia of a painter and a twelve-bore shot-gun. A bluff, florid man, with a red moustache of which Garibaldi need not have been ashamed—and was not, indeed, since John Ritchie had actually carried a musket at Calatafimi—and a military figure somewhat modified by the habit of *maccheroni*, he had abandoned Capri in August because he felt the heat and the tourists. From the moment of his elevation to Pogerola it became clear, from the facts that his paint-box remained packed and that he paid his way scrupulously, that he was neither an artist nor desperate. That he was mad went without saying. All foreigners were mad, more or less. But John Ritchie, it appeared, was less mad than most foreigners and quite surprisingly intelligible, since, during his service with the Redshirts and his sojourn in Capri, he had picked up a dialect, compounded of Genoese and Neapolitan, that could be understood, with a little perseverance, by nearly everyone.

He was living in Southern Italy for no other

reason than the excellent one that he liked it. He
liked the country, the food ; he liked, very much,
the wine, which he carried in vast quantities but like
a gentleman. He was generous and companion-
able. He had a sense of humour which showed
itself when the red moustache flew upward in a
quick, engaging smile. He was passionately interested, moreover, in the only things that really
mattered in Pogerola, the processes of agriculture
and husbandry, corn and wine and oil, and was
ready to lend a hand at any of them when the
uncertain season demanded it. Beyond all these
things, this ungainly Mid-Victorian knight-errant
carried with him a quite undeniable dignity, not
only in the regularity of his life, which ran much
more reliably than most of the local clockwork, but
in his outward appearance and dress, which never
varied from January to December, consisting of
strong shooting-boots, leather leggings, cord riding-
breeches of a perpetual texture, a jacket of green
Neapolitan corduroy with pockets each of which
would hold three brace of woodcock, a black
straw-hat, of the kind affected by Protestant parsons,
and a high starched collar constricted at its base by a
white Ascot necktie whose folds were held in
position by a grinning fox's mask in gold.

In more polite surroundings this combination of
costume might possibly have been considered
fantastic. In Pogerola it was merely regarded as
awful, in the original sense of the word, and as the
native integument of a species of foreign animal, as
proper to its wearer and as reasonable as are stripes
to a zebra.

It was his ecclesiastical headgear that gave John Ritchie his *contronome*, *"Capinero,"* the nickname without which, in Southern Italy, no personality is complete, while the three and a half inches of white linen collar, on whose shining surface its wearer could not tolerate a single speck, were responsible for his marriage to the druggist's sister, Concetta—and, as a consequence, for the existence of Paul—since Concetta, apart from her other allurements, was the only girl in Pogerola who had acquired the urbane art of starching and glazing. There was another excellent reason why, if he were going to marry at all, John Ritchie's choice should have fallen on Concetta. As soon as he had decided that he liked Pogerola and meant to spend the rest of his life there, the mad Englishman had set about looking for permanent quarters in which to establish himself, and found them, by an obvious process of exclusion, in the upper storey of the house in which his laundress lived, the shop of her bachelor brother Andrea.

It was the most considerable house in the village, commanding, in a social as well as a strategic sense, the plane-shadowed *piazza* in which all the vital movements of Pogerola's public life were concentrated. From his balcony, above the druggist's signboard, John Ritchie could look up from his *Daily Telegraph*, which arrived twice weekly by the carrier's cart, and wave good evening to passing friends or crack the somewhat salacious jokes for which he was famous. In Andrea himself the stranger found good company. With the exception of a certain Conte Ruffo, a mean little absentee landlord, who sustained in Naples the decadent shadow of a name which had long ceased to be illustrious, Andrea was by far the most considerable man in Pogerola. His shop was far more than a place where medicines were dispensed. It was the village club ; the centre of its political activities and dissensions in which John Ritchie, as one who had known Garibaldi in the flesh, stood shoulder to shoulder with his host. To that vivid, grey, round-headed little firebrand Andrea, John Ritchie was welcome if only because he was English and Protestant, and therefore anti-clerical. For the 'sixties were high days in Italy, and England had been the nursery of Mazzini's ideals. Pogerola, as the fierce little druggist explained, was somewhat provincial ; you might talk for an hour before a single idea succeeded in penetrating these rustic skulls ; in John Ritchie he had found, for the first time in years, " intellectual companionship " ; and when, as a consequence of her physical propinquity and her skill in laundry, the Englishman suggested marrying his sister Concetta, Andrea was over-joyed—not because of the social distinction which the marriage conferred, but because he was certain of having someone to talk to for the rest of his life.

They married. Andrea, who was mayor, conducted the proceedings himself to the delightful scandal of his uncle, the old priest Don Ambrogio. Within a year a son was born to them. The child was registered—not christened—under the name of Paul, and John Ritchie settled down comfortably to the joys of a late domesticity in a two-roomed

suite which the insularity symbolised by his white
hunting-stock and fox-headed tiepin insisted on
converting into an imitation of the rooms that he
had occupied in the garden quad at New College,
Oxford, thirty years before. From the cases which
had accompanied him on mule-packs to Pogerola,
he lovingly extracted a collection of decorative
oddments, a symbolical epitome of his career, from
which, apparently, his wanderings had never
separated him. They included a number of moth-
eaten otter-masks and rudders ; a leather book of
salmon-flies : a collection of bone-handled riding-
crops ; a torn red shirt ; two mangy Persian rugs ;
an elaborate oak pipe-rack carved with the motto
Manners makyth man ; a copper kettle ; eleven
silver goblets ; two glazed cases of shabby British
moths and butterflies ; one oleograph of Garibaldi,
one representing Queen Victoria flanked by her
consort in the act of opening the Great Exhibition,
and one of the Battle of Inkerman ; an ivory
filigree fan, presumably Indian ; a photograph
(Daguerreotype) of a lady in a crinoline armed by a
gentleman in the uniform of a colonel, both of
whose faces showed the agonised fixation in-
separable from that process ; and, finally, two
crowded shelves of books.

This library, which became the most potent
of formative influences throughout Paul Ritchie's
childhood was, perhaps, the only remarkable part of
his father's possessions. It began with a slender but
solid basis of English classics : old volumes of
Swift, Bunyan, Fielding, Smollett, with a sprinkling
of poetry—Crabbe, Blair, Young's *Night Thoughts*,

and a wine-stained, much-fingered *Don Juan*.
From this point onward, chronologically and
ethically, Paul's father's reading suffered an appalling
descent. Of the great Victorians not one was
represented, their place being taken by an astounding collection of pornography, mostly French—not
books that are deemed pornographic in the modern
genteel acceptance of the word, but a series of the
filthiest productions that ever fouled a press. It
was these, it appeared, that, apart from *Don Juan*
and the *Daily Telegraph*, had constituted the bulk of
John Ritchie's reading. Perhaps, in their unspeakable pages, an enquiring mind might guess at
the origin of the mystery which underlay this
distorted, expatriate career, the spiritual tides that
drove Paul Ritchie's father from the society in
which he was born and bred, to cast him ultimately,
like a piece of rotten driftwood, upon this remote
Italian upland. Who knows what dark abysses of
the soul that bluff and—if fantastic—apparently
sane exterior may have concealed? Certainly, as
far as anyone ever knew (and peasant eyes and ears
are shrewdly censorious) John Ritchie's married
life in Pogerola was a model of faithfulness and
propriety. Perhaps this was only because his
appetite for unpleasant adventure had been sated,
because he had reached an age in which he himself
felt the need for " settling down "; but, whatever
may have been the reason for his retirement into
domesticity, he commanded, in Pogerola, a little
more than the respect that is due to a sacred lunatic.
He lived, it appears, a normal and healthy life, an
outdoor life of the kind which peasants understand.

He was a good, if somewhat tyrannical husband, a staunch friend, and an amusing father.

III

It was in this guise, at least, that Paul Ritchie remembered him, when he stood on the steamer's boat-deck that evening, with the scattered lights of Naples going blurred before his rapt eyes, in a series of swift apparitions which flickered across his memory with a sort of arbitrary, mad inconsequence. If he tried to remember, memory denied herself; yet as soon as he abandoned the effort she rewarded him with revelations blinding in detail though evanescent as mountain landscapes flashed through a window thinned out of moving cloud. . . .

One moment he saw himself (if it were really himself?) a small child tottering out to the edge of the balcony that overhung his uncle's signboard and the *piazza*. It was evening. The cracked bell in the clock-tower jangled an *Ave Maria*. The plane-trees stretched a flat tapestry of leaves beneath him from which the setting sun reflected a rosy lustre. Even in those days the impact of colour had ravished his senses! And there, with a monstrous blue-green shadow moving before, over the white dust, his father came stalking toward him across the *piazza*, his gun on his shoulder, his burnt moustached face smiling like the red sun's disc beneath the tilted aureole of his black straw-hat. The pockets of his green corduroy jacket were bulging with quails (John Ritchie, to the amuse

ment of the village, never shot song-birds) and, as
he approached, he held up a handful of feathered
bodies and waved them for Paul to see. From the
back of the room Paul's mother was screaming at
him in dialect: " Paoluccio. . . take care! You'll
fall over the balcony. Quick! Come here!"
And she dragged him away, the benevolent amazon,
by the seat of his trousers. He could hear his own
screams mingled with his father's ringing laugh as
the cloud-curtain closed. . . .

And now he was sitting on his father's knee, his
clutching fingers conscious of the ribs of green
corduroy; his cheek aware of red bristles; his
nostrils of the odour of black tobacco. He was
stroking the soft mottled olive of the shot quails'
plumage, peering curiously at the shining agate
eyes, the sharp, bloodstained beaks. " When
you're older, you little devil, I'll teach you to shoot
quail. Not thrushes . . . ha? If I catch you
shooting a thrush!" And he pinched Paul's ear in
the violent way he had of showing his affection;
but Paul didn't dare to squeal, because his father had
told him that Englishmen were never cowards, and
that if he did he'd give him something to squeal for.
Paul must never forget, as long as he lived, that he
was English and that his Grandfather had beat the
Frenchies at Waterloo. John Ritchie always spoke
to his son in English and expected him to answer in
the same language. If he didn't, he got his ear
pinched to some purpose. " Come, drop that
monkey-talk!" his father would say. . . .

Now Paul was standing beside the arm-chair in
which his father sat and smoked, spelling out, word

by word, as far as the snorted clouds of black
tobacco-reek would let him see them, the lines of a
poem which John Ritchie had chosen for a text book.
It was *The Grave*, by Robert Blair, and had been
selected not out of any passion for the *macabre* but
because it happened to be the first to hand.   *Forbid
it, Heaven !* he read :

> *Forbid it, Heaven !—let not upon disgust*
> *The shameless hand be foully crimsoned o'er*
> *With blood of its own lord.—Dreadful attempt !*
> *Just reeking from self-slaughter, in a rage,*
> *To rush into the presence of our Judge. . . .*

Of course at the time Paul had no more idea what it
was all about than now, when the isolated verses
rushed back into his memory so clearly.   He
understood them as little as he understood the
ponderous leaders which his father compelled him
to read aloud from the *Daily Telegraph*, whose wide
sheets, redolent with the alien relish of stale printer's
ink, it was his particular and exquisite privilege to
unfold.   Those leaders were a misty epic, in which
two archangels, one bright, one dark, by the names of
Disraeli and Gladstone, went clashing to and fro like
Satan and Gabriel over the body of a darker fiend
named Bulgarian Atrocities.   The very mention of
Bulgarian Atrocities was enough to send John
Ritchie flying into a rage ; this oddly-named
monster was a partner in iniquity with the fallen
angel Disraeli, and Paul feared him even more
dreadfully than the fiend Apollyon.   Indeed, through
all Paul's early memories of his father, this read

ing of the English newspaper was associated
with violent meteorological disturbances that made
the whole house shake and quiver like that March
thunder which, his mother told him, was sent to
waken the serpents.

The last and most catastrophic of these tempests,
Paul would never forget. It remained stamped on
his brain like those patterns of trees which lightning
etches into the skin of its victim. It was on an
evening in June, when the plane-tree tapestries
wilted in the dying blast of a *scirocco* that had
scorched the mountains for three days. John
Ritchie came in hot and fierily irritable from his
vineyard ; the wind had burned the sap out of the
buds of his vines. He cursed his wife for the
climate, as if she, poor woman, controlled it. Then,
turning fiercely on Paul, who was standing timidly
waiting for his reading-lesson, he snatched the
bundle of papers from his hands and ripped them
open angrily, as though, perversely, he hoped to
find in them some further fuel for his rage. "Thank
God ! " he shouted. " It's come at last ! To hell
with that dog Beaconsfield ! Servia's declared war
on Turkey ! "

Shedding loose sheets of newspaper behind him,
he left Paul and his mother standing, and went
plunging down the stairs to tell the news to Andrea.
Concetta, economical soul, picked up the discarded
newspaper sheets methodically and folded them,
she patted Paul's head with a smile. " Your
father is nervous this evening. It's the *scirocco*,"
she sighed. And Paul, still dumbfounded by the
suddenness of this violence, crept to the balcony and

C

peered over it, straining his ears to catch the raised
voices that wrangled so rapidly in the shop beneath.
He supposed —and quite rightly, as it happened—
that all this to-do must be connected with that
villainous devil Bulgarian Atrocities. What he
didn't realise—what, indeed nobody realised—was
that a train had been lit in John Ritchie's explosive
brain which, within twenty four hours, was to blow
them all sky-high.

That evening, endlessly, as it seemed, the hot
debate continued in the druggist's shop. He
heard his father's voice, raised passionately, over-
bearing the quieter, more rapid tones of his uncle
Andrea. At one time it seemed as if the two old
friends were quarrelling. His mother went down
and joined them. He heard her protests added to
Andrea's ; and then, with a cold stab at the heart,
knew that she was crying. A sense of something
enormous, disastrous, rose up like a poisonous gas
and filled the room's dim silence with dread.
Bats came out, flickering through the tepid air that
bathed the plane-trees. Not daring to go downstairs, Paul stayed there, bewildered and nearly
sick with hunger. It seemed that everyone but
himself had forgotten all about supper.

For the next twenty-four hours, indeed, they
forgot about everything—Paul's existence included
—in the stir and confusion of John Ritchie's
departure to the wars. Neither Andrea's persuasions nor his wife's grief could move him from
his determination ; and when they saw that these
had failed, they both resigned themselves, with
Latin realism, to the fact that their strange relative

was mad in any case and that they might just as well save their breath and their tears as waste them on him.

It is difficult to say just what was the origin of this desperate decision in John Ritchie's mind. To dismiss it, as Concetta and Andrea did, as sheer mad Englishness, is merely to shirk explanation. He was, as Paul realised later, a man of passionate political prejudices, with whom any stick was good enough to beat a dog like Disraeli. He must have been, again, a creature of adventurous disposition with a taste for fighting, as was shown by his plunging, in middle-age, into the Garibaldine adventure. There remains, however, a third, and, perhaps, a more natural explanation : that this Servian campaign may have come to him as a God-sent means of escape from the domesticity in which, almost inadvertently, he had immersed himself. The isolation of Pogerola, where, from one year to another, he never encountered a man of his own race or culture ; the eternal monotony of Italian peasant-life, so romantically idyllic in theory, in practice so flat and stultifying ; the fact that, in eight years, he must surely have outworn the physical attraction which had united him to Paul's mother, combined with God knows what dark promptings obscurely hinted at by those scabrous bookshelves. . . . Was there more than a mad knight-errantry, Paul asked himself, in this sudden adventure ? A question that could not be answered. All Paul remembered—and this memory, perhaps, was more vivid than all the rest—was the morning that followed the storm's breaking, when his father

departed. The moment of farewell itself had
vanished utterly. All he remembered—and he saw
it, like so much else, from his vantage-point on the
balcony above his uncle's shop-sign—was the
sturdy figure of John Ritchie, dwarfed by his
gigantic bundle, setting out with strong strides
across the white spread of *piazza* made incandescent
by the noonday sun—a prepotent, vigorous figure,
which lessened and lost power as it retired, till, on
the last verge of vision, it turned and waved, for one
moment, a black straw hat. Paul, watching,
waved back excitedly from his balcony. Andrea, at
his shop-door beneath, was doing the same. No
other human being in Pogerola bade John Ritchie
farewell. In the dim depths of the room, where,
when his father had vanished, Paul turned his sun-
blind eyes, Concetta, his mother, lay moaning
desolately, with a linen apron clenched in her teeth
after the fashion with which the women of Pogerola
strive to check their cries in travail. That, too, was
a picture that Paul would always remember. . . .

IV

HE remembered also, but with an inferior distinct-
ness, the day—heaven knew how many months
later—when his uncle Andrea told him that his
father would never return. A martyr, Andrea
called him ; a martyr, whatever that might mean,
in the cause of Liberty, like those heroes who had
given their lives in the storming of the Janiculum.
In the mind of Paul, this tragic news excited nothing but a slightly awed interest. At his age new

impressions assail the brain with such tempestuous swiftness that old ones are quickly overlaid, and though, when he was reading his father's books, he still would think in English, John Ritchie had practically ceased to exist, so far as he was concerned, at the moment when his dwindling figure passed out of sight. The main change that his father's departure had imposed on his life had been the shifting of its focal centre from the upper room, in which the family had mainly lived, to the kitchen, downstairs, that was his mother's normal habitat, and the informal club-room which was his uncle's shop.

Paul Ritchie could see it now : a long constricted chamber with folding doors that, except in winter, were always open ; the narrow counter, the brass balances scoured with charcoal ashes to the smoothness of a worn coin : the drawers of medicaments with gilt inscriptions toned by successive coats of dirt and varnish to the hues of ancient pictures ; the phials of old glass enclosing syrups and tinctures of a ravishing brilliance ; the long bench, crowded with village politicians in hunting suits of green corduroy and thonged goat-skin shoes, and before them, always black-coated and professional, that vivid, grey, round-headed man, his uncle, endlessly expounding his violent political loves and hatreds. Paul used to sit there of an evening, his brown mop hidden behind the counter, listening to a hubbub of talk in which the great names of Mazzini and Cavour and Garibaldi and Victor Emanuel rose magnificently, accompanied sometimes by that of his own father : "My martyred brother-in-law," Andrea used to call him.

Paul sat and listened; and behind him, in the shadow of the unlighted room in which the family ate their beans and *maccheroni*, sat his mother— Concetta, as all the village knew her. She was a peasant of the mountains, and never pretended to be anything else. She did not try to understand her brother's politics any more than she had pretended to understand John Ritchie's. All day she sat and span and cooked and slaved for Paul and Andrea. It was she who polished the brass scales to their fine lustre, who swept and scrubbed the red-tiled floor clean of spittle and cigar-ends. By sunset her fourteen-hour day was ended. She sat there somnolent, like a Moslem woman behind her purdah, night after night, her wide skirts distended over the smouldering charcoal brazier—fine *carbonelli* of charred brushwood from the baker's ovens —that warmed her body and soul from below upward. She never spoke; yet Paul always knew that she was sitting there behind him; a large spare woman, with marvellous dark eyes and a beauty of skin that had withered prematurely, as such precocious growths will wither, into a brown flaccidity. Paul, eagerly listening, hoped she was asleep. But Concetta never slept out of her time; and when the cracked bell of the parish church tolled eight, so hesitatingly that each stroke seemed likely to be the last, she would murmur the two words " Paolo " and " bed," and he would steal obediently away into the darkness, leaving the *pezzi grossi*, the big bugs, to their talk.

A proud, a violent, a stubborn race, these Pogerolans. Even now it was remembered among

them that in those mountains the power of the
Lombards had been broken. From his hiding
place beneath the counter Paul heard wild stories of
death and violence, vendetta and brigandage.
These hunters, with their long-barrelled flint-locks,
would shoot at sight if their possessions were in
question. Theirs was an old world, cynical, and
incredulous of the new united Italy for which Paul's
father had fought. When they spoke of money
they still calculated their sums in Bourbon *scudi* and
carlini. And they spoke much of money. Paul's
uncle, that grizzled, vivid man, with his bristling
moustache and quick, fierce gestures, thought,
dreamed of it constantly. Even behind his political
ardours the idea of money smouldered. And, with
the thought of money, that of little Paul, his heir,
had gradually become synonymous.

It was for him, though Paul did not know it, that
his uncle hoarded gold and silver coins in a box
beneath the loose tile under his bed. Sometimes,
behind the curtain that was slung between them,
Paul would hear him clinking them over in the
middle of the night. It was for him that the druggist
drove his flinty bargains, accumulating land, strip
by strip, upon the sun-baked terraces ; adding here
a patch of vines, a group of twisted olives there, to
the little property which John Ritchie had acquired
for his diversion. Money and power. For himself he could not use them. He had found for
himself a position of assured bourgeois respectability
that carried authority ; yet, even if he were a lord
among peasants, he was still a peasant at heart, his
dreams deep-rooted in the fierce, thirsty soil.

Slowly, with infinite care and sacrifice, he had reached his present station. He clung there, grimly consolidating his forces. The next step would be Paul's.

The next step, naturally, was that Paul should become a doctor. Not that Andrea had any more respect for medicine than for incantations. He was a better doctor himself than many who could write degrees and titles on a plate, and knew it. A poor doctor, in his opinion, was in a worse case than many a rich druggist. But Paul would not be poor, and Paul, instructed in his own hard shrewdness, would have an advantage over half the students in the University of Naples. When Paul had taken his degree he would be able to wait, to choose his type of practice without a thought of *maccheroni ;* to establish himself in the independence of a city practitioner of the highest class, returning yearly to Pogerola in an aura of celebrity to collect his rents ; to found a family ; to show the miserable Conte Ruffo what the Riccis were made of. In his youth, wandering among the surrounding villages, Andrea had collected the fragments of a family tree. He never showed these documents to anyone, least of all to Concetta ; but this he knew—Ricci or Ritchie, what difference did it make ? The ancient blood was there—that in the sixteenth century the Riccis had been nobles. Slowly the wheel of destiny approached full circle, and Paul perhaps, or, if not Paul, Paul's children. . . Who knew ?

In his tenth year, when the other boys with whom he had played on the piazza were already doing man's labours with their mattocks in the fields or cutting chestnut pales for vines upon the upper slopes, Paul's uncle handed him over to the educational care of his elder brother, Don Ambrogio the priest. His action threw his boon companions of the pharmacy into a ferment, for most of them, encouraged by him, were fiercely anti-clerical. Andrea was playing with the accursed thing.

"Remember," they said, " the priests will teach him their roguery ; a young tree is easily bent."

Andrea waved them aside. " A young tree easily recovers its shape ; and if he learns their roguery now, so much the better will he be able to deal with it later on. No knowledge of any kind is as dangerous as ignorance, and all he need learn, so far as I'm concerned, is Latin."

Paul's mother said nothing, but, secretly, she was glad ; for though she knew that Andrea was anti-clerical, and accepted it, as she had accepted the same idiosyncrasy in John Ritchie, she always had a longing to walk in religious processions, as she had done when she was a girl, and feared the saints because of their incalculable power for mischief. Believing no more than her brother in the church's doctrines which, by this time, she had mostly forgotten, she never could feel quite sure that there mightn't be something in them. So, secretly, she would advise Paul to take an occasional sprinkle of holy water, just as she advised her neighbours, when Andrea wasn't looking, to swallow a pinch of the flowers of sulphur with which vine-leaves are dusted. She liked to think that, in the case of emergency, Paul was on speaking terms with both worlds.

Don Ambrogio, the uncle to whom Andrea
confided Paul's education, was a frail, doddering
creature of more than eighty years. For long
enough he had been too feeble to take an active part
in parochial work ; but partly out of pity for his
age and weakness, and partly because he never
asked awkward questions, and was too deaf in any
case to hear their replies, the village girls were not
afraid to confess to him, and their parents kept him
alive with small payments for masses and the
benediction of their houses at Easter. Also he
held the reputation, unique in Pogerola, of having
once been learned. This was one reason why
Andrea, in spite of the family feud, had chosen him ;
a second was the fact that Don Ambrogio suffered,
in winter, from chronic bronchitis, and that the fees
for Paul's instruction could be taken out in bottles
of cough-linctus.

These bottles Paul carried to his schooling in the
high, cobwebbed room behind the church which
Don Ambrogio inhabited. The old man would
seize them eagerly, for they were sweet; he couldn't,
in the ordinary way, afford to buy himself sugar,
and the bees which he once had kept had all died of
neglect. The linctus was cheaply made and Andrea
often laughed over his bargain ; but it is doubtful,
even so, if Paul got his money's worth ; for, having
taken a swig of the linctus, Don Ambrogio would
often nod asleep in the sun diffused by his cobwebbed window. Sometimes, too, in the middle
of a Latin lesson, he would lose the thread of what
he was saying. Then, to cover his confusion, he
would shake his skinny fist, mottled with yellow :

" But these accursed Protestants ! " he would cry,
and proceed to tell Paul of the enormities that
Nelson's English sailors had committed in Naples
before Murat came.   " Your father was an Englishman and a Protestant, poor damned soul !   And
Gioacchino Murat was an atheist, which is nearly as
bad as a protestant," he explained.   " The French
are always atheists, my son."

For all that Don Ambrogio earned his linctus
with a certain amount of Latin, and many hours of
Dante, with whose works he was more familiar
than with any Latin but that of the Breviary.
Paul's brains were quick ; sometimes, indeed, he
went too fast for his teacher, and when Don Ambrogio, tired of Virgil in Purgatory (as he called it),
fell asleep in his chair, Paul would draw him as he
sat, with the sticks of charcoal which, by this time,
he had begun to smuggle from his mother's kitchen.
The fine pallor of the old man's features, fixed in
repose as in death, his white hair trailing over the
black collar of his soutane, gave to a carbon drawing
the opportunity of completeness.   He drew that
sallow wasted face again and again, until he felt as
satisfied with his presentation as an artist can ever
feel ; he carried his sketches home in secret and
gazed on them with love.   But he did not dare to
tell anyone about them : not even his mother.

Now, in his twelfth year, the itch for drawing
would never leave him.   He suppressed and culti-
vated it like a secret vice.   Its practice was, of
necessity, furtive and dangerous ; for its materials
were scarce and must always be stolen.   Charcoal,
indeed, was plentiful enough in Pogerola.   Down

from the woods above the village came pack-mules
laden with it; but paper, even printed paper, was a
rarity now that the *Daily Telegraph* no longer
arrived, so that all Paul's life developed into a
restless search for blank, plane surfaces.

He drew on the chaste end-pages of his father's
scabrous books. He drew over the faded text of an
old Pharmacopoeia, which his uncle Andrea, who
knew it by heart, had ceased to consult for many
years; he drew on walls, on distant walls for
preference; he drew in the dust that lay on Don
Ambrogio's window-sill, in the smooth beds of
finely sifted soil that the peasants spread to receive
the olives shaken down in Autumn; he drew in the
early morning, before his uncle had stirred; he
drew in the dark, when only his muscles told him
what he was drawing. In every conscious moment
he was obsessed by the forms of things seen or
remembered; by lines of mountain, contorted
olive trunks, mysterious masses of stone and mortar
whose shapes tortured his brain until he had tried to
express them. All colour, too, inflamed him, as
well it might in an air of such dazzling, dry clarity
as that of Pogerola; but in the presentation of
colours his hands were impotent. There was a
moment of fierce hope succeeded by tragedy, when
he discovered the desiccated tubes of his father's
paint-box. Even so his greedy mind absorbed
and classified and remembered colour in its finest
variations.

This passion so engrossed him that, in the end,
his abstraction made him pass in the village for a
fool, the inheritor of the mad Englishman's eccen-

tricity.   The people shook their heads over him ;
but the subject was so delicate, and his uncle's
hopes so high, that none of the cronies in the
pharmacy dared to mention it.   Triumphantly,
and naturally, they put it down to heredity, Latin,
and the softening effect of Don Ambrogio's influence.

Andrea was in no hurry.   He didn't believe in
wasting money on forcing the acquisition of costly
knowledge that an unformed brain might easily
forget.   As Paul passed out of childhood into his
teens he still kept him at home in Pogerola, eagerly
watchful for any visitor from the outer world who
might be of educational value.   In his heart he was
satisfied that Paul would be sharp enough to hold
his own when serious work began ; in the meantime
he took the boy into his shop and made him gener-
ally familiar with the mechanical processes of the
chemist's art, the making of tinctures and infusions,
the smoothing of emulsions, the rolling of pills.

All this was a valuable part of the doctor's craft
which the schools, in their lordly way, neglected.
Often, as he had reason to boast, a visiting doctor
would have to come down from his high horse to
ask the chemist's advice.   Medicaments, after all,
were the most important part of medicine.   Andrea
believed in them implicitly.   When he stood with
his fine scales before him, measuring a gramme of
this, a cubic centimetre of that, his mind would glow
with a cunning satisfaction, following the potent
medicaments, in fancy, through his patient's blood
toward the obedient organs that each affected,
naively triumphant in the little stratagems that he
deployed.   " Ah, now I've got you ! " he'd cry to

some problematic liver as he measured his calomel.

Sometimes he tried to infect Paul with these militant enthusiasms; but Paul followed his arguments and instructions in a dream. The plastic masses of material from which his uncle's pills were made cried out to him for the imprint of significant form; the syrups and tinctures that he compounded suggested reactions not of physiology but of colour. How snow-like, magnesia flushed with cardamoms! How slumberous, how velvety were the brown glooms of laudanum! And those gay sulphate crystals of copper and iron: the blue of serene seas flashing down the gulf of Salerno, green of the young corn, vivid under wintry olives. . . .

V

On summer evenings, when, in the hush between the songs of *cicala* and *grillo*, the countryside released an odorous and tepid air, Paul would leave the pharmacy, where the cronies were already assembled, and set out eastward along the softened line of hills. This was the season of lovers, for the light faded late. The girls would walk together, arm in arm, murmuring in provocative, lowered tones broken by soft bursts of laughter. The boys would strut behind them, swaggering with loud, bold talk that was meant to be heard. Their voices echoed gaily as the dusk received them. And Paul was troubled by these sounds; for now he was over sixteen, and they suggested to him the

promise of a warm, indefinite content of soul that
was comparable to the feeling of tepid evening air
upon his cheeks. These sounds made his skin
flush and tingle, his heart beat faster; it was the
physical counterpart of the emotion with which
sudden revelations of beauty in form and colour
affected him.

But though he longed to draw nearer to the
source of these strange ecstasies, the careful seclusion
that Andrea's plans imposed on him made the first
steps impossible. He was different from the other
boys of his age who knew already the gay com-
panionships of the fields. He couldn't laugh and
joke and swagger as they did. All the emotions
that he knew were so closed and secret, that he had
never dared to release them in words. It was
easier for him to draw than to speak, and when he
came near to them the girls seemed aware of his
strangeness; they looked at him with shy side-
glances, as though they were frightened by the
preoccupation of his serious eyes; they would
whisper, and laugh, quicken their steps, and steal
away from him. Their difference took the softness
out of his longing and turned it into a feeling of
frustration, almost of hatred.

One evening as Paul climbed the mountain to
plunder a pocket of plastic modelling-clay that he
had discovered, he saw across the rose of sunset the
figure of a girl approaching. She came down the
stony path toward him, an enormous bundle of
brushwood balanced on her head; the track was so
uneven that every muscle in her body adjusted
itself to her steps, so that it seemed more curiously

alive beneath her summer clothes than any he had
ever seen. So slowly she came, with such an
exquisite balance, with so live and lovely a motion,
that Paul held his breath.

He knew her well by name : a girl of his own
age, Annina, the daughter of one of the cronies of
the pharmacy ; but this was not the Annina that
he knew. She was a rose, a flame ; her body a
vessel of transcendent workmanship enchalicing not
human blood but light. He could have cried aloud
for joy of the colour that was in her, of the form that
enclosed it. And her blue-green shadow thrown
on cold, lilac limestone was as lovely as her substance.

As soon as she recognised him she stopped and
smiled and called him by his name. She looked
around her, to see if anyone was near ; then eased
her burden and sat down invitingly at the path-side
with a sigh. Paul came and sat beside her. Rich
light enveloped them, Her neck was bare and
smooth as rose-tinted alabaster ; perfect as cold
alabaster, yet, when she breathed, warm and alive.
She seemed content to sit with him there, without
shyness ; her brown eyes were not afraid of him ;
she was so placid in the richness of light and life
that was in her, so gentle that Paul longed, and was
afraid, to touch her.

" Well, Paolino ? " she said at last.

Suddenly he grew bold. "Annina, I never
knew that you were so beautiful."

She laughed softly ; her eyes smiled at him
they were not brown, he saw, but golden ; and in
his thankfulness that she wasn't offended, confusion
seized him, so that he could say no more.

" Well, is that *all?* " she said.

All? It was nothing! He struggled with words that became formless and shrivelled away in the light of her puzzled eyes. At last the truth burst from him. " In this moment you don't seem to me like a girl at all."

She surveyed him with bewildered disapproval as he plunged deeper.

" You're so beautiful that I daren't even touch you. Annina, you're so lovely that I wish you could stay for ever like that." She smiled and was softened : " Not a girl," he said, " but an angel out of heaven. Some day . . ." He paused, but now she was eager to hear the rest.

" Some day . . . what, Paolino ? " she mocked him.

" I shall remember this moment all my life," he told her. " Some day I'd like to paint you ! "

" To paint me ? " She laughed out loud. Her teeth were dazzling in their perfection, her mouth as clean and healthy as a wild animal's ; there was an animal cruelty in her laughter. She picked up her bundle slowly, the curve of her body was like that of a poplar bent by wind, and straight as a sapling poplar she recovered. The line of it ravished Paul struggling to help her ; but now she wouldn't be helped. She spoke with her back to him, still veiling her annoyance with laughter.

" To paint me ! What do you take me for, Paolino ? I should think that's the first time a girl of Pogerola has had a thing like that said to her, upon my word I should ! "

" Annina, you don't understand," he was

D

calling helplessly. "Annina, I love you, I adore you!"

"Well, that's a funny way of saying it," she mocked him, talking straight in front of her and hurrying away. He had offended her. His clumsiness offered no remedy; for though she checked her pace to listen to him she would only answer with scornful proverbs.

"Why do you follow me like a goat?" she said angrily at last. "Do you want the whole village to see us? The mountain's one thing, but the village is another. Do you want me to lose my good name, running after me like this?"

Wretchedly he fell behind. Annina walked on into the last of the sunset. The light failed: the face of the mountain faded to an eerie greyness of lavender, and with it the magic faded from Annina's retreating figure. She became once more an ordinary girl of the village, swaying home at dusk with a bundle of brushwood on her head; one of those sly, alien creatures who watched him and mocked him out of the corners of their eyes. With a sense of failure and resentment, Paul trudged sullenly homeward. That was the end of love-making for him!

But it wasn't the end, by a long way, of Annina's story of his clumsy advances. That was too good to be wasted, since it reflected not only her own high sense of propriety but Paul's traditional queerness. For long enough the young people of the village had found a subject for joking in his mixed descent, his uncle's ambitions and Paul's lessons with Don Ambrogio, and since these themes were now wel worn, the knowledge of a new and more comical eccentricity was welcome.

Next Sunday night on the long lover's road, Annina provocatively swung past him, her arms linked with those of two girl companions ; and all Paul's heart came into his throat when he saw her, for, though he had decided to hate her, nothing could force him to forget that moment of transfiguration which, in the dusk, the swing of her walk recalled. As soon as she had passed him he heard whispers and laughter. He guessed what she was saying, and knew for certain that he had guessed rightly when, later, one of the girls who had been walking with her threw him a question over her shoulder : " Paolino, would you like to paint me ? "

Out of Annina's malicious indiscretion the joke spread further. Soon the boys caught it too. They called him " O *pittore*," the painter, and the word stuck like paint, for those people lived by nick-names, and the length of a man's nose might ticket his grand-children for life. It was the name above all others that Paul would have wished to deserve ; yet here in Pogerola it became an insult on every tongue that spoke it.

The story came at last to his uncle Andrea's ears. One of his cronies, a relative of Annina, told it with fat wheezings of laughter. The whole roomful laughed with him, for it wasn't often that they had the chance to do so at the druggist's expense.

" We thought it was doctoring you were after for him," they said ; " it seems the boy's taking a short cut behind your back. He's a public danger, Andrea, showing such an early interest in the

female figure. Like to paint them, would he?
Ha, ha, we know those pictures! Anyone who
wants to, can see that sort in Naples for himself."

The druggist went cold with fury. Differences
of opinion he could stand, but never ridicule, and
Paul, so it seemed, had made a fool of him. Annina's
cousin, finding that he had caught his old friend on
the raw, rubbed in the coarse salt of his wit throughout the evening.

As soon as the club had dispersed, Andrea went
in search of Paul. He hauled the boy from his
mattress by one arm and thrashed him with his fists
and with a dried cow's tail that he kept for the
purpose. Paul was taller than his uncle and wiry
for his years; but Andrea was like a small grey
fury; the anger that had smouldered under the
taunts of his cronies leapt up and consumed him.
If Paul's mother, stumbling out of bed, had not
flown to his rescue and flung her arms round her
brother from behind, there might have been murder;
for Andrea's violence, once released, gathered
strength like a spinning tornado and whirled his
senses away with it.

When he had finished, his own fury had battered
himself as much as the unfortunate Paul. He
flung the boy away from him. Behind the curtain
that separated them, Paul heard him panting and
cursing as he stripped to the shirt in which he slept.
Suddenly the oil-wick went out and there was
silence, for Paul's mother, in the next room, dared
not speak a word. Once before, in a political
quarrel, she had saved Andrea from his own
violence, and shame had made him hate her for it.

Hour after hour Paul heard his uncle tossing on his bed behind the curtain like a restless animal. In every matter of ordinary life Andrea despised his sister's opinion, and let her know it; yet always, in distress, he consulted her, if only for the fierce pleasure of violently disputing the opinions for which he had asked when they didn't fall in with his own. So, in the middle of the night, Paul heard him speaking; the partition was so thin that he knew she could hear him.

"Concetta, are you awake?"

"How could I sleep?" she answered.

"Did you hear what Antonio was saying about your son?"

"He's a child, Andrea."

"A child!" he snorted. "Have you no brains to understand? Of course not! Whatever the boy had done you'd stand up for him. Obstinate as an animal! Do you hear me?" Like an obstinate animal Concetta herself kept silence. "Is it nothing to you that he's made a fool of me, your brother?"

"Nobody can make a fool of you, Andrea, except yourself," she answered slowly. "Don't speak to me of animals. You yourself have behaved like one to-night."

"Cretin!" Andrea was muttering. "Here is this boy, whose future I've planned, whom I've treated as a son that I wish to be proud of, not only behaving like an idiot for all Pogerola to laugh at, but giving out behind my back—behind my back! that . . . in effect, that I'm a fool for my pains. Says that he'll be a painter."

"He must be what God makes him, Andrea."

"God? What the devil has God to do with it? What's God to you or me or him? What was God to his father—God bless him? Ah, yes—I might have known it; the priests have a finger in this! That brother of ours, Ambrogio! I'll go and see him to-morrow. If the old fox wasn't already as good as a corpse I'd make him one. This is a *dispetto*; they've put all this nonsense into his head to spite me; but I'll soon thrash it out of him. No fear of that; if your blessed God makes him a painter, he'll have made him a beggar as well. Remember that, Concetta, and tell him so from me."

"Now you are talking nonsense," she answered calmly. "There is no reason why Paolo should be a beggar. We are not poor people. We're not even dependent on you. There is the land to live on."

"The land!" Andrea laughed bitterly, "I see that nothing can change you. As long as you live, Concetta, you'll have no idea in your head beyond beans and lentils and olives. If you had your will you'd make a peasant of him."

"Like your father and my father before him. What's wrong with that? They were good honest men, both of them, and happier than you, Andrea. Much happier, too, than Paul's father. God gave them a long life and a full stomach and a decent burial. Nobody in this world has a right to ask for more, and I don't ask any more for Paolino. *They* never wore their brains out, scheming all night like you. What will be, will be; and there's an end of it; and if Paolino wants to be a painter, why, what's the difference of that from any other trade?"

"I'll tell you, I'll tell you," Andrea cried excitedly. "If ever you'd been to Naples, as I have, you'd know. Beggars and painters, there's little to choose between them! How do they sell their pictures? Just like beggars, Concetta. Standing up in rags at the street corners waiting to catch sailors and fools of foreigners. Daubs of Vesuvius with red fire spurting out of it; pictures of brazen, naked trollops that you'd be ashamed to set eyes on! What kind of a life do they lead with loose women and street-walkers? That's what a mother ought to ask herself before she talks about God making her son a painter. Riff-raff of the gutter such as you've never heard of!"

"Paolino's a good boy; I'd trust him," she answered fondly, but Paul knew from her voice that she was troubled, none the less.

"Then you're a bigger fool than I took you for," Andrea snorted. "Devil take the ignorance of women, they've no more sense than pack-mules."

"Turn over, my little one, and try to go to sleep. The *parroco's* cock is crowing," Concetta answered gently. In her heart she regarded Andrea as another child.

And he obeyed. Paul heard the creaking and commotion as the fiery little man lurched over; his own heart was warm with gratitude for his mother's gentleness and understanding. There was a steadfastness in her simplicity that calmed his spirit and took the pain out of his battered limbs. She trusted him. Oh love! Oh gratitude! Why

had he always been so timid with her? Why
hadn't he dared to tell her before of all those
shameful passionate aspirations? She would have
understood. He glowed to feel, for the first time
in his life, that he was not quite alone.

But still Andrea would not sleep. His ceaseless
tossing kept Paul awake until the hour before dawn
with its impatient clanging from the church's bell-
tower. Then suddenly his uncle started up in bed.

"I've said that he shall be a doctor," he cried,
"and I'll see myself dead and damned before he
takes to painting. Do you hear me, Concetta?
Do you hear?"

But by the silence that followed Paul knew that
the tired woman was asleep.

VI

THERE might almost have been something im-
pious and prophetic in that final challenge. One
evening, a week later, when Concetta returned as
usual from their vineyard, powdered, as a pale bee
smothered in pollen, with the sulphur that peasants
use for dusting their vines, and called to her brother
from the open doorway, Andrea did not answer her.
She called again; but instinct told her that this was
no ordinary silence. Terrified, she hurried in
behind the counter, and stumbled, in the dark, over
a figure huddled like a sack upon the floor. It was
Andrea. He lay where he had pitched over from
his chair, face downward like a child asleep; his
legs bunched up, one arm outstretched with fingers

clenched, as though he were shaking his fist at
heaven's face. She called him and caressed his
features. His forehead was cold under the stubborn grey hair. The fist was clenched so tightly
that she could not force the fingers open.

She ran to the door of the shop and cried out for
help. The little square had not yet awakened from
its afternoon drowsiness. Only under the languid
plane-trees a couple of dogs lay yawning with paws
stretched out in front of them. Then the bent
figure of Don Ambrogio came doddering round the
corner. She called him by name : "Ambrogio,
come quickly ! " but the old priest was so deaf that
he only wavered for an instant as though something
incomprehensible had momentarily troubled the
calm of his senses, then passed on his way. Concetta ran out and caught him by the arm so violently
that the poor old thing was almost overbalanced.

"It's Andrea," she said. "I think something
terrible has happened."

"Eh ? " said Don Ambrogio, "Paolino ? No,
sister, I haven't seen him."

She dragged the old man into the shop and
behind the counter. He bent and touched Andrea.
He rose and crossed himself. "Peace to his soul,"
he murmured. "Certainly it is finished. Courage,
my sister, courage ! "

In a few minutes the darkness of the little shop
was full of indistinct figures and whisperings. The
parroco and another priest were there ; Annina's
uncle ; enemies and friends commingled and re-
conciled in the stir of this excitement.

Concetta crouched beside her brother, wailing

and tearing her hair, and other women left their
evening cooking to share in this luxury of lamen-
tation. One old vulture, who made her trade of
death, was shrieking for men to carry Andrea
upstairs and lay him on the bed so that she could
attend to him. She put her lean arms round
Concetta's shoulders to drag her away from her
brother's body. Everyone was asking in low voices
how and when it could have happened.

The *parroco* shook his head : " God has struck
him suddenly. That is how atheists die." He
picked up his skirts about him and swept away.
Of the black-robed only Don Ambrogio remained.
He was so deaf that he could not hear what the
others were saying ; his frail white features looked
more like death than Andrea's face. He was lost
and childlike, vaguely wondering how he could
soothe his cough in the coming winter, since
nobody but Andrea knew the secret of that linctus.
Annina's uncle began to put up the shutters of the
shop.

When Paul came home dreaming through the
dusk he found the shop doors closed. He could
not understand, until he heard the women wailing
upstairs and pushed his way through the hushed
crowd in the kitchen to find his mother.

" Concetta, Concetta," they called, " here is your
son ! "

She looked at him wildly as though he were a
stranger.

For all his public protestations of unbelief they
buried Andrea under the cypresses of the *Campo Santo*.
It could not be otherwise, for in Pogerola there was

no accommodation for heretics, and the church could not positively affirm that his last moments had lacked the grace of repentance, even though the manner of his end had been awful and appropriate.

For a whole week, according to custom, no fire burned in the Riccis' charcoal-furnace. The neighbours brought Paul and his mother dishes ready cooked, roasted barley-coffee made with goat's milk, and baskets of fruit. It was the time of apricots and peaches and the first fruits—flowers, they called them—of the fig. These glowed in heaped platefuls in the darkened room. In secret, Paul was ravished by the opulence of their colours, the ripe fullness of their shapes. The neighbours, hanging in the doorway, were like adoring magi. "He is well," they said solemnly as they entered; "now he is in Paradise." Then they sat round in a circle, praying, gossiping and talking in proverbs; in Pogerola there was no contingency of human life or death that proverbs could not satisfy.

What they really wanted to know, one and all, was how much Andrea had left, and whether his documents were in order; for since he had acquired money Andrea had taken to lending it to small landowners whom he trusted, and many hoped that, in the unexpectedness of the catastrophe, these loans would be forgotten or evidence of them mislaid; but Concetta, even in her desolation, never lost her peasant shrewdness, nor gave a word or a thought away.

Slowly, methodically, with the devoted patience of ants whose world has been destroyed, she sat there, silently collecting, for the second time, the fragments of her life, so quiet, so serene, that it was only in her wounded eyes, as in those of a bereaved animal, that her misery could be seen. The loss of her brother, a catastrophe so immediate, affected her far more deeply than that kind of translation in which her husband—a stranger always—had vanished into the fog of the Serbo-Turkish war. Of the future she said nothing; not even to Paul did she breathe one word of what she was planning; but when the notary had found a purchaser for Andrea's business and the new druggist had haggled and paid his price, they moved westward along the hillside to a dilapidated cottage whose ruins were included within the bounds of the property which, at the time of their marriage, Paul's father had bought. To these narrow quarters she transported the fantastic decorations of John Ritchie's room, which she disposed on the walls in an order identical with that in which the vanished martyr had arranged them. It was an act of ritual piety rather than one of positive desire. When this was done she seemed happier. It was almost as if she and Paul were children together. Concetta had always been a peasant at heart. Her foreign marriage had distorted the stem of her existence. For her the life in the shop on the *piazza* had never been quite natural. Now, as in the days of her girlhood, before John Ritchie was dreamed of, she rose before dawn, and, with the dawn, was at work on the vineyard terraces. Paul got up with her, and there they would work together until noon reduced to silence every voice save that of the simmering *cicalas*. Then they would eat their meal in the shelter of a straw-hut and she would tell him stories that she had heard as a girl, stories of primitive cunning and love and vengeance, that seemed to him to belong to some earlier world, until she tired and fell asleep where she lay. Then Paul would slip away from her side and begin to draw.

For since the conversation which he had over-heard on the night of his thrashing he had never tried to conceal his passion from his mother. From the dismantled shop he had inherited a rich legacy of paper, and Concetta, almost as if she wanted to make amends for Andrea's perversity, showed herself childishly eager to see the work of his pencil ; she was half-proud, half-shy of it ; yet always more proud than shy. Her humility made him ashamed. It thrilled him with love and thankfulness to find that she didn't scorn his aspirations ; and yet the matter was so delicate, and she, for all her courage, so pitiful, that he dared not speak of his ambitious intentions, if only because they meant that he must leave her.

Nor did she speak of them, albeit she knew quite well what was in his mind ; for though the reactions of her instinct were quick, impulsive and usually right, this was a matter foreign to her inherited experience, proceeding from the English element in Paul's blood rather than the Pogerolan ; it demanded thought, and thought, with her, was an unfamiliar process, slow and laborious as the seasonal changes of nature.

Fortunately for Paul, she admitted that his creative passion was a thing outside the province of

her understanding, and that, whatever else it might
lead to, it unfitted him for the peasant's life to
which they had returned.   Andrea, with his educational schemes, had been partly responsible for
that.   She also knew that she couldn't solve
these temperamental difficulties by violence or by
repression as Andrea had tried to do, and all her
love for Paul, made more emotional by their late
disaster, urged her to sacrifice herself to his happiness.   So both of them waited without speaking;
and this rich season of peace and suspension, in
which the grape-clusters swelled and tarnished and
olives blackened into ripeness, seemed to Paul
symbolical of his own maturing purpose.   All
through his life he remembered the surpassing
silence and tenderness of those months.

Suddenly came thunder and rain.   They were
refreshed and awakened.   Autumn, in Pogerola,
was like a second Spring.   The sun-cracked terraces livened into blade and leaf, and dawns grew
sweet with the whimpers of returning migrants,
notes cool and liquid, falling like dew upon the dry
chafing of the *cicalas*.   Paul and his mother stripped
their vines and pulped the clusters; the cottage was
full of the slumberous smell of must.   No time for
thought in these days; for next came the olives,
bulging baskets with their heaped jet, basket after
basket to be carried down the slope to the mill in
Pogerola, and Concetta worked like a young girl,
singing with the other women as she went, with the
sun's tyranny past, and the thankfulness of harvest
in her eyes.

An old man named Alessandro, came from Naples

to make them an offer for their oil; a shrewd
wrinkled fellow, with young eyes, golden-brown,
like Annina's. For twenty autumns he had come
to drive his bargains in Pogerola, always young and
smiling, and Concetta respected him, because he
was rich and had been her brother's friend. All
through the summer she had been waiting to talk to
him about Paul, for he came from the city and knew
more of the world than people in Pogerola. He
sat cross-legged and smoked and sipped old wine
outside the cottage door, discussing Paul's future.
Paul, with moist hands, stayed within the house and
listened.

"His uncle wanted to make a doctor of him,"
Concetta said, "but Paolino is not like either of us.
He takes after his father; foreigners, as you know,
are different. He says nothing about it, because he
is a good son; but even when he's talking of other
things he thinks of nothing but painting. I want
you to tell me what you think of it. Andrea said
he would starve."

Alessandro waved his hand towards the yellowing
vineyard. "He need never starve," he said,
"while you have this. But it's true that you
need advice and help, Concetta; a woman like
you shouldn't live alone. If you thought of
marriage. . . ."

"No, I shall never marry again," she told him.
"In Pogerola men don't marry a woman of my age
for love. As far as the property is concerned, I can
look after it myself as well as any man. And
Paolo, though he does his duty, can never help
me in that way. He has learnt Latin; he can read

and write like Andrea. I can't make a *contadino* of him. Tell me, Don Alessandro, is it true that all painters are beggars ? "

" By no means," Alessandro assured her. " In every trade there are failures and successes, idle and industrious."

" Paolino will never be idle. It's a passion with him. His heart is in it."

" In that case, if he has a hard head for money as well, he may be quite as successful as if he were a doctor. In Naples there is an artist who has dined at the Quirinal, and painted the Holy Father in the Vatican itself. Well, nobody would call that beggary ! Then there's another great artist, a sculptor, I should say; Gennaro's his name. Now he's so prosperous that he never even puts his hand to a chisel. Not he ! He just sits in his villa at Posillipo with servants to wait on him, or drives down to Naples in his carriage and pair. He has workmen to paint the pictures and make the statues that foreigners buy, and a fine shop in the Toledo. No beggary there either ! Why, the amount he pays me for wine and oil would keep a small man in comfort. What's more, he'll make a tighter bargain than anyone in Pogerola, and you people take some beating ! Of course that one is what you call a genius, if you know the word, an artist in a million. Still, that's enough to show you it's a trade that has possibilities."

Concetta flushed with delight. One half of her fears was dissipated ; yet the graver half remained. She lowered her voice. "Is it true," she asked, " as Andrea has told me, that these artists consort with women and paint them naked? And with such women?"

It was true, Alessandro replied, in a sense quite true. But that was only in the beginning. One had to learn. And when once an artist had painted a successful picture—one that took the fancy of foreigners—he could go on copying it for years. It was the same, no doubt, with statuary. Besides, when an artist had made his name, the people whom he was asked to paint were of a social order who wouldn't dream of posing naked. Not they, they liked to show their jewels and their fine clothes! What was more, a sculptor or a painter of repute would confine himself to statues and pictures of great men, men of the very highest class, like Savonarola or Garibaldi (Concetta shook her head) or the Emperor Tiberio. No fear of moral corruption in that direction! "And then," he went on to explain, " there is human nature. . . .

" Take myself, for example," he said. " Now I, as you know, am a wine merchant. I travel all through the province, buying and tasting it. Gragnano, Falerno, Lacrima Cristi, Monte di Procida; I know them all—even this species of vinegar you make in Pogerola. Now, Concettina, I ask you a question: have you ever seen me drunk? Never! I'm too familiar with wine. And it's the same with artists and women: they see too much of them. Eh?" He emptied his glass with a triumphant gesture.

" And now I'll tell you something," he went on. " You women will never realise that your sons grow into men. And men want women: that's

the law of life. But—" and he put his finger
cunningly to his nose—" but women and all.the
other things that do a young man harm are a matter
of money. A full stomach, Concetta, and a full
pocket. If your Paolino goes to Naples keep him
short. That's what I told a customer in Gragnano
who's sending his son to Naples to be a doctor, and
that's the truth, as sure as I'm sitting here."

Concetta stealthily showed him some of Paul's
pictures, rude, isolated sketches of forms that had
entranced him. Alessandro scrutinised them with
an air of critical wisdom. " Yes, yes," he said,
" *Caspita* ! Why, that tree's an olive ; you'd know
it anywhere for an olive in Pogerola ; they'll
never learn to prune them rightly in this place.
Now, if they'd cut them low, as they do in
Bari. . . . Like this . . ."

She listened patiently while Alessandro smudged
the charcoal with his horny thumb.

" But if I make up my mind to let him go, Don
Alessandro, how shall I begin ? "

He laughed, refilling his glass. " This wine's
not so bad. When you talk like that I know
you've made up your mind already. That son of
yours can twist you round his little finger. You
mothers are all the same ! How to begin ? I'll
tell you. When I get back to Naples I'll see my
friend, Gennaro, the millionaire at Posillipo, the
one who keeps the grand shop in the Toledo. I'll
see if I can get your Paolino into his studio, where
he can see how the money is made. All he need do
is to keep his eyes and ears open and learn what
foreigners want and how much they'll give for it.

Then, when I go to Gragnano, I'll see my other
customer, the father of the boy who's going to be a
doctor. His son must be two or three years older
than Paolino, more, perhaps ; but he's a smart
fellow with a hard head, and if they two could lodge
together he'd keep the youngster out of mischief.
Lodgings come cheaper for two, and I know my
friend would be glad to keep down expense.
Yes, I'll do that, Concetta, for the love of you and
Andrea, and as soon as anything comes of it I'll
write and let you know. Only one thing you need
remember. Keep him short ! And now about
that oil. . . . It's a thumping good year in Bari,
Concetta ; you won't be getting the prices of last
November, nor anything like them."

Book Two

VITA NUOVA

Book Two

VITA NUOVA

I

THUS, in a series of scenes, words, colours, odours, rising unchosen, unbidden even, from some secret storehouse where memories kept their freshness unfaded, like painted figures in a Theban tomb, the past swarmed back into the brain of Paul Ritchie out of the darkness which possessed the steamer's upper deck. So bright in hue it seemed, so finely lit and focussed, with essential detail sharpened and compressed, that it gave him the illusion of a stage-play, a work of art, which, by ruthless selection, achieves a reality remote and yet more poignant than that of life.

The boy who stumbled through those scenes, the savage, eager and inarticulate peasant, with his low brows swept by tempestuous hair, and eyes that scowled alternate shyness and hostility along the street of Pogerola, he saw, objectively, as a figure having no spiritual continuity with his mature and urbane self. It seemed ridiculous that this fantastic creature should have been he; that the pangs of love and horror and passionate aspiration which this figure obeyed should once have moved himself. Indeed it was not so. Had not physicians told him that in a space of seven years each human body was renewed in its every cell? And, since those days, had not his own body suffered no less than six of these merciful metamorphoses? A seventh incarnation! The thought was strange, yet comforting. It encouraged him to turn his back on those early memories of Pogerola, from whose impact he had miraculously escaped with no deeper hurt than a gentle stirring of pity and melancholy; to face with a firmer front the moment which, for the last few days, he had most been dreading: the moment when this swirl of memories should sweep him up to the door of that dark house in the *Vicolo degli Angeli*, of which the starlit faience cupola of the church of the Carmine now warned him, like the beam of a lighthouse marking iron reefs. " It was not I," he kept telling himself, " it was not really I ! "

*   *   *   *   *   *   *

And so he came, the Paul of forty years ago, out of the clot of low streets, through which the boulevard now runs northward to the station, into the Square of the *Mercato*, where garbage lay littered as in a farmyard, and fishwomen screamed, and flies rose buzzing about his ears.

The ghost of Don Alessandro, the wine-merchant, walked with him—God knew how long ago old Alessandro had died! He hobbled along with a rapid motion that was like the tripple of a well-trained donkey, flickering his salutations to left and right; for Don Alessandro was an old Neapolitan, *viecchio 'e Napule*, and well known in the port; while Paul was breathless not only with haste but with wonder.

Naples was the first city he had ever seen; its
streets were paved not with garbage but with jewels,
the tall seventeenth-century houses awed him with
their magnificence; and, high above all, the bright
church cupola, jade against lapis lazuli of a dry
December, brought his heart into his mouth.
How should that heart be content with paper and
carbon when such gigantic slender miracles might
be wrought in stone? At once he was no longer a
painter, but an architect, a builder of great churches,
filling the sky with lovely gleaming domes.

"Come along, come along, come along!" Don
Alessandro panted. "That open mouth of yours
will catch more flies than *maccheroni!*"

Out of the sun, in the narrow lane, the air was an
icy draught that made them shiver; within the
archway a danker cold enveloped them. Paul's eyes
had never seen an entrance so impressive: a wide
span, beneath which the equipages of eighteenth-
century nobles had gallantly emerged; above it
a coat of arms and a ducal coronet. Yet time had
treated the house with little respect, scarring its
friable front of volcanic stone with hideous ulcer-
ations. To the right of the entrance some owner,
more pious than reverent, had chiselled a niche for a
blue-gowned smirking Madonna at whose feet lay
votive offerings of withered wild narcissus, odorous
in decay. Their harsh scent impregnated the air,
providentially masking a less tolerable stench of
humanity and sweet charcoal-smoke that rose from
a dark cavern which generations of sub-human
beings had excavated in the foundations of the
house. From the mouth of this subterranean

chamber the ragged and wasted figure of an old man grinned horribly at Paul and held out his hand for alms.

"Don't look at these beasts," Don Alessandro warned him, "or they will give you no peace. This is old Naples. Fine houses on the top, as you see; but underneath them, everywhere, these cellars—*fondaci* we call them—in which such people live. Beggars and cammorrists, murderers and thieves: God knows what rubbish you could find there if you looked! But nobody wants to look, least of all our brave policemen, and I, for one, don't blame them. . . . There must be thousands upon thousands of these *fondaci*. All the worst of our people drain down into them, like filth into a cess-pit. Sewer rats: that's what they are. Some day, when this accursed kingdom of Italy remembers the poor South, it'll have to disembowel Naples and stop them up. In winter, these horrors don't show their ugly faces; but when the warm weather comes, out they swarm, making the city disgusting and dragging in garbage from the streets to feed on. Like rats, I tell you, rats! Why, if I had my way I'd smoke them out with sulphur."

He paused in front of a warped wooden door and rang the bell. He rang impatiently, again and again; for, in spite of his good nature, this business of Paul's initiation was a nuisance. At last the door opened, cautiously, and a woman appeared. She was slight in figure and taller than Don Alessandro. By the cold light of the courtyard Paul thought her face sad and grave. It seemed paler, in this first encounter, by her contrast with the women of Pogerola whose skins were burned by sun and mountainous air. Her pallor was partly that of a living plant deprived of light, but partly that of a fairer, more northern race, as Paul realised when he saw the copper hair bound back, like a primitive saint's, from her smooth white brow. That brow was whiter, too, for the fine dark line of eyebrow, clean-curved like a swallow's wings, and the deep black eyes beneath them. She wore a kind of overall, black, and high at the neck, from the sleeves of which white arms escaped, skin smooth and firm, above a moulding of lithe muscle which contradicted the impression of fragility in her first appearance. Paul, whose brown eyes were active as a hawk's, judged that she was nearing thirty ; a woman far too old for a boy like him to think about, though the peculiarity of her colouring attracted his painter's curiousness. When she answered Alessandro her voice was modest, almost humble. There was an inflection in it that Paul hadn't heard before. Its strangeness, and the reserve that controlled it, attracted and scared him.

But Alessandro was too old, and too much of the world, to be frightened of any woman. Also he was in a hurry, and wished to get the business over.

" This is the house in which my friend Pietro Viva lodges ? The young doctor from Gragnano ? Yes, that's the boy. On the third floor ? Aha, that calls for a younger heart than mine. Though mine's young enough, mark you, when it comes to certain matters," he added, screwing up the wrinkles round his merry dark eyes till they almost disappeared. " Now the question is this. Here is

another young man ; a young man from the country
—innocent and gentle as a lamb, eh Paolo ?—who
comes here from his mountains to study painting."

She turned and gazed at Paul as if she were
wondering if Alessandro's words could be true.
This long-legged, rustic figure, glowering embarrassment at her, clutching his cap with clumsy
hands ; flushed cheeks, and dark eyes, at once
greedy and distrustful : could this, her glance seemed
to ask, be a painter ?

"He comes from Pogerola," Alessandro was
saying. "You've never heard of it ? Of course
not ; I might have guessed. Unless I'm mistaken,
signora, you come from Venice. Ah yes, I've been
there. Wherever there's wine or oil to be bought
and sold, there goes old Alessandro. But what am
I saying ? Lodgings ! That is our question. A
small room ; Paolo doesn't mind how small it is,
on the same floor as Pietro. And cheap, mark you,
cheap ! "

She answered anxiously : " Yes, there is a room,
a very small room, though, next door to Signor
Viva's."

"No doubt that would make things easier for
you," said Alessandro persuasively. "The young
men will be friends ; they'll take their meals
together. That'll be a saving of labour, won't it,
with all those steps to climb ? So that, with such a
combination, the room should come cheaper.
Remember the importance of this : he is only
beginning. A good, quiet young man who will
give no trouble. Say fifteen francs a month ? "

"You had better see the room for yourself," she

answered. " Then we will talk of money. If you'll follow I'll show you the way."

" By all means," Alessandro acquiesced politely. All through his speech Paul had noticed that the wine-merchant's little eyes were fascinated by the woman's white arms. Now, as she moved to the stairs, his desirous fingers stole out and touched one of them in the soft curve above the elbow. Her body was ruffled by a shudder of distaste which filled Paul with chivalrous anger. He was glad that she resented Alessandro's obscene touch. She hurried on ahead of them ; her clogs made a clatter on the marble stairs ; it seemed as if Don Alessandro were panting, like a satyr in pursuit, the house so lonely and she so unprotected that he must soon overtake her.

" This is the doctor's room," she told them—the climb had faintly livened her cheeks, but even with this access of colour, Paul decided, she was strangely pale—" and this one next door to it is free."

A bare room, long and barrel-vaulted, with a bed, a trestled table, and one chair. It was dark as a cellar ; for the window that occupied the end of the cylinder was closed and shuttered, and yet it smelt clean and dry. The woman passed before them, throwing open shutters and window, admitting a flood of air and light which poured in like a torrent that has burst its sluices, blinding their sight, searching the lime-washed walls, making a watchful spider contract its legs. On the flood of this white magnificence Paul's heart was tossed upward like a feather out of the depths into which the house's empty glooms had sunk it. When its overpowering impulse had subsided and his light-shocked eyes recovered themselves, he saw through the open window a greater wonder still : to the left the harbour, bristling with masts and cordage, motionless against a shimmering sea ; to right the bastions of the Angevin fortress, from which all Naples rose like a wave of stone to the crest of San Martino and Sant' Angelo's castle. Never, in his life at Pogerola, had Paul dreamed that the works of man could attain such splendour. Never had lonely mountains inspired him with such consciousness of his own dormant powers, such hope, or such desire. From that window's vantage-point all this glory was his to brood on, to absorb, to re-create. In the street below, crowds of men and women came and went like ants—like the ants he had watched in the vineyard, going and returning, pausing, for some momentary contact of their fine antennæ, then passing, intent on their unimaginable business—and he so high, remote, uplifted above them, that all their movements seemed to be in his power and by his favour. This was the home for him, he decided ; after that revelation no other would satisfy. Don Alessandro, meanwhile, went sniffing round like a pig in search of truffles, tapping the walls, shaking the table-legs, lifting the coarse linen of the bed and turning back the blankets.

"It's very small," he said dubiously. "Good for the winter, no doubt ; but summer will make a furnace of it. It doesn't surprise me, signora, that this apartment is unoccupied." He curled depreciative lips ; not because the room displeased him, but because, by a habit hardened into nature,

he never made a bargain in any other way. " An
ancient house," he went on, " and an unhealthy
neighbourhood. Sea breezes. . . . yes ; but then,
the miasma from the port, and such a population
of cut-throats ! Did you say twenty francs a
month ? Come, come, signora, let us be reasonable.
At fifteen, possibly. You mean, of course, that
service is included ? And bread and coffee in the
morning ? "

" The young doctor pays thirty," the woman
answered.

" Thirty ? God help us ! Well, some people
are made of money ; but this young friend of mine
has no rich father to help him. An orphan,
signora ! An artist ! You, who are a Venetian,
must know what that means. Suppose we say
fifteen ? "

She shook her head. " Twenty is the price. If
I wished to make it less I couldn't do so. The
master has fixed it."

" The master ? In that case I might talk with
him. You mean, I suppose, your husband ? "

" No, he is not my husband," she answered
firmly, " and I'm afraid you can't talk with him.
The matter is in my hands."

" If it had been eighteen," said Don Alessandro
regretfully, with a keen sidelong glance, to see if she
would waver. " Eighteen ? " he repeated, persuasively. A door slammed and echoed in the
basement below.

Suddenly the woman became agitated, as though
some mysterious fear or admonition had reached her
from outside their company. Colour mounted in

her white throat. She clasped her hands. The calm by which she had seemed possessed forsook her; she was stirred, spiritually, physically, like a water ruffled by wind.

"I must go," she said. " I am sorry. I cannot stay here." She hurried to the window, where Paul stood entranced, and closed it abruptly. He was conscious of a strange urgency in her movement. It seemed as if, for her, he no longer existed. She waited for them to move, impatiently, with clasped hands. Don Alessandro was curiously insensitive to these changes. He kept on quizzing her with his wrinkled eyes. " Eighteen ? " he said coaxingly : " eighteen ? "

" Please, please ! " She did not even hear him, and Paul, pained and disconcerted by his sudden expulsion from paradise, was seized with a panic fear that its future possession was slipping away from him.

" This is the room I want," he declared firmly. " Let's say no more, Don Alessandro, I'm content with the price." If it had taken half of his monthly allowance of sixty francs he would have consented rather than lose this God-sent opportunity. " If I may come in this evening ? " he added anxiously. Don Alessandro stared amazement at his rashness.

" This evening, yes," she answered. " But now you must go . . . quickly. I am sorry."

She closed the door and locked it. Disturbed and preoccupied, she hurried them downstairs, and disappeared from their sight without another word. Paul and Don Alessandro, the second still huffed at the way in which the business had been snatched ou

of his hands and their abrupt dismissal, stood for a
moment bewildered at the bottom of the steps.
From within the room into which she had passed
they heard the rasping of a voice, heavy and unpleasant in its suggestions of roughness, and then a
long silence.

"This courtyard is like a tomb," said Don
Alessandro with a shiver, "we had better go. It
seems that you can make bargains for yourself," he
continued resentfully; "but if that's the way you
make them you needn't ever dream of making your
fortune. To pay the figure that's asked you? It's
unthinkable! In another minute we should have
had the room for eighteen and saved a full month's
rent."

"She wouldn't have waited for it," Paul told him.
"You see how she got rid of us. What could we
have done?"

"You could have stayed there in spite of her,"
said Don Alessandro. "Were you frightened?
Two men to a woman? Ridiculous! She couldn't
have thrown us downstairs. And now a pretty
fool you've made of yourself. However . . ."

He emerged from the archway in aggrieved
silence. From the jaws of the *fondaco* the same
repulsive beggar thrust out his hand. Don Alessandro clutched Paul's arm.

"A fool of yourself," he repeated. "Now listen
to me. Do not make a fool of yourself in another
way. That woman's a Venetian, different from our
people here. Be careful: I know that type.
Those red, silent women, I tell you, are as crafty as
foxes: crafty, and lean, and hungry. Hungry's the

F

word. That woman could swallow a dozen of you, my poor child, at a mouthful. Be careful, I say. Mind you don't get entangled with that one or there'll be an end of everything."

At this, Paul laughed out loud. That woman, indeed? Why should Don Alessandro talk of women to him, who was in love with a vision of thronged shipping and curious house-roofs, with all Naples reared like a wave, and breaking in stone castles against the blinding sky.

II

THAT same evening his new neighbour, Pietro, the medical student, came swaggering into Paul's life. Viva was his name; sanguine and vivid his nature. His father, as Don Alessandro had told Paul's mother, kept him short. If he had given him length, Paul thought, then Heaven help Naples! He was as full of sap, as rampant, as robust as a Gragnano vine. A strong wine and a generous is that which flows out of Gragnano, and something of the force of that fluid ran in Viva's veins, declaring itself in the heat of an insatiable zest and energy and frank good humour. He burned, he radiated. When he was near him Paul's dreams and meditations wilted like young leaves in the breath of a *scirocco*.

From the first Paul deferred to him, for Viva was three years the elder by the ordinary measure of time, and older, in fact, by centuries. For in Paul, though he did not know it himself, the English blood of John Ritchie was always predominant, making him, by contrast with his neighbours—and even with his mother, seem vague and Northern, and quite incurably romantic. By Viva's side the mountain innocence of Paul seemed peculiarly young and callow. For Paul, not only the life of this new, fantastic city, but all life whatever, was still mysterious, fit subject for awe, speculation, romance. Wherever Viva went there was no more mystery, nor room for shadows. His mind cut like a scalpel through surfaces that Paul's timid mysticism would have respected, cut deep and fearlessly, till it reached the core of matter which, to him, was ultimate reality. His world was smaller than Paul's, but he was master of it; not distantly, as Paul possessed his, gazing down on it from his exalted window, but grasping what he saw with his firm, brown hands, throwing to the gutter everything that did not serve his purpose. Beauty meant nothing to Viva : power and knowledge everything. There was a cruelty in his zest ; but also a bravery that Paul knew to be beyond him.

Physically, even, Paul found himself dominated by this prepotent type. It was not that he was less well-formed than Viva, nor even weaker. He derived, in fact, on both sides, from tougher and more virile races; but in Viva the reactions and co-ordinations of mind and muscle were so swift, so finely balanced, so automatic in their certainty, that, beside them, all Paul's thoughts and movements seemed clumsy, rustic, lacking in definition. Viva was handsome too : his dark features were as fine and clear-cut as a cameo ; his eyes bold and insolent.

He had neither fear for men nor reverence for
women.   It was as though his anatomical intimacy
with both had filled him with a kind of contempt
for his own species.   If he was conscious and
appreciative of his own physical perfections, it was
only because of the powers of domination that they
conferred on him.   For this reason he cherished
and adorned them, contriving, in spite of his father's
meanness, a careful elegance in clothes that gave
advantage to his sanguine face with its crown of
crisp, undulant hair.   He wore a military moustache
which did not conceal the contemptuous line of the
lower lip : a full bow, strong and beautiful, but
never tender.   His whole aspect, indeed, was daring
and cavalier.   Although a tradesman's son, he was
expert in the code of chivalry, had fought two
duels with the rapier, and, scorning law, carried a
pistol in his pocket.   In every particular, physical
or spiritual, he was Paul's diametrical opposite.
Therefore, from the first moment of their meeting,
Paul adored him.

Pietro Viva, flattered, yet always laughing at Paul
and at himself, accepted this adoration for precisely
what it was worth.   That wise young man knew
the value of everything : a fact that Paul was quick
to realise when, on the first evening, he trailed
behind Viva, with straining ears, among the
compact crowd that surged along the canalised
course of the Toledo.   The noise nearly deafened
him, he was bewildered and excited by the swift
procession of so many faces grotesque or beautiful,
yet each with a secret to be divined.

Above all he was stirred and excited by the faces

of the women. In Pogerola he had never seen a
woman wearing a hat, nor skins unburned by
weather. The refinement, the delicacy, the exotic
quality of these Neapolitan faces challenged his
skill to give them expression : their distance, their
haughtiness defied him, affirming that they were
unattainable and himself an ill-dressed boor. In
the midst of the Toledo, where traffic was wedged
into a block, he found himself gazing full into the
eyes of one of these exquisites, and, as he gazed, she
smiled. Nobody but the transfigured Annina had
ever smiled at him like that. The smile drove him
into a panic ; he could not deal with it. Later, in
the cheap eating-house, where Viva took him to
dine, Paul confided to his new friend this em-
barrassing circumstance. Viva was glad enough to
talk about women. It was a subject on which he
felt he could speak with the authority of an
expert.

"A smile is cheap enough in Naples," he told
Paul. "It's reflex, automatic. The sweet in-
nocents can no more help smiling when you catch
their eye than a cherry tree can stop putting out
blossom in April. But it's one thing to see the
blossoms, my boy, and quite another to pick ripe
cherries and stuff your mouth with them. This
Naples is a devil of a place, I tell you ! Money,
money, money ! And the cunning of the creatures !
You may dress yourself like a duke, but it makes no
difference. The only part of your clothing that
really interests them is your pocket, and they can
see down to the bottom of that with their pretty
eyes shut. Of course they have adventurous

fancies, these ladies, as I've fortunately had reason to know ; but if you'll take my advice . . ."

The advice was so frankly brutal that Paul hastened to explain that his interest was merely theoretical and romantic. Timidly he quoted old Don Ambrogio's Dante. Viva stared at him : he hadn't quite realised, till that moment, that he was dining with an idiot.

" That excellent poet, my dear Paolo, lived in the sixteenth century."

" The fourteenth," Paul corrected seriously.

" What do two centuries matter ? " Viva laughed. " This is the nineteenth. A different pair of sleeves. The economic situation has changed. Tell me what this old mother of yours allows you ? "

" Don Alessandro will give me sixty francs a month."

" Not bad to begin with. And in this studio, this hole where you're slaving all day ? What will they pay you for that ? "

" Nothing. I go there to learn. It's supposed to be a privilege. There are eight pupils. We work away at the copies. The *padrone* keeps an eye on us and criticises our work."

" And sells it afterwards. I don't know how good an artist your Gennaro is, but he's a damned good business-man. Now listen to me, my friend ; you can't put romantic pictures into a frame of sixty francs a month, so don't imagine it. Your room will cost you more than a quarter to begin with. That leaves a franc and a half a day for food and diversion, which may be good enough in Pogerola, or whatever the barbarous place is called, but in Naples! Life, I may tell you at once, my dear Paolo, is not going to be a bed of roses. Possibly, if you're careful, you won't starve; but that's about as far as I'll go. You can't dine here to begin with. I'll show you a cheaper place to-morrow. Why, even I only come here at the beginning of the month when I'm flush. This is your last experience of gilded luxury, so make the most of it. Less than two francs a day. My poor boy, it's a crime! A beggar could pick up as much. You'd better make a fuss about it at once."

Paul shook his head. " If I did that I should find myself back in Pogerola. My mother believes everything that Don Alessandro tells her, and he says it's enough."

" Enough? Enough? The meanness of this old devil who skins our parents when he comes to buy their wine and keeps a mistress in *Torre del Greco* on it! ' *I* never drink,' he says: I've heard him say it; and I've seen him lying in the bottom of a cart like a sack of flour. I suppose he made that iniquitous bargain for you with Gennaro? How much has he made out of that? Don't answer me: ' Nothing.' He's a *cammorrista*, that one: he'd get a commission on his best friend's funeral. One thing I'll say for him: he knows good wine, and how to get it cheap. It's he who sells it to this place. Why don't you drink some more while you've got the chance? Come on, now! Waiter . . . another bottle!"

Viva emptied the last drains into Paul's glass. He himself had drunk enough to be generous, though, indeed, no wine was needed to make him

so : for Paul, at the moment was a guest, and Viva
sufficiently Neapolitan in his training to know that
for a guest no hospitality is too lavish.   When the
last drop was drained and Paul suggested paying his
share of the bill, Viva showed himself almost
offended.   What did he take him for ?   Weren't
they already friends, and Paul a stranger, and this
the first day of the month ?   " When I'm broke,"
he said, " and want money, you can be sure I'll ask
you for it."   He flung a handful of silver on the
table and left the waiter a whole franc for tip.
" More than half of my daily income," Paul thought :
in Pogerola people reckoned their purchases in
copper *soldi*.   It was magnificent, he decided, as
they emerged from the vinous odours of the
restaurant.   All things were magnificent that night :
not only his gay companion but this city of brilliant
streets through which they swayed, arm in arm,
with its high façades and wide spaces of darkness.
Even the cabs rolled by like triumphal chariots.
He remembered how, from the terraces above
Pogerola, the reflex of Naples could sometimes be
seen lighting the night sky.   Now he, the adventurous Paul, was the incredible centre of that core of
light : it was almost as if its fires emanated from the
activity of his dancing spirit, proclaiming its triumph
for Pogerola's benefit ; but nobody in Pogerola
would see it at this hour.

The contrast seemed so significant that he had to
remark on it to his new friend : " To think that in
my village everyone's asleep ! "

" In your village, by your leave, my dear Paolo,
they're never awake.   Here, in Naples, nobody

ever sleeps except for a few moments in the winter. In summer you can hear people chattering all night long. That's why you'll have to be careful. You'd better take my arm. Even if I *am* drunk—which I'm quite ready to admit—I'm a protection. You don't know the character of these streets down by the harbour. Why, in those country clothes of yours, you'll get your coat thrut . . . throat cut; they'll take you for a young carter come tramping in from the mountains with a string of donkeys. Or a *zampognaro*. Can you play the bagpipes by any chance? But seriously, Paolo, and speaking with all respect, these clothes of yours won't do. If you've enough money to get them out of pawn you can have a suit of mine, we're much of a size, although you slouch like a donkey-man. Peter and Paul; two brotherly saints. That's good! For God's sake mind your steps. There's a hole just here that'll shoot you down double-quick into the Roman sewers. Even when I'm drunk that's the one thing I always remember. Clothes, was I saying? In that awful rig-out, my dear fellow, you'll never get a girl to look at you."

With unusual eloquence Paul explained that he didn't want them to.

"Come, come, that's sheer nonsense," Pietro solemnly assured him. He became didactic. "Speaking as an eminent anatomist, I maintain they are a physical complement. Speaking as a physician, I say they're a necessity; and if they aren't there must be something wrong with you. Speaking as a friend, and man to man, I ask you: what else is there in life that really matters?"

" There's art," said Paul piously.

" But artists, notoriously, my dear Paolo, need women more than most men. Even your old friend, Dante, who, between ourselves, is a bigger bore than anyone except his commentators. Even an artist can't be different from everyone else, or nobody will buy his work ; and if nobody buys your work, why, what's the good of painting ? "

" It's good in itself," Paul asserted stubbornly.

" But quite impossible unless you're a gentleman of property, which isn't exactly your case on sixty francs a month. I'm sorry for you, my friend, but there it is ! Either you'll have to decide to become a normal civilised male, or else you'd better make up your mind to go back to Pogerola and keep goats."

The taunt threw Paul into a rebellious silence which lasted until they had crossed the *Mercato* and entered the archway in the *Vicolo degli Angeli*. As they approached the flights of marble stairway Viva took his arm in an attempt to soften by this familiarity the violence of his argument.

" You needn't take me as seriously as all that, Paolo," he said. " I never mean more than half of what I say. But still, that half's sound sense. I was as raw as you when I came here first. A fellow has got to adapt himself sooner or later. If he doesn't do it willingly he'll be kicked into it, and that'll hurt like the devil. You can't convert Naples into your blessed Pogerola at this time of day. I warn you for your own sake. You don't like it now ; but later on you'll thank me."

The foot of the stair was black as a pit. Suddenly a door opened ; the beam of an oil lantern swept the

court.   Behind it Paul saw the figure of the woman
who had received him in the morning.   Straighter
and paler than ever she seemed, and curiously
forlorn, with deep shadows ringing her dark eyes
and marking the composure of that sad mouth.
Though Viva and Paul stood full in the light of her
lantern, she did not appear to recognise them.   She
seemed as detached from life as though she were a
picture, framed there in the doorway.   As a picture
the set scene stamped itself on Paul's brain : that
guarded light, one ray illuminating the ivory
forearm on which Don Alessandro's little eyes had
gloated, another directed upward, sweeping through
the coils of burnished copper that were her hair.
Viva swept off his cap with a gallant, liquorish
gesture and smiled.   She saw, but her features gave
no sign of seeing.   They, too, might have been
chiselled out of ivory.

    Behind her they heard a sound of nailed boots
ringing on marble.   A man cleared his throat
raucously and spat, then suddenly an enormous
shoulder loomed across the light.   He lurched in
between them and the woman who held the lantern,
a vast figure in a hunting coat and breeches of bottle-
green corduroy, with a fowling-piece slung cross-
wise over his back.   He must have been very tall,
at least six inches taller than Paul or Viva, but his
neck was short and thick, and he carried his black
head low down between the shoulders, so that he
seemed, as he walked, to be impending over some
invisible prey, with bandy arms so long that they
almost reached his knees.   His forehead was fiery
red, with black brushes for eyebrows ; his nose

blunt and bulbous, his strong jowl covered with a beard crisp and curly, like the wool of a black sheep. And he came at them, out of the doorway, with head lowered like a charging bull.

Viva, surprised by the violent apparition, drew politely aside and wished it good-evening. The hunter answered with nothing but a snort. He swept past them with the deadly intensity of a bull that has seen red and charges to kill. Paul had the impression that if they had stood their ground they would have gone down like ninepins. Before he could recover from his surprise he saw the ground-floor door slammed to, and his picture of the woman with the lantern had disappeared. Then he heard Viva laughing weakly in the dark. Viva clutched his arm.

" That's a pretty sight for a man's who's drunk an extra bottle ! Is it just the liquor, or did you notice anything ? "

" Who is he ? " Paul whispered, " and what's he doing here ? "

" Suppose you knock at the door and ask Cristina, Viva joked. " She ought to know."

" Cristina ? "

" Cristina. *Cristo*, Paolo, don't be an idiot ! Pull yourself together ! The lady of the house. Didn't you and Alessandro interview her when you took your room this morning ? The one with the red hair and the ugly mouth. Of course, I forgot, you never notice women. She must have been a beauty in her day ; but that, my dear boy, was just the day before yesterday. It was her room he came from."

" You spoke to him.   You've seen him before ?
Not that it's the kind of face you'd ever
forget."

" Of course I've seen him before.   It's he that
Cristina calls her master.   No, if you take my
advice, you won't ask the poor soul about him.
The woman's a good sort, in her way, and if you
only mention his name she'll take fright and go as
red as her hair."

" What is his name then ? " Paul asked.

" You know," said Viva querulously, " you're so
damned literal.   *I* don't know his name, and you
can take it from me that Cristina won't tell it you.
He's her pet mystery, and heaven knows she's
welcome to him.   I call him the black hunter.
Before you've been here long you'll often meet him
on the stairs ; always the same great, dark brute,
with his shooting-clothes and the gun slung over his
shoulder.   If you've any sense you'll keep out of
his way and hold your tongue.   One word, and he
glares as if he'd murder you.   He *is* a murderer ;
I'd stake my shirt on that.   Sometimes he carries a
bag.   Don't imagine there's woodcock in it, and
don't go looking too closely at it, or you may get a
shock."

" But if he's so . . . friendly with her," Paul
persisted, " why did she stand like that : so crushed,
so terrified ?   She looked like a beaten animal,
Pietro.   I've never seen such a look before.   Is she
his mistress ? "

" I've told you she calls him her master.   I
daresay . . . Those lifeless, pallid women often
fancy a black brute for a lover.   Since you're so

interested, you might take the matter in hand and make inquiries."

" She looked so pitiable, so helpless. It's damnable, Pietro ! What could she do, a woman all alone, with a brute like that ? "

" Ah, now, my dear innocent, you're beginning to get romantic. If you feel so strongly there's no reason why you shouldn't try and comfort her, provided you relish the idea of a woman who might almost be your mother. Not that the thing's unheard of. Our little Cristina might easily teach you a thing or two. The humblest of God's creatures have their passions. Why not ? "

" My God, Pietro, can you think of nothing else ? "

" Of very little else," Pietro answered complacently. " I'd have you realise I'm a medical student. You know the song ? *Gaudeamus igitur juvenes dum sumus*." He sang the phrase at the top of his voice. It echoed indecently over the vaulted staircase as he dragged Paul up the marble steps.

III

THAT room, that bare room on the third floor of the house in the *Vicolo degli Angeli*, whose windows, thrown open at daylight, disclosed the prospect that had enchanted him on his first visit, became the central shrine of Paul Ritchie's life. It was the only real privacy that he had ever known. Behind its closed doors he found the solitude and seclusion that are essential to the development of an artist's dreams. To Paul it seemed dearer because its joys were, for the most part, so difficult to attain.

Every morning, as Don Alessandro had arranged, he left them reluctantly for the workshop at the back of the shop in the Toledo which supplied the material of that great artist Gennaro's business; a chilly room top-lighted by windows thick with dust, in which half a dozen of craftsmen and apprentices produced the plaster casts and painted panels which foreigners and sailors bought for souvenirs. Gennaro knew his trade-requirements backwards; by calculated eliminations he had reduced his studio's repertoire to a small number of models that were certain to tempt the most modest pockets. His statuettes, in plaster or terra-cotta, represented flower-girls, fisher-boys and tarantella-dancers, and were planned to face each other in pairs on either side of a mantelpiece. His pictures portrayed the same set of characters in brilliant colours against appropriate backgrounds, such as Vesuvius at night, in blood-red eruption, the blue grotto at Capri, and the traditional views of Naples with the great stone-pine on the Vomero thrown in. These subjects were painted on planed panels of olive-wood, imported from Sorrento, and strictly priced according to the area that they covered and the quantity of pigment used in them. The work was organised with a mechanical precision, and the duty of Paul, as the youngest and latest comer, was to fill in the sky and use as little paint on it as possible. Gennaro himself, driven in from his villa at Posillipo every morning, saw to these economies himself. He would smudge his finger over the edge of Paul's

skies to make sure they were not too thick, then
wipe it clean on the lining of his waistcoat.

A week of this useless monotony reduced poor
Paul to despair. He confided his troubles to Pietro,
who insisted on treating the whole matter as a joke.

" Gennaro's a wise man," he said : " he knows
his requirements and sticks to them ; and Don
Alessandro was right : when you know as much as
he does you'll be in a position to make your fortune.
You'd better go out to Posillipo on Sunday and
choose the villa that takes your fancy."

" But I came here to paint," Paul told him.
" That isn't painting. Anyone with a goat's
intelligence could do what I'm doing now. You
could do it yourself."

" A thousand thanks for the compliment," said
Viva gravely. " Evidently, in that case, you're not
cut out for making a fortune."

" Fortune ! If I were being paid, it'd be another
matter. I'm merely wasting time. The only
person who gains by my work is Gennaro. I want
canvasses, paints, an easel for myself. I want
money to pay models with. I want time. I tell you, I
might as well be pruning vines in Pogerola as living
like this."

" You want other things first," Viva agreed,
" notably a new suit of clothes. But I fancy I've
mentioned that little matter already."

Paul frowned. Viva's taunts on this subject
were becoming monotonous ; and yet he couldn't
resent them. Even in the descending scale of
eating-shops which they frequented as Viva's
monthly allowance dwindled, Paul's appearance was

an embarrassment which nothing but the student's complete lack of snobbishness condoned. He realised this more deeply every day. Already he was beginning to look at himself with Neapolitan eyes, to feel conscious of an uncouthness that he couldn't avoid, since even Viva's modest surroundings were a strain on his resources. He knew that the student friends, who generously accepted his company for Viva's sake and because of his odd Englishness, which they found amusing, could not help making excuses for this questionable companion. He had tried, with indifferent success, to become the complete Neapolitan. He had even endeavoured, pathetically, to make himself smarter, a process that awakened in him an agonising self-consciousness of his own unsuitability to the company in which he moved and was so happy. The realistic mind of Pietro defined the situation succintly :

"At Gennaro's you're earning and learning nothing. Therefore, in the first place, you are under no obligation to him. In the second, if you leave Gennaro, you cannot be worse off than you are now. You'll have gained, if you wish to be exact, twelve hours a day. Whether, in those hours, you can earn enough to make any difference is another matter."

"At any rate, I can try," Paul answered, confidently.

"Then why not do so ?"

"Because . . ."

There were a hundred reasons. His mother, to begin with, implicitly trusted Don Alessandro's

G

wisdom, and would consider any departure from
the plan with which the wine-merchant had settled
Paul's future as the first step to perdition.   In any
case there would be a devil of a row ; for Gennaro
was bound to resent the loss of anyone who painted
skies adequately and economically for nothing.
Alessandro, who had conferred this favour on his
customer, would lose the credit of the arrangement
he had made, and overwhelm poor Concetta
with reproaches.   It might even mean that all
supplies would be stopped.   Luckily, Paul remembered he had the money for his second month
in hand.

There was another and more important reason
for Paul's growing discontent with his present mode
of life.   Don Alessandro, in spite of Concetta's
confidence in him as the polished citizen of the
world and the trusted friend of Andrea, was not, it
appeared, the last authority on artistic education.
It is possible that he had acted with complete
honesty when he delivered Paul into the clutches of
Gennaro, the only kind of artist that he knew who
was also a prosperous tradesman.   But no sooner
had Paul found his feet in Viva's student society
than he became aware of the existence of another
opportunity for education : the Institute of Fine
Arts, the school of painting included in the ancient
Bourbon Academy.   Among the crowd of im-
poverished youths who frequented the eating-house
patronised by Viva's medical friends was a group on
whose lips he heard stray phrases that quickened
his pulse—talk of pigments and values and models,
all mingled with the names of the teachers of

painting whose influence dominated the Neapolitan
school of the day : the great Domenico Morelli,
Vincenzo Capri, Postiglione.

For a long while, his native un-Latin reserve
forbade him to intervene in this closed and, as it
seemed to him, enchanted circle, until, one day,
tearing himself away from the webs of unintelligible
anatomical jargon that bound him, he thrust himself
boldly into the midst of the other group, bewildering
them with a quick-fire of eager, innocent questions.

" I want to learn painting," he told them.   "What
must one do ? "

They answered him chaffingly at first, amused by
the intensity of this comic figure.   In the end his
trembling seriousness impressed itself upon them.
Their mysteries, it seemed, were really simplicity
itself.   The Institute of Fine Arts was an endowed
school, open to all.   There were no fees.   There
were even subsidies available for promising students.
All that he need do was to present himself to the
faculty of the Institute, with some examples of his
work that would show the seriousness of his
intentions.   If these were approved, the rest
followed automatically.   He would find himself
enrolled, as they were, with all Art lying open before
him, and no toll on his pocket beyond the provision
of his own materials.   Paul stammered his thanks
and left them, his head in a whirl—first with wonder
at the glory of the opportunity that opened before
him, next with a hot resentment against the stupidity
and ignorance of old Alessandro, which had
cheated him already out of a month of this new
splendour.   Without a word of excuse or ex-

planation to Viva, he hurried home to the *Vicolo degli Angeli*, snatched up a newspaper parcel of his Pogerola drawings, and dashed through the crowded streets to the Institute.

A frowsy door-keeper received him with evident contempt. Four hours of waiting in an icy corridor cooled his ardour. The light was failing and officials were hurrying home before he achieved the attention of a bored junior instructor, more supercilious even than the door-keeper, who signed to him, with a wave of a smoking cigar, to display his drawings.

" When he sees these," Paul thought, as his trembling fingers unwrapped them, " he's certain to change his tune ! "

Alas, he did not ! Languidly, with the cigar in his stained teeth, the instructor glanced through them—those sketches that were not charcoal drawings but dreams limned in heart's blood. He pushed them aside, one by one, with a taloned finger. At last, without a word of praise or condemnation, he picked up a pen, and began to write with scratchy deliberation. His name ? Paul Ritchie. Paolo Ricci, he wrote. His domicile ? Vicolo degli Angeli. He sniffed, as though the very words offended his nostrils. Occupation ? Paul stammered : " Painter." A flickering smile commented on his assurance. His Civil State ? The official looked up in surprise at his reply.

" You say you are English ? Is that true ? "

" My father was English. My mother is a Pogerolan."

" They were married ? "

Paul flushed with a sudden fury, hardly controlled. " Most certainly married."

The official pursed his lips dubiously. " Your nationality," he said, " makes the position a little irregular. However," he went on, with a glance at the discarded drawings, "I think that it may be arranged. In the meantime . . ." He scribbled instructions on another sheet of paper. " You will attend the classes that I have signified on this list. You can start the day after to-morrow." Paul took the paper with a thrill. He was burning to express his thanks ; yet thanks, it seemed, were not necessary. He stepped out into the lamp-lit dusk with a singing heart. He had reached the mouth of the *Vicolo* before he realised that, by this hour, Gennaro's workshop was closed. There would, he reflected, be the devil to pay !

Of course he knew well that he would never return to it ; but his shyness prevented anything dramatic in his defection. When morning came he simply did not go there. He spent the forenoon, and his month's allowance, in buying paints, pencils, boards, paper, canvas, and a number of the imperfect panels which Gennaro's foreman rejected. By the nicest calculation he found that this expenditure would leave him enough to live on for a month, if bread and dried figs and an occasional slice of cheese could be called living. His mornings, in future, would be free ; and in them he hoped to be able to produce some saleable merchandise with which to augment his pittance. The rest of the day would be dedicated, with the fervour of a religious convert, to his new, his high adventure.

It seemed to him already as if his life were crowned by triumph. Viva and his student friends celebrated Paul's emancipation in a boisterous night.

It was with a tremor of the acutest joy that he opened the shutters of his room next morning. Like an exiled prince he took possession of his kingdom. He locked the door. As he sat at the window, munching the bread that he had stowed secretly in his pocket at the restaurant overnight, life seemed to him so pregnant with possibilities of fame and glorious achievement that it almost frightened him. He walked to and fro, under the white barrelled vaulting, approaching the moment when he should take his pencil in hand as though it had some sacramental significance. Then, with a spoiled panel propped against the bucket that served for his ablutions, he began to paint.

He painted Vesuvius at night, in blood-red eruption ; but Paul's Vesuvius was not the Vesuvius of Gennaro. He painted it as he had seen it on nights of North-East wind, the great plume dissipated at the moment of its formation into a lurid, threatening veil, blown downward, over the brilliant city ; the mountain grey, sullen and secret as some nocturnal monster risen from the sea. It was a picture that Gennaro would have consigned at sight to a bath of turpentine ; but as it grew beneath his fingers Paul was so possessed by rapture that he forgot to eat. He was no longer himself, no longer an uncouth country lad, toiling, with flushed cheeks, in a Neapolitan garret. He was an inspired creator ; he was part of the vision

that he created. Out of the tissues of his unconscious body the mountain's shadowy bulk took
shape ; the fire that glowed in its sullen plume was
the fire of his own ardent mind.

In the early afternoon a sudden knock on the
door made him jump into his skin again. It was
Don Alessandro, hot with Gragnano wine and anger,
breathless with the exertion of three flights of stairs.

" What's this ? " he cried, " what's this ? Illness ?
Idleness ? You don't look as if you were ill.
Signor Gennaro has sent me a message. What are
you doing here ? "

" I have left Gennaro's," Paul explained, with a
composure that astonished himself. He could not
even look at his visitor ; his eyes kept returning,
like birds scared from their nest, to his beloved
picture. At last he saw what was wrong : the
confusion of values with which he had been
struggling for two hours ! If only this vinous old
fool would give him the chance to correct it ; now,
at this moment, when everything shone clear !

" You've left Gennaro's ? " Don Alessandro
spluttered. " By whose permission, I ask, by what
right have you left Gennaro's ? You must be mad.
Without one word of explanation ! And now you
stare at me with that brazen face. You must
explain."

There was nothing to explain. He put the matter
exactly as Viva had put it.

" No obligation ? " Don Alessandro cried.
" Please understand you are under the obligation
of my word : my word, which has never been
doubted in all the province—in all Italy, in all the

world! I gave my word that you would work there for a year."

"Without consulting me, Don Alessandro."

"Consulting you? *You* . . . ?" The idea was monstrous. "And who in the name of Christ are you, that you should be consulted? A bargain's a bargain when I make it. If folk don't stand by their bargains the world will come to an end. When they can say that Alessandro's word is not his bond . . ."

"It was an unjust bargain, Don Alessandro, and anyway, I had nothing to do with it."

"If only your poor uncle could hear you speak. My poor friend, Andrea! Already you are in Signor Gennaro's debt for a month's instruction."

Paul laughed. "It's little enough I could learn from him."

"Then that," said Don Alessandro, "must have been your own fault. Perhaps you have less talent than you imagine."

"An idiot could have learned my job in twenty-four hours. I assure you, you could have done it yourself, Don Alessandro."

"An idiot? I? Is this meant for insolence?" Even Don Alessandro's anger subsided beneath his offended dignity. "Evidently neither here nor elsewhere have you been taught respect to your elders and betters. You are young and strong, and have me at a disadvantage at the top of these cursed steps. What? You'll be saying next that *I* haven't helped you, that *I* haven't used all my influence to put you in the way of an honest and artistic living. This is the way you repay me. Enough. . . .

More than enough! To you I will say no more. But to your poor mother . . ."

Paul knew what Alessandro meant: He was going to tell a long tale to Concetta, and Concetta was bound to believe it. He tried to put the threat out of his mind, to continue his interrupted picture. He set to work fiercely. To his amazement something of his own volcanic indignation found its way into his treatment of Vesuvius. This strained sense of working against time and fate put him in a good humour again, which was rather disappointing, for he had made the discovery that when his mind was distracted by anger his style was freer; a thing to be remembered. He worked until the light failed, and then threw himself on his bed and slept so deeply that Viva had to thunder on his door to wake him.

" I thought you'd committed suicide," Viva said. " If ever you contemplate doing anything of that kind please ask for my advice as an anatomist beforehand: the majority of suicides are so amateurish. What have you been doing?"

" I've been working," said Paul, " I've finished a picture. Do you want to see it?"

" Spare me that on an empty stomach, my friend," Viva answered brutally. " Come out and get some food."

Paul shook his head. " No more restaurants for me!" he said. " My dinner is bread and figs until I know how things are going. You needn't be alarmed. Even my poor uncle used to say that an artist must starve, and starvation's better than growing fat with Gennaro."

"Well, there's something in that," Viva answered solemnly. "As a physician I'm convinced that we all eat too much and drink too little."

"*You'll* never die · from the second of those indiscretions anyway," Paul laughed. "Goodnight."

IV

FOUR days later there came a letter from Pogerola. Concetta had evidently dictated it in a fever of alarm, but in its fine calligraphy Paul recognised the hand of Don Ambrogio, an origin which was confirmed by a postscript exhorting him not to miss hearing Mass on festivals in the church of *Santa Chiara*. The receipt of this letter so pricked him that he finished three pictures on end, while thinking over the terms of his reply. Even when he had answered it, he knew that he had not made himself understood. How could he convince thick heads in Pogerola, for whom Don Alessandro represented an extreme of urbane acuteness, that the wine-merchant was not the last authority on artistic education, and that his great artist Gennaro knew as much about it as a fish-hawker? How could he persuade them that he was working harder, and to more purpose than ever before, in the Fine Arts Institute? Only an appropiate gesture could convince. He achieved it with reckless daring. "There is no need for you to send me any more money," he wrote. "By the end of this month I shall certainly be supporting myself."

It was magnificent; the written word assured
him that it was true, and gave him a vicarious sense
of independence and elation; but, as the month of
trial on short commons drew towards an end, the
boast seemed nearly as empty as his stomach.
Viva and his medical friends were always ready to
take Paul back into the fold from which he had
strayed into dubious artistic backwoods. At heart
they were kindly and generous; often they invited
him to eat and drink with them; but frustration and
solitude made him proud and roughened his tongue,
so that they ended by letting him go on his way,
treating him, good-humouredly, as the grotesque
that he was. Try as he would he could never
really be one of them. The wine which took the
others out of themselves had, on Paul, an opposite
effect, making him more self-contained and English
than ever.

All afternoon he worked at the Institute. In the
morning he painted panels which he hawked all
over Naples, offering them to every shop-keeper in
whose windows pictures appeared. If they had
resembled Gennaro's he might easily have sold
them; but although the subjects were in order,
their treatment was so irregular that nobody would
take the risk of buying them. The shopkeepers
spoke to him kindly; there was something sym-
pathetic in the appearance of this lean young rustic;
they were even ready, at times, to give him advice.

"Now if you would only realise," said a smart
salesman in the *Via Pace*, "that when a foreigner
buys Vesuvius, what he wants to show his friends
is a mountain spouting fire. The smoke that you

have painted might just as well be cloud. Fire, and plenty of it, my boy. Something like this." And he flourished a typical example of Gennaro's Vesuvian series. In the top left-hand corner of blue black sky Paul noticed the smudge of Gennaro's niggardly finger and an inequality in the panel that he himself had filled with stucco.

"Yes, yes, I know," he murmured. "You see, I painted it." The shopman laughed. Evidently, Paul was joking.

"I painted it," he repeated.

"Then why in heaven's name . . . ?"

And then he met Kalisch.

Kalisch was an Austrian Jew, a lean old man in spectacles, who lived and ate and slept, like a slow-moving spider, amid the dust of a basement shop on the *Riviera di Chiaia*. Each day, as Paul passed its dirty windows on his endless wanderings, he saw the old man crawling about among his stores of rubbish or eating his dinner from a dirty newspaper. He sold, or offered for sale, antiquities ; and indeed any object that stayed for long enough in his care acquired a patina of grime and dust that gave it an appearance of authentic age. Paul approached him as a last resource ; for sometimes, behind the bleared window panes, he had seen oil paintings suspended. As he entered the shop Kalisch's watery eyes surveyed him with disapproval. His lips were covered with crumbs, for he was in the middle of his mid-day meal.

"I have pictures for sale," Paul told him.

The old man took them from him and examined each with care, flicking away the bread crumbs that fell on them with a red-silk handkerchief. He spoke at last with his mouth full, mumbling bread between his words.

" These are not old," he said, " Do you know who painted them ? "

" I did," said Paul, his heart fluttering.

" You painted them ? H'm. You have talent of a sort. I like them. But I can't sell them. This one's not bad."

He held up the veiled Vesuvius that Paul had painted in his first flush of anger and freedom. Paul's heart warmed to him : he wanted to tell the old man how and when it was painted. " You look hungry," said Kalisch. " Sit down with me and eat."

When they had finished the Jew took off his spectacles and smiled at Paul with his weak eyes.

" I should like to keep this picture," he said, " not because I can sell it, but for myself. It's a poor picture, but it's clever. I can see that you want money. Well, so does everybody, including myself. Trade has never been so bad in all the forty years I've been here. So I can pay you nothing. Nothing ! You understand ? But we will make an exchange. If there's anything in the shop that takes your fancy—up to the value of five francs—you shall have it for your picture. H'm ? "

A pathetic ending to high hopes ; and yet it seemed better than nothing. Among Kalisch's rubbish there were many beautiful things that Paul's greedy eyes detached from the grime that surrounded them. He passed from one to another eagerly. Kalisch moved mumbling behind him,

approving his comments, yet always on the watch
lest something should disappear into Paul's pocket.

"It seems you have taste as well as talent," the
old man said. "That is a thing that cannot be
taught, and much the more valuable of the two.
You might be useful to me. H'm? Naples is full
of good things in unlikely places, and I am getting
too old to find them. Keep your eyes open, my
son. When you see something good and cheap
you shall come and tell me about it. I will give you
the money to buy it and a small commission for
yourself. H'm? Yes, we'll do business together.
H'm?"

Beneath his shrewdness and his guttural grunting
speech, the old man was so kindly that Paul was
driven to a confession of the embarrassments into
which his rash gesture of independence had thrown
him. Kalisch listened without the least sign of
sympathy.

"Your stupid friend the wine-merchant spoke
wisely," he said at last. "You cannot paint
pictures that are original, like these, and eat. I
say original; but, remember, that's all I say. You
have talent—not genius, mind you. That's a
different thing. But you still have to learn to
paint. As far as the mechanics of painting are
concerned, the Institute is not bad. In ten years
time, it is possible that you may paint a good
picture. Possible . . . h'm? In the meantime
you must work, and you must live. Now it's clear
that you cannot live by painting things like this;
but if you paint bad pictures for a living your talent
will suffer. It is impossible to do good work and

bad in the same medium. H'm? Therefore you
must do something in another medium at the same
time. Not things of which you are ashamed, for
they corrupt the soul."

"I'd sweep the streets," said Paul, "if it would
help me to learn to paint."

"It wouldn't," said Kalisch. "Now you are
talking foolishly. I thought you were more
intelligent. Foolishness and talent, unfortunately,
are not incompatible. Still, if you are wise enough
to listen to me, I'll tell you something."

Spiderwise, he crawled to the other side of the
shop. As he went his skinny fingers touched
things as though he loved them, and held them up
to his rheumy eyes. From a high shelf, that
seemed to strain his crooked back intolerably, he
took a wooden casket and handed it to Paul. It
was a Florentine box with a smooth, illuminated
surface of parchment smoky and yellow with age.
In texture and colour, it gave an effect of mellow-
ness, almost of beauty. Paul handled it with
mystification. He could not conceive of its being
any earthly use.

"No, it is not useful," said Kalisch. "And
except for the parchment covering it isn't old. I
don't even consider it beautiful, myself. But
people have a passion for buying boxes in which
they think they can put something, God knows
why! It's a part of human nature. Even when
they're dead folk want to be screwed into an
ornamental box, h'm? And these—I have had a
number of them—are very saleable. Easy to make
too, if you put your mind to it. All that you want

is a box, a piece of old parchment, some glue, and a little imagination.   I'll lend you this one to use as a model, and if you make me five others like it I'll pay you twenty francs apiece.   A hundred francs in all.   H'm?"

"If I could find the boxes . . ." Paul began.

"If you could find them!" Kalisch snorted. "You cannot find them; but any carpenter will turn them out for a couple of francs.   As for the parchment, here is some to go on with." He pulled out a ragged portfolio stuffed with pages torn from monastic missals, loot of the suppressed monasteries of the Campanian coast.   "These pages," he said, "we sell for one franc each. They're getting scarcer of late, I don't know why; but you can always pick them up in shops like this in Naples.   What did I say for the picture?   Was it four francs?"

"Five," Paul corrected him timidly.

"Five francs," the old man repeated, counting out five sheets of parchment as though he could not bear to part with them.   "Now this is work that you can do at night.   At night you make boxes for me; during the day you work at the Institute or spoil canvas at home.   You'll never sell any pictures.   When you've finished them you can scrape the canvasses or panels and use them over again; but if that makes your young heart bleed, you can show them to me before you destroy them, h'm?   Now go and find your carpenter, and whatever you do, be careful of the model.   Remember, that's worth fifty francs!"

"I thought you said twenty," Paul suggested.

"Twenty to you. Fifty to me. That's the difference, h'm ? " said Kalisch.

With this the surprising commerce in illuminated, parchment-covered boxes began. Those were great days for Paul, for fortune perversely favours the prosperous, and his mother, always inclined to tenderness, and moved, by the present of an expensive shawl which Paul sent her, to believe that her son was making good, renewed the allowance that the indignant Alessandro had persuaded her to suspend. Spring was already in the air. From Paul's miraculous window he could see long drifts of blossom, first almond, and then peach, invade the vineyards on the slopes above Posillipo. The South-West wind broke in torrents of spring rain, scouring Paul's window-panes, washing the landscape into clear brilliancies, enlarging the sky with cloud-shapes that gave it a soaring vastness. And he was happy in the absorption of work whose very promise was an attainment.

It was a life of sheer asceticism. All through the morning he painted for himself ; now, for the first time, without a cramping restriction of material. In the afternoon, he worked at the Institute ; when the light failed, he turned to Kalisch's illuminated caskets ; and even this work was no drudgery, for every day his mechanical prowess increased. His eyes found a new skill and delight in adapting the beautiful monastic illuminations of capitals and musical clef-signatures which graced the torn missal pages to his schemes of formal decoration. His boxes, maybe, were not works of art. At least they were triumphs of a minute technical ingenuity

H

which supplied the diversion of a mechanical task
and absorbed a mind already too swollen with high
imaginations.   He was far too busy in these days to
see much of Viva.   Apart from the students who
sat working beside him at the Institute, he scarcely
spoke to a living soul.   His room was a complete
hermitage, entered by no feet but his own and
those of the mysterious bronze-haired woman
Cristina, who contrived, by some secret knowledge
of his movements, to make his bed and lessen the
confusion of his belongings during his absence.
Week after week went by without Paul's setting
eyes on her.   Her presence was as unsubstantial as
that of a ghost—a fragile appendage of the black
hunter whose ringing footsteps Paul sometimes
heard on the stairs.

Kalisch approved his work ; what was more, he
sold it and was always eager to buy more.   This
puzzled Paul ; for whenever he chanced to enter the
shop in the *Riviera di Chiaia*, he never saw the
shadow of a customer.   Kalisch, indeed, handed
out his money and his parchments so readily that
Paul began to suspect that he was being under-
paid.

For the best part of an evening they argued a
readjustment of prices, and in the end, reluctantly,
the old man raised his scale of payment from
twenty to thirty francs.

The visions evoked by this new affluence nearly
turned Paul's head.   He decided to abandon work
for the rest of the day and enjoy the city sights that
his labours had long denied him.   It was a soft
spring evening ; all Naples seemed to be taking the

air in his own holiday spirit. At the hour of the *Corso* the streets were thronged with sleek-skinned horses, and bright equipages full of dark women in their arrogant elegance. It was a vision so rare in its refinement and costliness, so poignant in its contrast with his own condition, that Paul, the intoxication of Kalisch's ten francs' increase still buzzing in his head, was carried away by a sudden desire to be master of the power and luxury and pride that squeezed him into the gutters of the *Toledo*.

In that moment of exultation, indeed, all things seemed possible ; but to it there succeeded another in which he saw himself as he really was : an entranced peasant, gaping at the unattainable. The truth was difficult to believe, until a humiliating vision of his own shabbiness, reflected in a plate-glass window, reinforced reality. Then he grew angry with himself and scornful of his ambitions, so angry that he refused to look any longer at the taunting reflex, and stared deliberately past it to the shelves of the shop-window. There, in a place of honour, he discovered the secret of Kalisch's munificence : three of the boxes that he had finished a week before set in a row !

Trembling with fury and shyness he entered the shop and asked the price of them. The shopman, an elegant with bejewelled fingers, glanced at him contemptuously. " The antique caskets ! A hundred francs each," he said, as though he grudged the effort of speaking to such an apparition.

" I made them," Paul blurted out. " I made them last week."

The shopman stared at him. "You must be mistaken. These things come from Florence."

"I made them, here in Naples. If you'll take them down I'll show you my initials : P.R. You can see them for yourself. I know where you get them," he went on hurriedly in his anxiety to be heard. "You bought them from Signor Kalisch, in the *Riviera di Chiaia*. I can make three a week. He buys them from me. But if you don't mind, I'd far rather supply them to you direct. I've two more, ready finished. I can bring them to show you this evening."

The shopman's eyes were still incredulous. He looked Paul up and down, taking stock of his poverty. "How much ?" he said.

"Fifty francs," Paul stammered, magnificently daring.

"I'll give you forty-five. Provided, of course, that they're the same quality."

"In half an hour," said Paul.

"In five minutes we shall be shut. Bring them here to-morrow morning."

Viva, and Viva's student friends were sharers of Paul's fury and of his triumph.

"To-morrow," Viva said, "you'll have to go to the *Riviera* and pull the old swine's beard. If you like I'll come along with you to see fair play."

"I'll never set eyes on him again," Paul answered bitterly.

"You're a queer devil, Paul. There's something wrong with your spirit. It must be the English in you. Now if *I* were in your shoes . . ."

"He did me a good turn when I most needed it ;
now it's finished and we're quits."

"You beat me altogether," Viva grumbled.
"Call that a good turn? Well, now you're a rich
man I hope to goodness you'll begin to live up to it.
As it is, you're worse than a Franciscan. Poverty
and chastity. . . . My boy, it's your bounden duty
to expand. Three boxes a week at forty-five
means more than five hundred a month. You
could run to a mistress on that. Think of it ! And
for God's sake, before you live another day, do get
some clothes less suitable for donkey-driving and
more like a civilised man's . . ."

They laughed together, dined sumptuously, and
drank a litre of wine apiece. Under its influence,
and remembering the horror of his own reflection in
the shop window, Paul promised to reform himself
in Viva's image. Next day he did so ; a little too
closely, perhaps, for Viva's Neapolitan type was one
that lent itself more to physical elegance than his
own, and Viva's tailor's ideas ran to uncomfortable
restrictions.

Working in his barrel-vaulted room, Paul in-
variably relapsed into Pogerola home-spun ; but
when the band of students went out at night he was
as exquisite as any of them, his cheeks shaved and
powdered, his wild hair trimmed and perfumed, his
shoes polished to an irreproachable lucidity by the
bootblacks under the arches of the *San Carlo*.
Only his obstinate shyness of women in any but a
pictorial relation separated him from the manners of
his companions. For long enough they chaffed
him on the subject ; but Paul was too stubborn to

be moved by chaff, and, in the end, they gave him up as a bad job.   And still, although as Kalisch had sombrely prophesied, he never sold a picture, the work went well.   It seemed as if the personal confidence that his prosperity gave him extended itself to his art.   His faith in himself, his enthusiasm, never failed.   He was a happy young man.   And now his artistic imagination began to catch fire from the work of others—not only from those somewhat shrill echoes of French impressionism which his instructors painted, but from the pictures in the dank and echoing museum and incense-clouded churches.   It was in those impressionable days that Paul Ritchie contracted that passionate admiration for the great Neapolitans—Caravaggio, the prolific Luca Giordano, and Ribera (called Spagnoletto) which Jacob Levine took credit for recognising in his maturer work.   It was the element of the grandiose and the macabre in their paintings that particularly fascinated him.   And life, in the near future, though he little suspected it, was destined to press his young art into their sombre mould.

V

BAD times fell on Pietro Viva.   His bright and dissolute good-nature had not endeared him to his professors, and with his failure to pass examinations at Easter the academic world collapsed about his ears.   For two years he had been gaily accumulating debts that he could not pay.   His father, a red, gross farmer from Gragnano, came storming up the stairs and left him like a thrashed dog. The debts, or as many as he confessed to, were paid in anticipation of his allowance. "*I* live on bread and onions and *maccheroni*," said the farmer. "It's time this flaunting in cafés was stopped. Now you shall live as I do, and as your grandfather did before you. This is your last chance, so make the most of it."

In these conditions Viva was singularly, pathetically helpless. His smart clothes were not made to cover an empty stomach; his fine physique demanded a nourishment of gross and expensive pleasures. His realism was strangely unadaptable. Without the stimulation of rich food and women and gay companions, his company became anything but gay. He wilted; he grew harsh, bitter, and even careless of his appearance. Paul was amazed at his queer lack of resilience, for he had always imagined that Viva was stronger and more independent than himself. He took pity on him, though it was a difficult and delicate business to pity Viva.

He proposed, as Don Alessandro had prudently suggested many months before, that they should keep house together. It would cost, he argued, a very little more to feed two people than one. The expense of service, to begin with, was practically the same, and one that he would have to incur in any case if he took his meals at home. He assured Viva that he had long been wanting to make this change, that he had no time to spare for eating in restaurants.

"You crafty little devil," Viva growled. "Do

you think I can't see what you're after? *I* don't want your charity, thank you!"

But he took it all the same. They ate in Viva's room; by this time Paul's tunnel was too cumbered with canvasses, boxes, frames and parchments to hold another table, and Viva had two chairs. The woman Cristina cooked for them in her basement and carried the food to table: bread and black coffee at seven, one dish at mid-day and another in the evening. When Paul first asked her if she would do this it seemed as if she took fright.

"I don't know: it's impossible to say," she told him.

"You mean you must ask your master first?"

"Yes, I should have to ask him. Perhaps. If I dare . . ."

"I'll ask him myself, if you'd prefer it," said Paul good-humouredly.

"Oh, no, no, no!" she cried. "You won't do that? Promise me!"

"It seems," he told Viva, "that all these matters are governed by an elaborate etiquette. You'd think she was a duchess, she's so particular about them. I'd no idea that housekeeping could be so dramatic."

"That black hunter is a figure of melodrama: I've always said so," Viva declared. "I sometimes positively doubt if he has any existence when I'm not in liquor."

But Paul had no doubt. On the marble steps of the tenement-house, the hunter had been much in evidence of late. Twice in one week Paul had opened his door to find this enormous bottle-green figure charging down on him, with head lowered, arms swinging, and red eyes staring out with a buffalo fierceness beneath his craggy brows. What he could be doing on that high landing, with nothing but attics beyond, was past guessing. But there he was, as large as—or rather larger than—life. Not only at nightfall, but at any hour of the day, one might look to meet him, with his sack sagging empty or bulging with sinister fulness. When Paul saw him coming upstairs or down, he would step aside to let him pass and give him an automatic good-day, which was never answered by anything but a bull's snort. Often as he sat at work he would hear the nailed boots ringing on the flags.

The day after he had made this proposal to her, Cristina came knocking at Paul's door. She looked much younger, almost childish with excitement; the sunlight gave her skin a golden tinge as if a frail cold fire were burning inside it; it occurred to him that, as a girl, she must have been pretty.

" I can come," she said eagerly. " He says I can cook for you and bring you your food. Because there are two of you," she added with a solemn innocence.

" *You* weren't afraid of us ? " Paul joked her.

" I wasn't afraid of *you*," she replied with a blush.

He hardly knew if this were a compliment. Viva, immensely flattered by the distinction, assured him that it wasn't.

" Why, even there," he said, " you see you've got no chance." It set him at his old game of showing, in Paul's presence, how easy and familiar he could

be with women, and proving that even Cristina
must fall a victim to his charms. But this time
Paul had the laugh of him, for Cristina appeared to
be quite unmoved by his graces. She regarded
them both with the same gentle composure whatever
Viva said or did.

"There must be something wrong with that
woman," Viva declared, proceeding to medical
details that Paul couldn't understand. "I don't
believe there's a drop of good red blood in her body.
Look at her arms, how white they are."

Viva often looked at Cristina's arms. Paul had
noticed this in his case as in that of old Don Alessandro. He looked at them himself, for their form
was beautiful, and under their golden lustre there
glowed, though Viva hadn't noticed it, that frail,
cold fire. Paul thought of them, instinctively, in
terms of line and colour; but Viva's interest was
not so purely medical as he pretended. Cristina's
indifference challenged his reputation as a conqueror
of women, and since his opportunities of gallantry
were now restricted by lack of funds, he settled
down to a leisurely but careful siege.

Paul knew nothing of this; for Viva had been
clever enough to see that Cristina disliked attentions
in public. In these days Paul's painting so engrossed him that, when Viva returned to meals, he
could not bring more than half of his intelligence to
table; the other half remained suspended in the
clouds of glory from which his work emerged. It
came as a shock to him when he realised, a few
weeks after their housekeeping had began, that
Viva and Cristina were not on speaking terms;

that her eyes were always averted from Viva's, that she even shrank from contact with him.

"What have you been doing to Cristina?" he asked when she left them alone.

"To Cristina? Nothing," Viva answered irritably. "I told you before that there was something wrong with that woman." He became cryptic: "I have made . . . investigations. I was right."

"It's evident," said Paul, "that your investigations offended her."

"The woman's a fool, a half-wit. She's not a woman. I wish she'd cover her damned arms up; they make me sick. What the devil are you laughing at now?" he burst out, irritably.

"Better luck next time, Pietro!" Paul chaffed him.

"Well, try it, and see for yourself. You're a queer pair, the two of you. You're just about her kind, if the truth were known."

Whether this were true or not, the fact remained that Cristina and Paul got on very well together. In a little while a change in Viva's duties at the hospital prevented him from returning to the house at mid-day, and Paul took his lunch alone in his companion's room.

Heaven knows what the black hunter would have thought of this arrangement! Probably Cristina didn't dare to tell him; but when she came gently tapping at Paul's door and called him to lunch, she was strangely soft and tremulous, as though she knew that she was running some desperate risk. Often, as he settled down to table, she stood there in the open doorway and talked with him, shyly at first, as though she feared that such familiarity might offend him, but later, when she began to realise what a boy he was, with a naturalness that equalled his own.

So, while she stood with ears strained to listen, and Paul sat and ate, they drifted by degrees into a queer companionship which was like that of two children. It was gay and trivial, interspersed with little jokes of their own invention; for Cristina, when once her timidity was overcome, had a quick and whimsical humour, un-Latin, like Paul's own; so that each of these mid-day meals became a pastoral idyll, remote and isolated in time and space, in which, by a sort of convention, they separated themselves from their different circumstances, and became for the time united in a child's-play that banished loneliness—for each was lonely—and took no count of differences in age or sex.

The transfigured Cristina of these moments had no relation to the woman who served them when Viva was present. Physically, even, she seemed different. When she was talking with Paul her grave mouth grew soft and younger; her body lost its rigidity; her brown eyes melted in tenderness; even her voice changed. She was a leaden landscape suddenly smitten by dawn; her eyes awoke like grey water when sunlight dances down on tawny pebbles. All in a moment, incredibly, Paul saw her thus.

" My God, Cristina," he cried, " you're wonderful. I must paint you like that. Why didn't I see it before ? "

Then colour, like that of a dying sun, swept over her; and when it had gone there was no beauty left. She was grave and rigid again; there was no more light in her.

"Why did you say that?" she answered dully, bitterly. "Of course you can't paint me. Do you want him to kill me?"

It was the first time that the shadow of the black hunter had fallen between them. She was so intense, so nervous, so painfully apprehensive, that Paul tried to pass it over with a laugh.

"Don't be so ridiculous," he told her. "He's just a man like any other man, this Goliath of yours. I'm not afraid of him. Tell him that David presents his compliments, and may he have the honour of painting the lady in the basement in return for a portrait of his elegant self? In hunting-costume, of course. No extra charge for the sack."

"Oh, don't, don't," she cried passionately. "Don't joke about it. You're talking like a fool. You don't know what he is."

"Well, that's your fault, Cristina. Why don't you enlighten me?"

"I can't." She put her hands to her eyes. "Why have you ruined everything like this?"

Paul had never before been forced to deal with such a situation. The contrast between his own mild amusement and Cristina's sudden passionate-ness impressed him with the duty of putting her at her ease. He remembered Viva's observations on the woman's strangeness. Probably Viva was right.

"You needn't be shocked like that," he said. "I

only want to paint you. I haven't the least intention of making love to you."

He rose from his chair; but when he approached her she took violent fright and hurried from the room. It was inexplicable. Women, evidently, were far more complicated than he had imagined. No doubt, in similar circumstances, Viva would have known exactly what to do. He would have to consult Viva on the point. On second thoughts he wouldn't. Viva would only laugh at him, and scoff at the clumsiness of his imaginary overtures. That was ridiculous. He had no intention of falling in love with Cristina, as Cristina herself knew perfectly well. But he did want to paint her: the leaden landscape made suddenly awake; that grey river-water revealing golden sands. . . . Some day, he supposed, he would learn how to deal with women.

VI

"What ever have *you* been doing to Cristina?" Viva asked him that evening. " I never saw such a sullen pair of eyes."

" They're not sullen," Paul said; " and yet it's true that you can't tell what's behind them. They're like the eyes of a stray dog that stare at you from a distance. You can't invent thoughts for them or guess whether they're looking at you with shyness or hatred or just bored indifference."

" And as far as I'm concerned," said Viva, " I've no wish to."

It was only by degrees that Cristina's confidence returned; and now Paul knew better than to talk of painting her, or of anything else that might trail the shadow of the black hunter across their sky. Little by little they slipped back into their familiar relationship. It even seemed as if Cristina were anxious to make amends for her unreasonable fit of panic. When Viva was away she prepared him little unexpected delicacies of her own country, and brought them to table with a timid excitement, an anxiety to please that was pathetic. In all domestic matters she had an intelligence amazingly sensitive to his changing moods, so skilled, so tactful, that she knew what he was wanting before his dreamy mind had realised it. She mended his worn clothes; she washed and ironed for him. Even his chaotic studio showed traces of her unobtrusive care. When April came she put roses at his bedside, and once a snowy branch of bitter-cherry blossom. He found it blooming there, miraculously, when he returned from breakfast in Viva's room, and scolded her mildly for her extravagance.

"They're nothing," she said, "and yet they make country-people like us feel at home."

"I don't see any mention of these in the bill," he said. "You've no idea, Cristina, how rich I am nowadays. I want to pay for them."

But this she obstinately refused. "You don't see," she said, "that they give more joy to me than to you."

"You'll live to regret it," he said. "You're spoiling me. You're like a mother to me."

"Yes, like a mother," she happily agreed.

" You've never told me about your mother, Paolo. I wish you would do so."

He talked about Concetta and the life of Pogerola. She listened, standing, with grave eyes, so quietly, that he began to think he was boring her.

" No, no," she said. " Go on telling me. It's like a dream to me, a good dream. I never had a mother myself." He pressed her to explain. " I was brought up in an orphanage in Padua," she told him. " There were three hundred of us, all in little grey frocks and straw hats. The sisters were very kind to us, but that, of course, isn't the same thing. Go on, I like to listen."

" But when you left the orphanage ? " he said.

" I was sixteen. I came with a family to Naples. The woman died . . ." She stopped suddenly.

" And then ? "

" That's all," she said dully.

" My dear Cristina, you stop just when your story's getting interesting."

" Interesting ? " she answered bitterly. " No, that's the end of my story."

Paul stood smiling at her. " I suppose," he began. . . .

" You can suppose nothing," she interrupted hastily. " Paolo, don't pester me, and don't smile like that. It's no use. I shall never tell you. Never, never, never ! "

She retreated to the doorway, a grave and tragic figure. All the sweetness and youth had gone out of her ; all their strange intimacy had vanished. She fled from him, precipitately.

Yet, even when she was gone, Cristina's image

troubled him. By slow degrees, imperceptibly, her presence had penetrated and established itself in his solitary life. Without his knowing it, her forethought and her attentions had become essential to him. Her silence was a necessary background for his spoken thoughts, thoughts that he could not speak to Viva or any other soul in Naples. He even talked to her about his work; explained his pictures to her, expounded his triumphs, and excused his failures. In her company he found that he could think aloud. She listened so subduedly, and the vehemence of his enthusiasms was so intense, that he was able to imagine that she understood him.

She did not understand him; but her mind was so quick, and so adaptable, that, by a swift repetition of some phrase that she had caught from his ardent exposition, she was able to convince him that she did. Then Paul would glow like a furnace, and her face would catch part of the fire that was in him in a flush that was half triumph and half shame for her dangerous deception. It was enough for her that Paul should be happy.

One day when he carried his week's work to the shop in the *Toledo* a surprise awaited him. The shopman, who had always welcomed Paul, received him coldly.

"We don't want any more of your boxes," he told him. "We have made a large purchase of some others at a third of your price."

"But you commissioned five more," Paul said, "and here they are."

"No use to us," said the shopman. "We're

I

overstocked already. You can see for yourself."
He handed Paul a sample from a heap displayed on
the counter.

"But these are inferior to mine," Paul assured
him. "The work is rough, the designs are banal,
there's no imagination in them. Look, they are
all the same."

"That may be so," said the shopman, " but
customers don't notice any difference. They sell
just as well, which is all that matters to me. I am
a shop-keeper, understand, not a patron of art. If
you can produce the same thing at our new price
we might possibly consider another order in a
month's time."

Paul stood there dumbfounded. Slowly he
began to wrap up his work in the handkerchief in
which he carried it. His mind was hot with anger
and indignation. The shopman had turned away.
Paul followed him obstinately.

"Would you be kind enough to tell me," he said,
"where these things come from?"

In his heart he suspected Kalisch.

The shopman swung round on his heel; there
was an avaricious light in his eyes.

"Well, that is hardly your business," he said,
"but since you're an old client of ours I'll tell you.
They come from the studio of Signor Gennaro in
this street. Possibly, if you use my name, he
might employ you. You might even take the
things you have there to him."

Then Paul burst out laughing. This vengeance
was poetic. He carried his boxes back to the
Vicolo degli Angeli. For a week he struck work

living on his capital, which was little enough, for of late he had been extravagant, financing Viva as well as himself. At the end of that week he realised that this would never do. Once more he made a pilgrimage of humiliation to the shop in the *Toledo*. The shopman took his boxes at a reduced price and promised to buy more.

"I agree with you," he said, "that your boxes are better than Gennaro's, and occasionally we meet with a customer who discriminates. Probably in a week or two the price will go down again. Gennaro tells me that he is sending dozens of them to Rome and Florence, and the bigger the production, the cheaper the article."

It seemed to Paul as if circumstances were assembling to crush him from every side. Still, he must live; and so he set himself to meet the new and desperately narrow conditions cheerfully. He needed all his courage to do so. Another trial lay in wait for him. Whether he owed it to Gennaro's manufacturing developments or to nothing but a malicious fate, he never knew. The price of parchments rose so suddenly and disastrously that in a few weeks his profit had shrunk to a figure that made the work a slavery. All over Naples he tramped in search of cheaper parchment. And then, more devastating than the rise in prices, the actual supply of parchment began to fail.

"There's only one thing left for you," Viva mocked him. "You'll have to go down on your knees and ask a favour of old Kalisch."

"I'll starve first!" Paul flamed.

"Probably," Viva agreed. "And so, by the

way, shall I.   That is an unfortunate coincidence," he added, petulantly.

Hour after hour, day after day, Paul sat savagely painting in his little room.   Once, in the past, he had discovered that anger tapped a flow of new inspirations ; but now his resentment was a dull and stultifying weight, a sullen, crushing burden, as though the air he breathed had been turned into lead.   Whatever distraction he essayed, there was no escaping from it.

Strangely enough he had never troubled Cristina with his confidence.   It was no business of hers ; he was proud and she could not help him, although, as he knew well enough, she could not fail to see the physical signs or feel the spiritual repercussions of his distress.   From the first he had realised that it would be necessary to restrict and simplify his meals.   He told her to do so.   In the hot weather, he explained, a man could live on next to nothing, like the beggars in the *fondaci*.   It pained her to see how little he was eating.   Skilfully she tried to tempt his appetite with new delicacies.   He didn't even notice them when they came to table, or talk to her, as was his wont, while he was eating.   All through the day he was listless, silent and absorbed. At night, when he returned from the Institute, he no longer worked at his boxes.   As soon as dinner was over he went out with Viva into the city, returning long after midnight.   In the morning when Cristina called him to breakfast his face was clouded.   And then, at last, he went out at night no longer.   He was ashamed to show himself in the city, for he had been forced to sell his clothes.   She missed them, when she came to brush them in the morning, and wondered what he had done with them; but Paul's looks were so gloomy and savage, his temper so uncertain, that she dared not speak.

At last, unable to bear the mystery of his strangeness any longer, she opened fire: "Paolo," she said, "I am tired of seeing you like this. It's becoming impossible. I speak to you: you don't answer; you stare at me as if you hated me; you won't even talk about your painting. I bring you food; I think all day about it; I might as well be feeding cattle for all the notice you take. If only you told me what has changed you, I could bear it. Oh Paolo, tell me, tell me!"

She spoke so rapidly and with a passion so surprising that he made her a rough answer: "At any rate it's nothing to do with you."

Her face clouded with pain.

"No, no, I don't mean that, Cristina," he said hurriedly. "I didn't mean to hurt you. I only meant that if I'm as you say I am, it isn't your fault; that there's nothing in my churlishness that need affect you or trouble you."

"How can I live here beside you," she cried, "and not be affected? You, with your painting, Paolo, are so superior. You live in a world of your own, and are so wrapped up in it that you think you can trample on everybody's feelings. You don't even know when they're under your feet. That's why you're born to break people's hearts, you artists! The pain that you give them doesn't affect you; it doesn't interest you. It isn't that you're cruel: you're just proud and blind."

In the fury of her emotion this woman was almost
eloquent. A second transfiguration! She stood
with her head thrown back, her hands clasped over
her breast. The blood rushed into her white neck
and cheeks like flame. Flickers of that cold fire
enveloped her. The sight was magnificent. It
took Paul's breath away.

"My dear Cristina! . . . " he stammered.

She broke in eagerly :

"Tell me at once, Paolo," she said. "Is it a
woman?"

"A woman? My dear Cristina . . ."

"I knew it. I knew it!" she cried. "That's
Viva's fault. I know him too well . . . too well.
He's driven you into it. God, how I hate him, the
pig! It's lucky I haven't killed him. Who
knows? There's still time . . ."

Paul rose at once in his friend's defence.

"Pietro has nothing to do with it. You go too
fast. Upon my soul, Cristina, you look like a
murderess."

"You make me feel like one," she cried. But
her tone was quieter. "Tell me, Paolo, who is
she?" she asked, with a white intensity.

"For God's sake calm yourself, Cristina. Of
course there is no woman. You might have
known it. What time have I for women?
Why, you are the only woman I ever speak
to."

"Is that true, Paolo?" she gasped. "Is it
true? Oh, Paolo!" Her voice was pitiful in its
entreaty, faltering into a dazed silence. "Yes, yes,
I might have known," she went on more calmly,

almost resentfully. "Then tell me, please, why are you so mysterious?"

"Why, there's no mystery whatever," he told her cheerfully. "I'm on the rocks, that's all. That's what a painter's life is said to be like. All ups and downs. And I'm not hardened to it. When I came here first I had no money, as you must have guessed. Then things went well. An Austrian Jew in the *Chiaia* showed me how to make some. I became as rich as Crœsus."

"Crœsus?" she echoed blankly. "Ah yes, I know. Those funny boxes."

"They weren't as funny as all that," he said, "but that's beside the point. No boxes: no more money. There's all your mystery!"

"But is that really all?" she asked bewilderedly. "Oh Paolo, why didn't you tell me that, and save me all this suffering? I have some money. A little. . . . Please let me lend it to you. It's no good to me."

He shook his head. "Your money won't solve my trouble, Cristina," he told her. "It goes far deeper than that. You can't expect me to live on what I borrow from you. I've got to make a living out of my brains. For the moment I'm beaten; but soon I shall find some way. You need have no fear of that."

"I want to understand all this," she said solemnly, "so please be patient with me. You mean that they won't buy your boxes any more? I called them funny, Paolo; but they are very pretty boxes all the same."

"Thank you for the delayed compliment,

Cristina." He smiled and bowed to her. She couldn't bear him in this mocking mood. Either one must be serious, or else. . . . " Indeed you're right," he went on ; " they weren't so bad ; but circumstances prevent my making any more of them. It is a matter of materials. There's no more parchment to be bought, except at ruinous prices, and so . . ."

" Parchment ? " she interrupted. " Tell me : what is parchment ? "

It was in moments such as this that her simplicity astonished him ; but her seriousness checked his smile.

" The skins with which I used to cover my boxes," he explained. " Leaves out of old missals. Surely you must have noticed them ? "

" Oh, those ? " she cried. " Is that all ? Oh, Paolo, Paolo, why didn't you tell me before ? And if you had these—these parchments, would you be happy again ? "

She was so eager, so childishly excited that he couldn't think what she was driving at. " Oh, Paolo, wait one moment, only one moment," she said. " Oh, my poor child ! If only I'd known ! "

In a moment she was gone. Paul, mystified, followed her to the door. The landing was empty, and when he peered over the iron balusters she could not be seen. Where she had disappeared to he couldn't imagine. Her exclamation, her eagerness, her sudden vanishing, were unreasonable, mad, fantastic. Standing alone on the empty stair-head he felt like a fool. Suddenly he heard the slam of a door on the landing above and raised his head.

She was coming down the attic stairs with her face
on flame, with joy and laughter in her eyes.   She
came breathlessly to his side.

"Not here . . . Oh, Paolo, I'm so happy, so
frightened," she laughed.

He followed her into Viva's room.

"The door," she whispered ; "close it.   I've
told you, I'm frightened."

He obeyed her and when he returned, she took
from her folded apron two sheets of parchment
and thrust them into his hands.

"Is this the kind you want ? " she asked him
eagerly.

He stared at them in amazement.   Two pages
torn from a missal : the rich and lovely workmanship of the fifteenth century, as fresh as though that
moment it had left the monastic illuminator's hands.
Only once or twice in all his searchings had he
lighted on such virginity.   For the moment he
could think of nothing but the maker's skill and
grace.   He handled the pages reverently.

"Ah, they're no good," she whispered, " and
I hoped so much that they would please you.
I'm sorry, Paolo.   I thought . . ."   Her voice
faltered.

"Cristina, what are you saying ? " he cried.
"No good ?   But they're marvellous . . . marvellous.   Too good, if you like !   Can't you see for
yourself how beautiful they are ?   These twining
tendrils of vine, those branched candelabra ? "

He smiled at her and saw that her brow was
anxious, her lips tremulous, her eyes bright with
tears.

" Really and truly, Paolo ? " she said. " You mean it ? You're not saying these things just to please me ? "

" Of course I'm not saying it to please you. It's a miracle . . . a miracle, Cristina, and you are a witch. But how in the name of Satan . . ."

" Oh, Paolo," was all that she could say. The swift alternations of fear and hope and disappointment had tried her too much. She smiled, but tears ran down her cheeks. Laughing and crying at once she stretched out her hands to him in a gesture that seemed that of a bewildered child. " Oh, Paolo," she said, " I'm so frightened, so glad . . . so glad ! I'd do anything, anything in this world to make you happy. And now you are happy ? Tell me, Paolo . . .?"

Laughing he took her hands in his. She leaned towards him with her eyes half-closed. His fingers slipped upwards over her white forearms. They were warm, and incredibly soft. This contact moved him to a strange giddiness. The blood sang in his ears. He was no longer master of his hands. They seemed to be possessed by a life of their own, to have become the receptive organs of some sensibility through which new and disturbing stimuli flickered into his brain. Of themselves they wandered onward over the smooth contours of her upper arm—so soft, so satiny, so glowing—and, as they did so, it seemed as though all the ardour of Cristina's breathing body came out to meet them : a warm passivity, drawn willingly against him, and then enveloping him. Her hot cheek lay upon his own. Languidly she turned her head. Her lips were on his. She shuddered. Like a storm-tossed living tree she shuddered, and was still.

Only for one moment. In the next his whirling brain recovered itself. It awoke to a consciousness, sudden, and piercingly clear, of his surroundings; of Viva's room, one table littered with medical text-books and human bones, on another the fragments of his unfinished lunch; of the two sheets of illuminated parchment that had fallen to the floor; of the window's vast panorama of Neapolitan house-roofs, bleaching in the sun; of a small mirror on Viva's dressing-table, in which, as in a miniature carefully composed he saw the image of himself with the body of this strange woman in its arms.

Once more the blood rushed up into his head. This time it carried with it a flood of astonishment and of shame that turned his heart to ice. His fingers relaxed their grip of Cristina's shoulders. Through his mind there blew a chilly draught of fear, of distaste, of wonder at the demon that had taken brief possession of himself. Was this the adventure of which Viva and his student friends were always boasting? No, this was not love! Or, if it were love, this discomforting physical enthralment, it had withered in the moment of its birth. He did not love this woman. She was a stranger; she was nothing to him. Yet she still lay in his arms, her eyes closed, her lips upon his cheek, in a rich, somnolent content. Was it possible that she, so joined to him, had not felt some vibrations of the revulsion that ran through him? Could she be so insensitive as to imagine

that he loved her? If that were so, her insensitiveness became a claim for pity. At last she opened
her eyes; they were soft, appealing; she smiled out
of the richness of her deluded content, and pity,
stronger than any emotion that had preceded it,
save in that moment of mad possession, swept his
mind bare of any other emotion. He thought of
her goodness, her humility, her isolation; of the
scorn with which she had rejected Viva's base
proposals, of all the endless kindness and devotion
that she had shown to himself; of the eager
elation, the joy, the pride with which she had
brought her parchments to him; of the desolation
of that house in the *Vicolo degli Angeli*, of all the
mystery and terror that concentrated itself in the
figure of the black hunter. Thinking of these, his
instinctive revulsion seemed to him a crime, an
insult to her innocence, her pitiful loneliness.
Those eyes that smiled at him and dwelt so con-
tentedly on his were like those of an animal in
their innocent trustfulness. He could not bear to
look at them with a refusal in his heart. Gently he
released himself from her; so gently that still she
could not understand what the movement implied.

"I am so happy, Paolo, so happy," she said.
She laughed softly. "I don't know what happened
to us," she said. "I don't think I knew what I was
doing. I was frightened—about your parchments,
I mean—and when you were silent for so long I
thought that they were no good to you after all.
You see? And then when I knew that it was only
your funny ways, why, then I was so happy that I
thought my heart would break. It would have

broken of itself, Paolo, if we hadn't kissed each other. And now . . . oh, now I feel as if all this life had been blotted out, as if I had become a little girl again—you know?—in the days when we used to go out picking the flowers of St. Joseph on the hills in spring-time. Yes, just like waking up early in the morning in spring. You've never heard the birds in my country, Paolo, so you can't imagine it. Here in Naples I don't think any birds exist."

As she spoke her voice took to itself the tones of a dreamy, vernal softness that was intolerable to Paul. Her words were gentle, pleading; her hands stole out and touched him as she spoke. Her fingers wandered in a soft possessive ecstasy over his features. Rather than wound her by failing to respond, he stooped and picked up the parchments from the floor and re-examined them awkwardly. She came to his side once more and peered at them. It seemed natural to her to want to be near him, and Paul was grateful for any diversion that might resolve the emotional stress of the vein in which she had been speaking.

"You didn't say that to please me, Paolo?" she said. "They are really what you want?"

"Can't you believe me? I might sift the whole of Naples and find nothing so perfect."

"Ah, Paolo, if only I'd known before!"

"You're a worker of miracles, Cristina. A white witch. How did you do it? Tell me, where did you get them from?"

She shook her head pitifully. "Don't ask me, Paolo, my dear one. Must I tell you the truth? You've been kissing a thief. I stole them."

" But where ?   And how ?   And from whom ?
You must tell me !   Make me your confessor,
Cristina."

" No, no, I daren't," she murmured.   All the
old fear came back into her eyes.   He had seen that
look before and knew its origin.   " I think I was
mad," she said.   " Just mad with happiness.
Now I daren't think of it.   Oh, Paolo, dear, don't
ask me . . ."

" But you've told me already," he cried, triumphantly.   " Your master, the man we call the black
hunter !   But how in the name of goodness . . .? "

" Don't, don't ! " she whispered.   " For God's
sake don't even speak of him.   You, of all people on
earth ! "

Her face grew blank and crushed with misery ;
there was no happiness, no possibility of happiness
in it ; her eyes communicated a fear so desperate
that Paul himself became afraid for her.   He spoke
solemnly :

" Cristina, you have no right to run any risk for
my sake.   If these parchments are his, it's better
that you should take them back to where you found
them.   There's a certain dignity. . . . How can I
profit by things that are stolen ?   If I might pay for
them it would be different."

" No, no," she cried, with a sudden renewal of
passion.   " Of course you can't pay for them.
How could I even speak of it to him ?   Besides,
they are mine . . . mine.   I have a right to them.
Nobody can dispute my right.   Haven't I paid for
them a hundred thousand times ?   Take them, take
them, Paolo !   They are nothing."

He could not agree with her. "You're wrong, Cristina. I don't think you understand. Not that they're actually valuable by themselves ; the value's a small thing ; but—how shall I put it ?—their condition, their workmanship, everything about them make them. . . . I was going to say unique, but that's not the right word. To put it quite crudely, they're likely to be missed. And then . . . for your own sake . . ."

"No, they will never be missed," she assured him emphatically. "Not even if I had dared to bring you a dozen more. Oh, Paolo, I beg you, think no more about it, and above all, don't think of me. Why, even now . . ."

She stopped suddenly and stood transfixed like a wild animal that has caught the scent of an enemy. The silence of the empty house was intense enough to breed fear of itself. Paul felt compelled to break in on it ruthlessly.

"Why do you stop ?" he said. "Cristina, you're so mysterious. You mean that there are more, many more ? "

"Yes, there are many more. But, please, don't ask me ! "

"Then our friend is a collector ? "

"A collector ? I don't understand."

"And in this house . . .? " he persisted.

"Oh, Paolo, don't torment me. Be merciful, be kind ! " She stood before him entreating, with clasped hands. "Now I must go," she said. "Already I've stayed here too long. This is the time at which he often comes here. Good-bye . . ."

But still Cristina did not go. She waited. And

Paul, a little puzzled and cold, knew what she was waiting for.   Of his own accord he could not give it, for that moment of strange madness had passed irrevocably.   Not even as a duty, as payment for a debt incurred, could he move to meet her.   An obstinate inhibition, that the pleading in her eyes could not melt, froze his body.   Not even pity now . . . He felt himself hard and unresponsive as steel, and feared that she must be aware of his hardness.   Swiftly, softly, she crept again into his arms, and, for one moment, pressed her lips to his unwilling cheek.   It was as if she did not realise his rebellious coldness, as if her own glowing warmth sufficed for both.   Sick with the consciousness of his own baseness, thankful that she did not perceive it, he submitted to her embrace.   They parted. One moment she stood at the doorway with rapture in her face.

"To-night," she said, "I shall reach paradise without need of stairs."

Book Three

PURGATORIO

K

Book Three

PURGATORIO

I

SHE went. . . . For all the rest of his life Paul
Ritchie was to remember that parting ; the ominous
sun-drenched silence of Viva's little room ; the
figure of Cristina standing in the doorway with
arms outstretched, and on her features the transfiguration of a beautiful saint. " To-night I shall
reach paradise without the need of stairs," she had
said. Those words, that voice, had a strange power
of persistence, outlasting all others, even the most
moving, that he had heard in forty years of a laborious
life. There, through the darkness of the steamer's
upper deck, they returned to him with a devastating
clearness, defying the passage of time as completely
as if their syllables had been stamped indelibly on
the ether that still, as then, enveloped the gleaming
cupola of the *Carmine*. Again and again, in spite
of himself, Paul Ritchie was forced to hear them :
those symbols of an exalted, unapproachable
happiness, of a cruel, irremediable despair.

By an extreme effort of will he succeeded in
launching himself out of that vortex into the hardly
less violent flood of memories that followed. It
was a passage full of blackness and terror, with the
roar of nearing rapids in his ears ; and yet he knew
that, whatever suffering, whatever humiliation it

cost him, he must go through with it. It was the
penalty of this rash, deliberate return ; the last and
bloody-footed league of his appointed pilgrimage ;
an act of penance, of atonement, of lustration, by
which, if ever, the hauntings of the past might be
appeased and dissipated.

*   *   *   *

He saw himself standing behind the closed doors
of Viva's room. On the table beside him lay the
parchments that Cristina had stolen for him : the
means of his salvation, the evidence of his shame.
For though the gift had come to him of her own free
will, he felt that he had retained it under false
pretences. His sternly scrupulous nature, that
legacy of his father's Northern blood, assured him of
this. It rebelled not only against the idea of
handling and profiting by the possession of stolen
goods, but against Cristina's obvious misunderstanding of his feelings toward her. "They are
mine. . . . I've paid for far more than that," she
had declared ; but the assertion was one that he
couldn't conscientiously accept, and even if he
accepted it, there remained the false conception of
his relation toward her that her last words implied,
the ghastly misunderstanding of their two embraces :
the first an act of madness, committed in a moment
of exaltation and prolonged by heaven knew what
weakness in his physical nature ; the second an
outcome of no emotion more passionate than pity
for her misguided innocence.

"She loves me," he thought ; and the sudden
magnificence of his own unconscious achievement

made his head spin.   Without word or deed he had
accomplished the conquest in which the skilful and
sedulous Viva had failed.   " But I do not love her,"
he told himself.   " She is older, much older than
the woman that I should love.   She is not beautiful,
as I imagine beauty."   He remembered with distaste
the unpleasant discoveries at which Viva had
hinted.   " She is soiled, polluted, second-hand,"
he thought ; " the mistress of that black bull of a
fellow whom she calls her master.   How can I
hesitate ?   Of course I do not love her ! "

Yet, in the midst of this assertion, he did hesitate.
He remembered, in a mixture of ardour, shame and
discomfort, the waves of blood that had beat in his
ears and blinded him, the silken smoothness of the
skin that his fingers had caressed, the sweet and
penetrating warmth of Cristina's yielding body, the
enervating softness of her lips on his.   " That isn't
love," he cried ; but even as he protested, her
grace, her humility, her lonely, pitiful childishness
reproved him.   He was haunted by the pleading
gentleness of her eyes.   " Are you cruel enough to
deprive me of the only happiness I have ever
known ? " they seemed to ask him.   " If you are
as cruel as that, Paolo," they said, " I would rather
be dead."

All through the burning afternoon, while he
worked at the Institute, he struggled with these
problems, but could not solve them.   The South
wind seemed to have borne a heavy stupor of
middle Africa upon its wings ; the gulf was like a
cauldron of molten lead : there was no power of
life or thought beneath the sky's oppression.   It

seemed as if, in some subtle way, his whole nature
had changed.   As he worked in the crowded
classroom, he became conscious, for the first time in
his life, of something more than a study of lines and
planes in the form of the nude model that posed for
them.   Her body, which hitherto he had almost
taken for granted, became invested, in spite of
himself, with the attributes of Cristina's ; its curves
awakened hot memories that centred not in his eyes,
but in the trembling hands which held his pencil,
amplifying the knowledge of things that had been
hidden from him that morning.   His eyes were so
greedily intent that he could not draw, and a panic
seized him lest this intrusive emotion should ruin
his growing power.

"If she comes to me again to-night," he thought,
"I will make my position clear to her.   It's better
to do so at once than that we should live another
moment in such an atmosphere of falseness."

But Cristina did not come again that evening,
and as the hours wore on Paul's first scruples seemed
to lose their strength.   The hard, realistic strain of
peasant blood that his mother had given him
reasserted itself, bringing his thoughts back to the
stage of frustration and hopelessness with which the
morning had begun.   There, on Viva's table, lay
the parchments that solved his material difficulties.
No scruples troubled Cristina, the person most
intimately concerned.   Why should they trouble
him ?   For himself, he had acted honourably.   He
had offered to pay for any that she brought him.
That, she said, was impossible ; his honourable
offer had been refused.   There were so many

parchments where these came from, she said, that
she could have brought him a dozen more without
the least danger of their being missed. Where,
where? And in the name of heaven, why?

That was a question which some queer taboo
prevented her from answering, and though its
pursuit fascinated and puzzled him, after all, it was
none of his business. No doubt, in the course of
time, the matter would straighten itself out. In
time he might even induce her to let him pay for
what he used. He found a feeble satisfaction, but
satisfaction none the less, in the prospect of this
virtuous atonement for a venial and purely tem-
porary sin. He took the parchments away into his
room and began to work on them.

But though the renewal of mechanical activity
engrossed him, the larger and more personal
question of his relation with Cristina continued to
give him trouble; and here, again, his way became
smoother than he had expected; for always, in the
depths of his mind, like a smouldering fire, there
lay hidden the memory of his instinctive response
to her embrace. He knew nothing of women;
he had always been afraid of them. Viva and Viva's
student friends were forever taunting him with his
ignorance and timidity. Let them continue their
taunts! He could bear them, and even with secret
satisfaction, if this strange business reached its
natural end. Knowledge and courage would have
come to him without his seeking them. A woman
whose virtue had defied all Viva's skilful ruses had
come, of her own accord, to his arms: a conquest
very different from Viva's sordid loves! He'd

have the laugh of them yet. As he mused on this triumph, his hands intent upon the growing work, that smoulder in the depths of his mind quickened to a flame.

And even if, in his soul, he did not love Cristina, even if these uncontrollable flickerings were something other than love, what right had he to refuse her devotion, her generosity? She was so childlike, so honest, so free from all guile. So pitiful.

Once more that treacherous word aroused in him a sense of obligation. What right had he to treat her innocent emotions with scorn? For they were innocent. Like a child awakening early on a spring morning, she had said. If she had been the wife of the black hunter it would have been another matter. She was his mistress, and only that by Viva's prurient account. For herself, she had never admitted it. Whenever she had spoken of her " master " it had been in frightened whispers that implied darkness, mystery, terror—anything but love : which made it all the more reasonable that her weakness should be cherished and protected, her desolation solaced, her sadness mitigated by any gleam of happiness that he, her only friend and more than friend, could bring into her sombre life. Now that he knew that such a thing was possible, it was his duty, as a human being, to provide it. Slowly, but thoroughly, after the manner of young imaginations, he was beginning to recreate and sentimentalise the figure of a woman who had smiled on him, clothing it with virtues and graces, with a beauty, even, that her presence would have denied. In that wholly virgin soil the seed throve valiantly as the miraculous beanstalk, touching unimagined altitudes in a night.

When Viva came in, tired and disgruntled, that evening, he found Paul still working in the imperfect light.

"I'm starved to death," he said, pitching his hat into a corner. "Nothing to eat since breakfast, and damned little then, and that cursed professor of surgery biting my head off all day. Hello . . . what's this? *Cristo!* you don't say that the tide's turned? Have you stolen some parchment, Paolo?"

Paul laughed out loud. Stolen. That was the word, though Viva didn't know it.

"Two sheets," he answered. "Three boxes. We'll have a good meal to-morrow, my son."

"To-morrow be damned!" cried Viva. "I'll find credit somewhere to-night. This calls for a bottle of wine. Give me my hat."

Paul tossed it to him. It was stirring to see the rapidity with which Viva's chilled spirits expanded like mercury in a finely adjusted clinical thermometer. When he had gone on his foraging errand Paul lit two lavish candles, and set himself feverishly to recover lost time. So absorbed was he now that there was no room in his mind for anything but the joy of swift, sure craftsmanship, all warmed by the glow of Viva's careless good spirits. Within an hour Viva returned, his pockets triumphantly bulging and a bottle of wine in either hand.

"I've fished out that slut Cristina," he panted, "and in a quarter of an hour the *maccheroni* will be ready. I broke the good news to her that your luck had turned Paolo. You'd have thought that, being such a special fancy of yours, she'd have been pleased to hear the news—the grocer was, I can assure you!—but not a bit of it! Sullen as a dog, she was. That woman hasn't a spark of life or feeling in her : no wonder she's never managed to catch a husband."

They dined. Viva ate voraciously. The meal was coloured with his boisterous humour. Cristina waited on them. A strange, subdued Cristina, made mothlike, ghostlike, by the still shine of candlelight. Like a dark moth she hovered, softly, in the shadows ; her white hands fluttered to the lighted table and were gone. Viva, refreshed and stimulated, forgot his grudging, and tried to draw her out of the dusk into the vivid lightning-flickers of his conversation. Perhaps he still had hopes of making a conquest ; but for that end, at least, he might have spared his scintillations. Cristina was more silent—more sullen, he would have called it—than ever. Only, out of her silence, her presence spoke to Paul more clearly, more piercingly than words.

All through the meal he was conscious of her warm immanence, and, as the unaccustomed plenitude of food and wine inflamed him, there followed a sense of triumph in the secret which Viva, for all his smartness, couldn't penetrate, of pride in the assertion of his new-born manhood. This festival was his and Cristina's, Viva was their guest, their dupe. Once, when Pietro wasn't looking, he raised his glass to her. Out of the darkness she answered him with no word, not even with a smile, but with a look of gentleness that gave her, suddenly, all the beauty with which his imagination had dowered her in her absence. When, late that night, Paul tumbled into bed, his body and mind still quivered in a strange, exalted confusion.

II

WITH daylight came the inevitable reaction. Paul was still sleeping when Viva entered his room to growl good-morning before he carried his sore head and bleary eyes to hospital. The hot *scirocco* still dragged its languid tail over the African sea ; the morning air fainted beneath its moist oppression; even the water with which he swilled his sleepy eyes felt dead and tepid on the skin. Before he had finished dressing Cristina knocked discreetly on his door to tell him that breakfast was ready. When he entered Viva's room she was standing, waiting for him.

At the sight of her, in that clear morning light, her figure clothed in the black overall that he knew so well, his damped spirits suffered a sudden shock. This was the Cristina with whom for months he had been familiar, the awkward, silent woman of their first encounter, never, for one possible moment, the creature whose presence had thrilled him and whose memory had inflamed his passion on the night before. A gust of wonder, almost of distaste, blew through him. He grew shy, ashamed, fearful lest his averted eyes should show her what he was feeling.

Perhaps, indeed, she was dimly conscious of his embarrassment; for the smile with which she greeted

him was timid and subdued, and her voice, when she
spoke of ordinary things, had a note of strain and
diffidence in it. He turned his back on her, in an
access of clumsy self-consciousness, as he began to
eat. She watched him from a distance. He
would have been happier if she had left him alone.

"You slept well, Paolo?" she asked him quietly,
at last.

"Moderately well," he answered, afraid that any
word of his might lead them into paths of danger.

"You drank too much Gragnano. I was
watching you. With Viva it doesn't matter—he is
more coarsely built, and will go on drinking whenever he has the opportunity till he dies. But you,
oh my Paolo, with you, it is different. I would
have tried to warn you if I had dared. But I am so
timid. You'll never know how strangely shy I felt:
as if we had never set eyes on each other before. So
shy, so tender, so happy! Then, when I went to
bed, I lay awake thinking about you, Paolo, hour
after hour. I told you, didn't I, that I should sleep
in paradise? This morning, somehow, it is
different. I can't think why, for neither of us can
have changed. Perhaps the blessed saints will not
allow us too much of heaven for fear that we should
die of happiness."

Indeed, it was different. It seemed monstrous to
Paul that he should be unmoved by her words; for
there was nothing in them that did not speak of
love, of gentleness, of goodness, of all the undeniable
virtues that he could not accept from her. He
could not accept them, he told himself; yet had he
not already accepted and used the parchments that

she had stolen for him? Could he take one without the other? And was not her generosity more acceptable in the first case than in the second? The damnable falsity of his whole position stifled him and made him dumb. He could not thank her; he did not love her; and yet, without those leaves of parchment, the fruits of her devoted dishonesty, he could not hope to live, nor, what was equally important, to fulfil the passionate destiny of his art. For more than a fortnight now he had not touched a canvas; the thwarted lust of creation burned in his brain and fingers. Here, in Cristina's munificent kindness, lay the power to assuage that passion: an inexhaustible store of the materials by which he lived. Beggars, they said, should not be choosers. A single word of tenderness from him would not only make life and art together possible, but also fill her empty existence with the joy of service and sacrifice.

Paul could not speak that word. Never since the day of his arrival in Naples had he felt more impotently miserable. Cristina, apparently, did not guess his misery, or, if she guessed, was too simple to interpret it rightly. The workings of a young man's heart were unfathomable, shadowed by strange moods; a woman gained nothing by probing too deeply into them. Her part was less complicated than that. It was enough that she should give him love, sympathy, devotion to the last that was in her, and if these failed the fault would lie with destiny rather than with herself.

Deftly and sweetly she accommodated herself to Paul's incomprehensible mood. She left him to

finish his bitter meal in silence; he could hear
her moving in his room next door, singing softly
to herself as she reduced the disorder of his restless
night and set his table ready for the morning's
work. And Paul sat on stubbornly over his unfinished breakfast, half hoping that, when she had
finished, she would have sufficient tact and sensi-
tiveness to leave him alone. He heard the door of
his room close quietly behind her. A long silence
followed, and with a feeling of precious relief, he
compelled his thoughts into the direction of the
unfinished task which awaited him in the adjoining
room. His hopes had overrun themselves. Suddenly, stealthily, Cristina re-entered. She was
standing at his elbow. Her voice was low and
breathless as she leaned close to him:

"Look, Paolo," she said. "Look, I have
brought you these. Tell me quickly if they are
right. If they won't do I'll change them. I'm so
ignorant that I don't really know for certain what
you want."

She thrust before his eyes a sheaf of seven pages,
enough to keep him busy for a week. The parchment, in its ivory innocence, tempted his greedy
eyes.

"Cristina," he stammered. "Oh, why have you
done this?"

"Because I love you, Paolo," she laughed softly.
"Isn't that reason good enough?"

"No, no. How can you say so? Of course I
can't take them. You know that they're not yours
to give."

"But haven't I told you, my dear one, that

there are hundreds . . . thousands ? If I brought
you as many as these every morning they'd never be
missed. Nobody will ever know, my darling, but
you and me."

He laughed, in spite of himself, at her innocent
guile. "But we are supposed to be honest people,
Cristina, which makes it impossible. Surely you
can see that ? "

For a moment her conviction wavered, but only
for a moment. "In love," she declared magnificently, "such things do not count. They're
nothing compared with what I'd be ready to do
for you. Besides, what is it ? A few francs more
or less ! "

"In principle . . ." he began.

"Ah, principles ! " she cried. "That word's
beyond me, Paolo. But look," she went on, as in
the flush of a new and important discovery, "don't
you see, if there is any wrong, it's I who have done
it, not you ? So that you, my dear, are absolved.
Isn't that simple ? Now you can put your dear
conscience to sleep again. Now you can take
them, Paolo ? "

The childishness of her casuistry was disarming ;
but still his will resisted, supported not so much
by the weight of honourable scruples—for the
matter, as she had half persuaded him, was a small
one—but by an obstinate and sinister premonition
that if he yielded to her persuasions at this stage
he would commit himself to a falseness without end.
He struggled to find words for a refusal that would
not wound her too deeply. Cristina, seeing him
waver, swiftly changed the angle of her attack.

"I see that you want to make a fool of me," she said, with a sudden, bitter intensity. "Ah, Paolo, how cold, how calculating, how inhuman you are! Do you think I can't read you? Well, let's admit the truth, the last word of it: that you despise me as a light woman, a wanton, a fool of a wanton, who has set out to catch you with a bait that she's stolen. Isn't that what you're thinking? It is, I know it; and that's why you don't dare to answer me. Oh, but what lies you imagine, how cruel, how unjust you are! Now you shall hear the truth. I'll tell you everything; and even if you don't believe me you shall listen. From the beginning . . ."

He would have protested his innocence of the thoughts she imputed to him; for whatever else there may have been in his mind, there was no scorn in it; nothing, indeed, but a vague, instinctive misgiving that he stood on the verge of some situation that threatened incalculable disaster to his peace of mind. He would have explained; but even as he opened his lips the flood burst over him.

"From the beginning . . . Ah, you know nothing of what goes to make a life, even a life like mine. I've told you about my childhood, a word here and there. Up in the mountains of Venezia. I come of country-people, like yourself. In winter there was snow: mile after mile of it, so white, so sparkling; and an air that made your body tingle. But that is a dream. What I remember is spring. The flowers . . . Oh, Paolo, if you had only seen them! Such a big greenness, and the bees making honey, and little swallows chirruping and sitting huddled up together under the eaves : long sloping eaves of wooden clatters such as you've never seen. My father would never shoot the swallows. Mother told me so. He kept a baby wolf in a cage . . . And that's all I remember of him. The holy sisters never talked of any father but God in the orphanage at Padua. Many of the children there hadn't ever had a father : I suppose that was the reason. I think I must have been very miserable in the orphanage at first, just like a lost lamb, and the other children so cunning and so much at home ; but all that's so long ago tha I almost forget about it. Only the cold I remember. Blue, stony cold. We used to rub our hands in the morning to thaw them before we could feel the beads of our rosaries. Oh, how the needles used to slip through our shiny fingers ! Our little souls and bodies were all frozen up together so that we couldn't think ; only sew, and sew, and sew . . ." Her voice slowed and softened in the monotony of her memories, until she was silent.

" Why am I talking about Padua ? " she went on suddenly. " That's all past history ; it means nothing to us. A woman came to the orphanage to look for a servant. I was stronger than most of the other girls. I was always a strong one, even at thirteen. I suppose that was why she chose me. She ran her eyes over me like a cabman buying a horse. She was a fat, sad woman, with no life in her. She looked so cold, so cruel that I was frightened to death of her ; though, really, I needn't have been scared at all. You see, she had just lost her husband and come up to Padua from Naples

L

because her sister lived there. She took me away from the orphanage. We drove to the station in the rain—all the cabs with their hoods up, and the people crowded under long colonnades. We travelled all night in the train. She slept with her mouth open and snored, but I could do nothing but cry and cry and cry, very quietly, so that the other people in the carriage shouldn't hear me. Think of it! I'd never been in a train before; I was half dead with fright and loneliness. If the carriage had run off the lines in the night I shouldn't have minded. Dear, dear, how distant it seems!

" Afterwards I knew that even if she had heard me crying she wouldn't have comforted me. Her own unhappiness made her blind to everything else. You see she was going back to Naples—to Torre del Greco, rather—where she'd been happily married for twenty years, coming back to the emptiness of the house where they'd lived together, she and Gargiulo—that was her husband's name— with no company but the wretched red-haired little orphan she'd picked up in Padua. Her own life was finished, poor dear, and why should she think of me?

" But she did, Paolo; she did, later on. For three years that woman was like a mother to me. Partly I suppose, because I was a Northerner like herself, and her own daughter Caterina was a Neapolitan taking after the husband. It was a quiet life a Torre; but the sun used to shine as I don't believe it ever shone in Padua, and we had plenty to eat In spring, when the peach-trees were in blossom we used to take a walk in the evening, up towar

Vesuvius. The Signora Gargiulo walked slowly, leaning on my arm. She was too heavy to go very far. Ah, the sweet evenings!

" And on summer nights, Paolo, there were fire-works; the people at Torre are proud of being very religious. One *festa* after another, all summer long! We had a balcony that looked out over the gulf; you could sit and see the rockets and fire-balls bursting all along the shore, and on these evenings of *festa* old friends of the Signora's husband —he'd been a haulier—used to drop in and drink a bottle of wine with her and watch the fires. That used to brighten her up like nothing else, dear soul! She had a way that put men at ease; they knew that she understood them, and they respected Gargiulo's memory. I think she could easily have married again if she'd fancied it. She had money in the bank, besides land and the house that we lived in. ' But then,' she used to say, ' I've lived my life. This is the day of the young ones, Cristina.' She had an old proverb to fit everything, so that you almost knew before she spoke what she would say next.

" The men who came to the house were very kind to me too. You see Signora Gargiulo treated me like a daughter. She knew that young girls like flattery, and encouraged them. I was young and pretty in those days, Paolo, and red girls like me were rare in Naples. ' One of these days,' she used to say, ' before I'm gone, we shall have to get you married.' ' No, no, I shall never leave you,' I told her. Then she'd shake her head. ' Don't be so sure, my child,' she'd say. ' That is a matter of destiny.' *Destiny* . . . *He* was one of the friends of her husband who used to come and visit her. You know who I mean?"

She paused, a little anxiously. Paolo assented.

"I liked him, too," she went on. "I must speak the truth, Paolo; I liked him as well as any of them. He used to come down with his gun in the autumn and shoot quails in the Gargiulo property. He would cook them, and eat them with us. Ten years ago . . . You see he was much younger then, far younger than any of the others; thirty-five, perhaps. He was dark and strong and manly; he looked you straight in the face, and his eyes held you. He looked like a fighter. And he did fight : for me, too. He used to take my part against the old woman's daughter. Caterina, her name was. Oh, but I'm wandering—I've told you her name before! Caterina was jealous of the way in which her mother treated me; she couldn't bear to see me used as anything but a servant. And she was jealous, also, because *he* looked at me, although she had a husband of her own in Castellamare. He knew that too. He has eyes in the back of his head. I think he had a passing fancy for Caterina as well. Well, anyone would do for him, as long as it was a woman; and just to make Caterina wild he'd play me off against her, like the devil he is. It was just a good joke for him; he loves to make women jealous; it's half his joy in life.

"And I, little fool," she continued, bitterly, "was so flattered that I hadn't the wits to see why Caterina hated me! But when her mother died, I knew soon enough! It came quite suddenly—

the end, I mean.   Of course her breath had been
bad for a long time.   Her legs were all swollen,
and they said it was the fluid that had reached her
heart.   I was with her when she went, all alone
with her.   I'd never seen death before—nor since,
thank God!—when my own mother died I was too
little to know.   But this time it was terrible.   I
ran out into the street crying; people must have
thought I was mad.   I'd only lived with her three
years, but she'd become everything to me, all I had
in the world.   Then I sat in the corner of the room
and cried.   Some women came in to lay her out;
the police were sent for to put on the seals, but
Caterina was there before them.   Can you believe
it?   Even when that poor thing was lying dead
Caterina was tearing the mattress to pieces, looking
for money.   She was far too busy to take any
notice of me; but when I saw her behave like that
I could bear it no longer.   I flew at her in a fury.
'How dare you, how dare you?' I cried.   'You
shall not touch her!'   Terrible, in that dark room,
with her own mother lying there dead, and Caterina,
her mouth twisted, her eyes blazing with madness
to get at the money!   I caught her arm and tried
to drag her away; but she was stronger than me.
She fought like a cat and forced me down on the
floor, then threw me into the corner of the room.

"'You little snake,' she said, 'what business of
yours is it what I do?   At last she's escaped from
your clutches, you bastard brat!' she said.   'How
do I know what you haven't stolen already?   You
with your creeping ways and your thieving blood!
I'll have you stripped, if you're not careful, to see

what you've got hidden on you; I'll have you
searched by the police. You came into this house
like a beggar,' she said, ' and a beggar you shall
leave it, trust me for that! Why, even your clothes
are not your own. What's this that you're
wearing?'

"She came down on me like a hawk and tore my
apron from me. It wasn't really mine, that is true;
but her mother had always let me wear it in the
afternoon. 'Now go,' she said. ' Get out of this
house at once, and let me never see your ugly white
face again!' She pulled me on to my feet; she
was as strong as a man. She pushed me to the
door. I fell on the stone stairs. First death, and
then this . . . I was as helpless as an idiot. Then
she began to kick me—I think she must have been
mad with hatred. She was screaming at the top
of her voice and the neighbours stood and stared.
Not a friend, not a single friend, and Caterina
shouting her filthy insults after me. They made
way for me to pass. ' Where can I go?' I said.
' I've nowhere to go. Oh, let me stay here a
little!' Caterina came flying down the stairs behind me. The people were laughing at both of
us, but she took no notice. ' Out of the house,'
she shouted, ' out of it! Where can you go?
Why, into the street where you came from. Go
there, and earn your living as your mother did
before you!'"

Cristina drew her breath sharply, as though the
insult still had power to wound her.

"Paolo, I didn't even know then what she meant.
If I had known, I think I should have snatched up

a knife and killed her. I heard someone saying it
was a shame, but nobody raised a finger to help me.
Cowards! They were all cowards, like the people
are here. Caterina came up close behind me with
her claws lifted, and I rushed out into the street.
The light outside was blinding, after the dark house,
and my eyes were dazzled with tears. I ran along
the street crying aloud; but people only turned
and stared at me. Why, anyone could be murdered
in the streets of Torre and no one turn a hair!
I ran and ran; I didn't know where I was going.
I didn't care . . .

"Then somebody caught me by the arm. It
was *he*. You know . . . I must have looked like
a mad dog running through the street. 'Why,
Cristina, my little Cristina,' he said, 'whatever's
the matter with you?'

"'She's dead, she's dead; the mistress is dead!'
I told him. I could think of nothing else. 'She's
dead, and Caterina has thrown me out of the
house.' He quickly let go of my arm and crossed
himself. 'Dead? My God!' he said. 'And
where are you going to now?' I told him what
Caterina had said. He laughed. 'The jealous
devil! That's our Caterina all over,' he said.
'But where are you going to, seriously, Cristina?'

"I told him that I'd spoken the truth, that I
didn't know.

"He made up his mind in the quick way that
he has. 'Well, then, I'll tell you,' he said. 'You're
coming with me. Do you understand what I say?'

"I didn't understand. At that moment I think
I'd have gone with any living soul who had spoken

a kind word to me. He called a cab and helped me into it, and told the driver where to go. I suppose we must have driven for miles and miles, but I remember nothing : only my crying, that nothing could stop, and the smell of his cigar, and the sun . . . the blinding sun. We drove through the barrier of the *dazio* and into Naples. He paid the cabman in the *piazza*, just outside here. We walked down the *Vicolo*, to the door of this house. I've been here ever since."

Again she was silent ; then turned her eyes on him pleadingly :

" Ten years, Paolo," she said. " I was only sixteen . . .

" At first he was very kind to me. Not even the devil could have been anything else to such a miserable creature as I was. He left me all alone in the house. He'd just bought it cheap—you see his father had died a little before, and he'd become very rich—partly to let in lodgings, and partly as a warehouse. He kept the ground floor for himself and for me. And I was really fortunate, in a way. It was fate. If I hadn't run into his arms, so to speak, at that moment, heaven knows what would have happened to me. Perhaps I might have become what Caterina suggested ; I was so utterly innocent. And in those days, you know, he was much younger, and quite gentle with me. He used to treat me . . . how shall I say ? . . . rather like the little wolf that my father kept in a cage : I was a little wild animal, just kept there to play with in spare moments. But always the cage . . .

" And of course he made love to me, Paolo. I

was terribly shy and scared of him ; but that, too, was only part of his play.   From the first he forbade me to talk to any of the tenants—oh, yes, even then he could be frightening at times—so that he was the only living person whom I ever saw.   It was amusing, yes, and rather exciting too, to have a house of my own to look after.   I took a strange pride in it ; working, working away to forget my unhappiness.   The place was so old and dirty when first I came here.   You can have no idea how I scrubbed and scrubbed at the floors.   He used to laugh at me and tease me too, pretending to find dirty corners that I'd neglected.   But sometimes he got angry and impatient to see me working, because, when he came, he expected to find me waiting for him.   And sometimes he'd joke with me about other things, though I didn't know he was joking.   'When are you going to marry me, Cristina ? ' he'd say.   Not that he ever intended to marry me.   I didn't know till long after that he had a wife already in his other house.   If he had really wanted me to marry him in those days, I'd have done so.   I supposed that everything was all right ; that we should be married later.   I thought of it often, quite seriously, just waiting for him to speak the word.   And then . . ."

She stopped dead of a sudden.   " Paolo, don't look at me like that, or I can't go on telling you. You don't help me at all.   You don't say a single word !   You're just like a stone."

He couldn't even help himself, poor lad.

" I wasn't looking at you, Cristina," was all that he could stammer.

"Oh, yes, you were," she cried; "but no matter. Whether you like it or no, you've got to hear. When I told him that I was going to have a baby, he wouldn't believe it. He went off in a fury, and brought back an old woman, a midwife, out of the *fondaco*. She came in mumbling and chewing fennel seeds. I can smell her breath and her rags when I think of her now. He tramped the room, up and down, till she'd finished with me. 'All my good wishes,' she said, 'let's hope it will be a man.'

"If black looks could have killed her! He took her by the shoulder and dragged her into a corner. I could hear them whispering together. She was trying her best to bleed him, the old scarecrow, laying it on about the danger, the police, blackmail from the chemist. 'My sister,' she said, 'my own dear sister's in prison for a job of that kind at this moment. It's not so safe in these days as it used to be . . . It'll cost you two hundred francs. Not a *soldo* less!'

"I listened, and just at first I didn't guess what they were after. Then suddenly I knew what they meant. I'd heard enough talk in Naples for that— they wanted to kill my baby, Paolo, they wanted to kill my baby before it was born! I jumped up and ran to them. 'You shan't, you shan't do it!' I shouted. 'It's my baby, it's mine! You've no right to touch me, any of you. I won't swallow anything you give me, not if I have to starve myself to death!' The old woman grinned at me and waved her hand. 'Eh, wait till you know as much about child-bearing as I do; then you'd change

your tune, you little fool!' He shut her mouth
for her. I'd never seen him in such a black fury
before. Then he turned on me; stormed at me.
He was the master in this house, he said, and I'd
got to do what he ordered. I'd do anything else,
I said, anything but that! It was funny . . .
When I knew that what I'd suspected was true, I
wanted nothing in the world so much as the baby.
Heaven knows what I said: I went quite mad, I
think. Something in what I said must have maddened him too. He caught me by the neck and
sent me spinning across the room. I think I must
have struck my head somewhere and lost my senses.
When I came round again the two had gone.

"After that day I don't think I was ever happy
again: for, up till then, I had been happy, in a way.
I expected so little, Paolo. How many nights I
lay awake wishing I was dead! When once he'd
got over his first annoyance, he was a little kinder;
but never the same as before. It might have been
worse. I suppose some men would have turned
me out of the house. He didn't do that, thank
heaven! Of course I was useful to him. If he'd
got rid of me he'd only have had to get someone
else to take care of the house and have paid them
for it, so it was cheaper to keep me. And though
he hated the thought of the baby coming, he used
to come and visit me just the same. I had to put
up with that; I couldn't stop him coming. When
he was with me I used to make myself think of
something else: queer things—it sounds foolish
when I tell you—like the snow in Venezia and the
peach-blossom behind Torre and the sisters in the

orphanage.   Some days he'd come and go without
speaking a word.   He'd give me a look as if I
filled him with disgust.   And sometimes, when he
lost his temper, he'd beat me like a dog and leave
me to cry by myself for hours and hours.   And if
he saw a speck of dust in the house he'd rave like
a lunatic and swear I was lazy.   I used to feel so
tired, so tired in those days . . .

   " And then my baby was born.   I was all alone
in the house.   I had to crawl to the window and
cry to a woman in the street.   It was a girl, Paolo ;
but the poor little thing never breathed.   So tiny !
I only saw it for a moment.   Oh, but it's silly of
me to cry like this.   It was so long ago . . .

   " The neighbours said I was a lucky girl.   Perhaps they were right ; perhaps the baby was lucky
too, to have died before she was born ; but if she'd
lived I shouldn't have been quite so lonely through
all these years.   Sometimes I used to tell myself I
was foolish to stay here ; but one life, it seems to
me, is very like another, and I've grown used to
this one now.   It's what the old woman at Torre
would have called my destiny.   The house keeps
me busy ; I have enough to eat ; then, two or three
times a week he still comes here.   That's what I
dread.   Although I've known him all these years,
I can never guess what his temper's going to be
like.   Sometimes, when he's tired out with hunting,
he's too lazy to notice anything much.   At others,
particularly when he's been drinking, he comes in
angry, as ready to beat me as to look at me.   Then
it's hell, Paolo, hell !   I can't be certain, you see.
That's why I tremble and turn to ice when I hear

him coming. You never know. One moment
he's smiling; the next he's like a wild beast. I
think he believes it's best to keep women frightened.
And he's so jealous, too! Why, if he ever caught
me speaking to one of the neighbours he'd flay me.
When first I dared to ask him if I might wait on
Viva and yourself . . . No, I won't tell you what
he said . . .

"And that's my life . . . or rather that was my
life, Paolo, until you came here. Perhaps I
shouldn't have told you? I wouldn't have told
you, my dear, if it hadn't been burning my heart
out all night in the darkness. I used to watch
you, at first. You were such a strange creature,
so different from ordinary men like your friend
Pietro. I couldn't understand you, and I wanted
to understand. Because . . . somehow . . . you
didn't belong to this part of my life. When I was
near you I seemed different; I felt as I used to
feel—but I've told you—when the birds began to
twitter in the spring, as I used to feel at Torre
when first I came there. All the rest—it was as if
it had slipped out of my life, leaving nothing that
wasn't happy and beautiful. Oh, Paolo, Paolo,
you've made my heart so young. And last night
when you kissed me . . ."

She clung to him with closed eyes.

"No, no, you can't love me," she whispered, "I
know it's too late for that; but if you pity me,
Paolo, I shall die with shame. You know that I've
not been asking for your pity? Swear to me that
you'll never pity me, Paolo! Once and for
all?"

She would not be satisfied till he had given his promise.

"Neither love nor pity," she said. "All that I want is that you'll not despise me, even though I deserve to be despised : just that, and that you'll think of me kindly. As though I were your sister, Paolo : your friend and your sister. I'm not too old to be your sister, am I, Paolo ? "

"Of course you're not, Cristina," he assured her.

"If only you knew what happiness it gives me to hear you speak my name. I'd grown to hate it ; but now you make it sound beautiful. You will always call me by my name ? You'll never guess what happiness these small things can give me ! So now we are friends ? " she added, eagerly. "Friends. Let me hear that word."

"For always, Cristina."

She sighed luxuriously. "The freedom, the relief ! If I hadn't told you everything I could never have felt as free as this." She spoke solemnly : "This day I have been born again. Imagine it ! Now I shall never again be lonely. Even when he comes, I shall be able to think of you. And now that we have no more secrets, nothing can come between us. Paolo, we shall be so happy. And I shall help you, and you'll know why, and never question me ? " She pointed to the parchments that lay on the table. "About little things like this, that can hurt nobody, but give your poor Cristina so much joy ? "

He could not answer her. That was another matter.

"Why do you hesitate ? You needn't be

frightened," she persisted. "I am the only one who has need to be frightened, and I'm not afraid any longer."

Still he was obstinately silent.

"And if your dear conscience troubles you," she said, "we'll find a way to soothe it. Listen, Paolo! I cannot see you starve and go thin like this. You took the other pieces from me : why not take these? When you have made your boxes, you'll have plenty of money. Isn't that so? And with that money we'll buy some others and replace them. You see, you see? Isn't that a splendid plan? Nobody need ever know how wicked I am. Only you and me. Why did we never think of that before? How stupid we've been!"

She was so gay and breathless with the ingenuity of her stratagem that he was forced to smile. "If that is understood . . ." he began.

"Of course it's understood, my foolish child. The time we've wasted over your tiny scruples! But now that's all over, and you will work, and I shall be watching you, and both of us will live happily for ever and ever." She paused and lifted her eyes to his with an appealing shyness. "And sometimes," she whispered, "Paolo, you will kiss me?"

He could not refuse. That kiss, so timidly demanded, and almost grudgingly bestowed out of the pity which Cristina had begged him not to give her, set a seal upon the contract of conspiracy to which Paul now found himself committed. The first step, with all its strained emotional accompaniments, was the hardest; but even when Paul had grown used to accepting an unashamed passion to which that house, the scene of her sufferings, and the imminent shadow of the black hunter gave, by contrast, an air of dizzy and perilous intensity, there were moments in which his powers of imagination failed him, in which, with a devastating, humiliating clearness, he saw their relation objectively : himself a callous, calculating, cold-blooded failure, basely profiting by the generosity of a woman whom he did not love, living comfortably, like a pander in a brothel, on the proceeds of her shame ; and Cristina, bereft by the same chill realism of the transfigurations that her warm devotion sometimes gave her, a wan and anxious woman, the black hunter's discarded mistress, urged by an ugly, unaccountable hunger, to seek her satisfactions from the nearest available victim.

He saw her thus, and shuddered with his old spiritual distaste ; but even when he shrank from her, her physical presence moved him, and though his reason fought stubbornly against illusion, his own figure in that picture was so false and ignoble that hers, by comparison, seemed full of truth and innocence, and for this reason doubly painful. He told himself that even in his diagnosis of her motives he had not done her justice ; for, if that were just, she might far more profitably have set her desires on Viva, whose advances, in point of fact, she had rejected. This flattering preference was enough, in itself, to turn so young and so imaginative a head as Paul's. It showed Cristina's passion as a personal triumph. It imposed obligations which, in a revulsion of feeling rather than reason, created the new illusion of a tender, loveless creature, whose heart the sardonic forces which she called destiny had conspired to lacerate. And how should he, by no means blameless, presume to add his cruelty to theirs ?

There were other reasons, he shamefully admitted, against his rejecting her overtures : above all, the fury of creative art which ran in his veins like madness, and, but for her help, would have died of sheer starvation. The first release of this thwarted energy declared itself in a spate of imaginative power that transported him to the seventh heaven. In all his new creation there was the clarity of vision, the swiftness of execution, the precipitate urgency that is the mark of work conceived under spiritual stress. It seemed to Paul that at last his art had found itself. The mood was too precious to be broken by anything so unimportant as a scruple of conscience. Once broken, its continuity might be lost for ever. He would have given his soul to retain it. Perhaps, he reflected, in those brief instants when reflection was possible, that was what he was doing.

So be it ! Now, every morning, when Viva had gone to his hospital and Paul sat alone at breakfast, tenderly brooding over some unfinished canvas, Cristina would glide, as silent as any ghost, into the room. This was the hour for which she lived, the hour that Paul dreaded, and hated himself for dreading. Cristina entered timidly, like a shy animal, that experience has taught to be wary of unexpected anger. When she saw him rapt in the contemplation of his work she dared not speak,

M

for his painting, as always, remained a mystery to
her.   It was for him to descend from his high
clouds and speak to her.   He compelled himself to
do so, guiltily ; and when she answered him, she
would speak in whispers, her ears strained to catch
the iron ringing of the black hunter's hobnails on
the floor below.

Sometimes the conflict of his emotions made
Paul dumb, and she would stand before him pitifully, her mouth moulded in an anxious, a tenderly
solemn smile.

" I am afraid you have not slept," she would
whisper.   " Paolo, what can I do with you ?   You
never think of yourself.   Last night I came upstairs
and listened outside the door.   You were still
working away—don't deny it !—long after midnight
I know you are over-tiring yourself.   Your eyes
look all black and sunken.   Why won't you listen
to me ?   Why should you work yourself to death
like this ? "

" Because at night I am a tradesman, Cristina,"
he said.   " My painting is a luxury for which I
have to pay since no one else will pay me for it.
Yesterday it got hold of me so violently that I
played truant half the evening, and had to make up
for it at night.   Canvas and paints cost money.
To-day I must start work on a new set of
boxes."

He spoke the last words with an uneasy laugh,
to conceal from himself the shame that was hidden
in them.   Even at this stage his cowardice would
not allow him to be honest with himself.   It was
not in her nature to acquiesce in this language of

hidden meanings, although her mind was sensitive
to understand them.

"What? Are your parchments finished?" she
said. "How careless of me to have forgotten!"
Then she would slip her wooden clogs from her
feet, stealing, bare-footed and cautious, to the attic
above, returning, breathless, with the parchment
sheets that she had taken from her master's store.

"These are all right?" she always anxiously
asked him.

And when he took them from her she would
stand mute, flushed, expectant for the embrace with
which her theft—for somehow their flattering scheme
of a repayment in kind had never materialized—
was paid. In this exalted ritual her spirit took fire.
She was refreshed, rejuvenated, as by the elements
of a mystical sacrament. She sought to prolong
its fervour, to make endless the moments in which
her body was pressed to him and her lips burned
upon his. Into their short duration she compressed
the gathered intensity of all that lay hidden beneath
the silences, the dull, inadequate words of the
intervals between them. They were so charged
with passion, half desirous, half maternal, that
Paul was shaken, by sheer force, out of the indifference which his reason imposed on him. They
left him shattered; no longer master of himself.
He was a little afraid of them; no less shocked by
his own unwilled response than by the transfiguration, the rapt, beatified saintliness of Cristina's
smile, from which he shrank as desert hermits may
have shrunk from diabolical visions.

And even more intolerable to his imagination

was the glow of joy, the flushed and radiant childishness with which she left him. If he could have found the courage to tell her that each of these bartered kisses was a lie! He was a coward, as he readily confessed, solacing himself with the conviction that at least he had given her happiness, that for this reason the base exchange was justified.

It almost seemed as if the conditions of their bargain were defined and understood. Sometimes, in the abstracted brooding with which his work enveloped him, he would take the parchments that she brought him without fulfilling his part of the compact or even thanking her. Then she would stand at his side, unwilling to leave him, yet too proud to demand her wages in words, until her silent presence compelled him to perform the duty from which he shrank, and filled him with hatred, not for Cristina, but for himself.

His negligence made her crafty. With the same silent persistence she began to withhold her gifts until payment had been made. If she had been immodest in her demands or made them openly, if she had reproached him for his lack of answering fervour, if she had appeared less pitifully dependent on his kindness, her attitude might have spurred him into active opposition and refusal. But Cristina, in her simplicity, was like a child who craves the assurance of a good-night kiss at bed time, and these embraces were as innocent as those. Sometimes Paul wondered if they could continue to be so innocent. A time might come when Cristina would not be satisfied with so little. He dreaded its coming; for the fear haunted him that

he might not always be able to answer for himself.
And always, behind these qualms of the spirit,
though neither chose to confess it, the imponderable
menace of the black hunter darkened the sky.

III

AT Midsummer, or rather on the day of St. Peter,
the village's patron, Paul paid a hurried visit to
Pogerola. For several months the letters which
old Don Ambrogio wrote at his mother's dictation,
had been imploring him to come and see her. The
carrier's cart toiled upward through the chestnut-
woods from the verge of which Pogerola, half
hidden in greenness, looked incredibly shabby and
shrunken to Paul's eyes. The whole effect of his
visit was somewhat ghostly; he trod the remembered streets ungreeted, anonymous, for none of
the villagers whom he met had wit to recognise in
this spruce Neapolitan, with his dusty black shoes,
the hobbledehoy who had left them a few months
earlier.

Even his mother seemed awed by his changed
appearance, and Paul, for his part, was no less awed
by hers. Since the death of his uncle Andrea she
had lived to herself entirely, her interests all concentrated in the care of her little property. Her
life, which had been modified for a time by her
marriage with the mad Englishman and those
memories of him that were preserved by the
reminders of Andrea and Paul, had relapsed, with
the death of the one and the departure of the other,

into the primitive state in which her forbears had
lived. In her solitude she had formed the habit
of talking to herself. Paul heard her mumbling in
the kitchen as she fanned at her charcoal furnace, a
gaunt, ageing woman, barefooted, in whose
weathered features there remained little of the
swarthy distinction that had attracted John Ritchie.

She had changed so much—unless it were he who
had changed—that she seemed to Paul little less
alien than those old-time acquaintances who had
failed to recognise him in the street. Deliberately
though he tried to do so, he found it impossible to
establish points of contact with her. Each belonged
to a different species—one would almost have said
to a different race; and perhaps this was actually
true—perhaps, in his mixed composition, the
physical and temperamental elements of John
Ritchie's blood were now preponderant, their
differences aggravated even by this short separation.

Certainly, in those days, he felt more at home
amid the ghostly reminders of his paternal past than
in her company. The most homely thing in the
house was John Ritchie's library. Paul returned to
it eagerly and found, with a thrill of triumph, not
only that he had not forgotten how to read English,
but that his sharpened intelligence discovered a new
wealth of meaning in what he read. The face of
Concetta, as she watched him, darkened sadly.
Those books, she had long been convinced, were
works of the devil; this son was not really hers,
but a reincarnation of all the strangeness that had
belonged to his father. Who knew at what moment
the paternal madness might not seize him ? Per-

haps she knew more than she had ever admitted of
John Ritchie's past. Perhaps it was some associated prompting of alarm that made her question
him so shrewdly, when they sat in the dusk that
evening, about his life in Naples. Of Viva she
knew already ; old Don Alessandro, in a flying visit
to Pogerola, had told her about him—a steady
young man, it appeared—Paul smiled to himself—
but what about the others, the students in the
Institute ? Was it true, as Andrea had said, that
the models posed nude ? Was their life as irregular
as everyone declared it to be ? Paul had spoken
of men friends ; was it possible that he knew no
women ?

Not a woman in the world, he assured her, then
checked himself suddenly, and blushed, remembering Cristina. But the dusk hid his blushes, and
Concetta, reassured by his confident tone, went on
to develop the theme of her counsel in these
matters. When he married, she said, he should
marry a girl from the village. As usual there was
a proverb to meet the case. " A girl of your own
place," she said, " is like wine in a glass : you see
what you're drinking. A girl from outside is like
wine in a black bottle : who knows ? A girl from
the city is like wine in a goatskin : be careful !
God knows what you'll find inside when you've
carried it home." And then, as though the subjects were not even remotely connected, she went
on to talk about Annina, the girl whom, some years
before, Paul had wanted to paint. A clean girl,
she said, and the father a friend of Andrea's. What
was more, an uncle of Annina's had lately returned

from America, with money to spare and no inclina-
tion to marry. Paul might do far worse than keep
Annina in mind.

He smiled, and evaded the subject. On the night
of the *festa* he had caught one glimpse of his old
flame walking with her friends, and wondered how
in heaven's name he had ever admired her. She
had thrown him—or his clothes—a glance that
acutely embarrassed him. The girls of Pogerola,
dressed up for St. Peter, seemed strangely uncouth
to him after so many memories of slim, Neapolitan
elegance. Why, even compared with Cristina . . .
It was strange to think how, at this distance, the
image of Cristina returned to him; how lonely
he felt, in his mother's company, for the sound of
her voice, the gentleness of her lowered eyes. The
thought of her filled him with an odd, inexplicable
nostalgia. When he went home to Naples after
three days, feeling as if he had turned his back on
Pogerola for the last time, with an unexpected
present of money from Concetta in his pocket, it
was the prospect of his meeting with Cristina that
thrilled him most of all.

Her face, when she greeted him, lightened like
a flame. "I thought you were never coming,
Paolo," she said. "Each moment has seemed like
a year to me. Can it really be you?"

They kissed, and this time, for Paul, the embrace
was a willing one. In his absence it seemed as if
she had really grown younger. The ease, the
luxury of being himself, with no need for explaining,
the familiar aspect—even the smell of the room into
which he crept back like a snail into its shell, filled

him with an elation whose warmth she was quick
to catch.   They ate and talked together that evening
with the light-heartedness of two children.   When
she bade him good-night her eyes glowed with a
happiness that, in itself, was beautiful.

Next day Paul threw himself into his work with
furious enthusiasm.   Not only in the impetus that
renewed prosperity had given to his art, but in the
comforts which it provided, these were halcyon
days.   Viva, whose spirits had wilted under poverty
like the leaves of a tropical tree transported to a
temperate clime, burst out again into his natural
efflorescence.   The change in their financial condition had been so sudden that he couldn't feel
satisfied until it was explained to him.

" Why, in God's name, be so mysterious about
it, Paolo ? " he said.   " If it's true that you've made
a compact with the devil, why not confess it, so
that I can prepare myself to face the final reckoning ?
Or if you've merely been cutting throats for the
cammorra, let me protect myself by making friends
with the police."

He always laughed at Paul.   It was their habit
rarely to speak in earnest, though the types of their
humour were as different as German and Greek.
But even while he was joking, Viva's eyes, sharpened
by the habit of clinical observation, were quick to
notice anything unusual in Paul's room.   One night
they swooped, hawklike, upon the latest sheaf of
parchments which Cristina had brought him.   He
picked them up and examined them closely.   Paul,
wondering what he was after, peered over his
shoulder .

" Curious . . . This is curious," Viva murmured.
Paul had not noticed anything curious about
them. Now, his attention quickened by Viva's
eyes, he perceived that they were different from
any that he had used before. The parchment was
thicker and whiter than that of the thumbed missals
to which he was accustomed ; its script was of an
unusual character ; the text in a Latin full of long
and unfamiliar words ; the pages numbered, continuous, flat, as if they had just been torn from a
bound volume. Viva, following the letters with
a pointed finger-nail, was murmuring the Latin
words of the title as he deciphered them, translating
as he went :

" *Regimen Sanitatis Salernitanum :* The Sanitary
Regimen of Salerno. Paolo, this is too good to
be true ! It's written in verses. You see?
Rhymed couplets. Just wait a moment ! Let's
get the dedication right first. *Anglorum regi scribit
schola tota Salerni :* To the king of the English
the whole school of Salerno writes . . ." He
turned on Paul excitedly : " Good heavens, Paolo,
do you realise what you've got here ? "

Paul shook his head. The school of Salerno
meant nothing to him ; much less the king of the
English.

" Well, then, I'll tell you," Viva cried. " This
is more in my province than in yours. The School
of Salerno was the first School of Medicine in
Europe—possibly in the world. It was founded in
the twelfth century by one of the Norman dukes,
the conquerors of Sicily. Roger was his name.
Ruggiero Salernitano. Look, you can see for your-

self! I forget the details, although I'm supposed to have learned them. Anyhow, this Roger—the first great patron of medicine, mind you, in Europe —decided to collect and record all the medical science of his time. All the physicians of the middle ages gathered at his court. Constantinus Africanus came over from Carthage. Mesue, too, an Arab : the great authority on antidotes. Useful, as you can imagine ; poison was the fashion in those days ! All this accumulation of wisdom was summarised in the *Regimen*. I seem to remember that copies of it exist in some museum. Copies ! But this . . . who knows, Paolo, if this sheet that I hold in my hand isn't the first page—the first three pages of the original ? " He shook Paul's arm. " Lord ! What's the matter with you ? Are you so wrapped up in your damned painting that you don't see the importance of this ? Don't you realise, my poor dear fool, that if you could find the rest of it it would fetch a million ? There isn't a moment to lose. Where did you find it ? "

Paul found himself hedging. In spite of his intimacy with Viva, he couldn't confess his infamous contract with Cristina.

" They come from all kinds of places," he said. " It's difficult to remember . . ."

" Difficult ? My dear Paolo, you *must* remember ! " Viva cried. " Don't you see that a discovery like this would set all scientific Europe on fire? It would make millionaires of us. Look carefully at these margins ! I'd swear that these sheets have been torn from a bound book. Why, if you tramped Naples for a month and ransacked every

shop where you've bought parchment, it'd be worth
your while.   Pull yourself together ;   forget your
silly daubs, and get to work at once !   Remember,
a million is waiting for you ! "

Through all the rest of the evening, Viva went
flaming on, girding at Paul's guilty placidity,
ardently planning the extravagances in which the
prospective million should be spent.   By bedtime,
in spite of the shame which made him feel like a
felon, Paul's imagination had taken fire from
Viva's.   As soon as he was alone in his own room
the visionary million expended itself in channels of
which Viva would never have dreamed.   He saw
himself tasting the great galleries of the world :
Rome, Florence, Paris, Amsterdam, Antwerp,
Madrid.   He saw himself frequenting the studios
of modern masters, whose names waved like banners
before him, whose pictures he had never seen ; he
saw himself received by them as a brother, initiated
into the arcana of their dreams, the secrets of their
technique.   The horizon of the little room in
which these visions were born expanded, widened
illimitably.   The whole world opened out before
him.   A million, said Viva !   Now he was not
only an artist, but a wealthy patron of art.   He
fingered the enticing pages ;   he gazed at them
reverently, as if they possessed a talismanic virtue.

The arrival of Cristina with a bedewed carafe of
water brought him back to earth.   Still shaken by
his excited imaginings he approached her.

" Cristina ! "   She   turned   timidly.   " These
parchments. . . . Where did you get them from ? "

" From the same place as the others," she

answered calmly; "from the attic. I took the first that came to my hand; I didn't dare to stay long. Why, what is the matter with them? If they won't do, I'll go and change them, Paolo."

"There's nothing the matter with them," he answered. "On the contrary, I find them unusually interesting." Her eyes, which had been momentarily puzzled, cleared with thankfulness. "I want you to try and remember," he continued, repressing the emotion that unsteadied his voice, "exactly where you found them."

She raised her head helplessly: "I cannot possibly remember that," she said.

"But you must . . . you must!" he persisted. "At least you can remember if there were others like them?"

"No, no. I've told you. I didn't even look. I took the first."

He pressed her: "You tore them out, separated them from a bound book?"

"Paolo, it's no good asking me. When I go up there I'm so frightened that I hardly know what I'm doing, much less remember. Besides, the attic is so dark. The dark terrifies me. It feels as if it were full of spirits, Paolo."

"Cristina, you're talking like a baby. You, a grown woman! It's ridiculous! Now close your eyes; imagine yourself back in the attic, and try to remember what you did, all over again."

She obeyed him, mechanically, for a moment, and closed her eyes. "No, Paolo, it's no good. I can't; it's quite useless," she told him. "But what is the matter? Tell me!"

He would not be beaten. " You have the key ? " Submissively, she felt for it in her apron pocket. " Then you must take a light and go and look for me. Examine these carefully. Try to remember what they're like. You see, the parchment is thicker than usual, the pages larger. All I want to know for the present is if there are many others of the same kind."

She gazed at the leaves which he held before her. There was no sign of recognition in her eyes. Out of shame, or sheer reluctance, she was silent.

" Can you remember ? " he urged her. " The shape of the letters—the margins ? "

She shook her head. " I'm sure that I shall not remember. You see, Paolo—" she hesitated— " you see, I cannot read. In the convent they taught me a little : but now I'm afraid I've forgotten ; it's gone out of my head."

" In that case I must go with you myself," he declared. " We are wasting time."

" You, Paolo ? " she cried. " Oh, never, never . . ."

" Why ? Your spirits don't frighten me, Cristina," he assured her.

" Never," she repeated. " You've no idea what I suffer whenever I go there. I creep in like a mouse. That is the one room in the house that he's concerned about. Nobody in the world, he says, must ever go near it. Such threats ! When he gave me the key to keep, he promised he'd cut my throat like a pig's if ever I entered it. You laugh, but you don't know him, Paolo. He meant what he said. Supposing he came by surprise ! He might come and find us there together at any moment. We should be caught; we couldn't escape him. His strength . . . you don't know what it's like. Those long arms, they're like steel. Those hands . . ." She shuddered and clasped her own. " Why, Paolo, he's so strong, he could crack us like two walnuts in his fingers ! "

As she spoke, her eyes stared, her face blanched with terror. But by this time Paul was too fiercely wrought up with eagerness to let her go. He took her in his arms, half out of pity for her distress, half hoping that he might still persuade her.

" What I ask you is nothing," he told her. " It's useless to explain. All that I want, if you won't help me, is to see for myself. No harm will be done. I've no intention of damaging his property. As for the danger . . . I'm sure you exaggerate it. Come now, Cristina, I shall be with you."

She shivered violently. " I daren't, I'm too frightened," she whispered.

It seemed that, whatever he said, he could not reassure her. She stood with clasped hands, her eyes staring before her. Suddenly, as if, in that silent struggle, her fears had resolved themselves, she put her face to his and kissed his lips.

" Paolo," she said, " there is nothing that I would not do for you, not even this. Come, let us go there at once."

" Cristina, you're splendid," he cried. He was flushed with triumph. " First, a light."

He took a candle from the table. She watched him solemnly. The calm anguish of martyrdom was in her face. He put his arm about her pro-

tectively. Together they passed on to the landing
and up the last, narrowed flight of stairs. She went
beside him lifelessly, like a martyr going to the
stake. Outside the attic door they stopped.

" The key ? " he whispered eagerly.

She produced it. Her hand shook, she fumbled
as it approached the lock. " The candle . . .
nearer ! " she whispered. But, as she spoke, they
heard, in the dank pit of the staircase beneath them,
the sound of a fist of iron beating on the lowest
door. Hobnails rang on the flags in impatient,
uneasy movements. A harsh voice roared : "Cristina ! " Before the echoes of the knocking had
died away she had blown out the candle ; she was
gone. Like a moth, like a ghost, she fluttered away
down the stairs. New echoes floated upward.
The black hunter was cursing her, asking her
where the hell she'd been. He grunted, and
snorted like a bull. His voice rasped angrily.
Paul, flattened to the wall like a lizard, heard
Cristina answer her tyrant with a nervous laugh.
Her voice sounded strange to him, the voice of
another woman ; there were tones in it, cavernously
magnified by echoes, that he had never heard before.
He heard the sounds of a scuffle, a cry of pain. The
door of the basement opened and slammed like a
gunshot. Paul, his hands and forehead stony cold
with sweat, clung to the attic staircase with the reek
of the extinguished tallow in his nostrils.

That night he could not sleep for the thought of
Cristina ; Cristina's softness, bruised in the iron
bands of the black hunter's arms. Imagination
magnified his vision of her courage, the reality of

the danger that she had courted for his sake. He
was ashamed to think that he had imposed this test
upon her for the sake of Viva's damned million ;
beside the baseness of the kiss with which she had
yielded to him, the baseness of all their other kisses,
shameful as they were, seemed negligible. To hell
with Viva and his money ! To hell with all the
visionary ambitions that he had built upon it ! The
Codex of Salerno, if it existed, might rot in the
attic for ever, for all he cared ! He had a feeling
that Viva's materialist enthusiasms had betrayed him
into a cruel, a monstrous meanness. God knew he
was despicable enough already ! The realisation of
this last infamy determined him to be done with all
the rest.

IV

It was easier to make such resolutions in the
solitude of night than to perform them. Next
morning, Cristina knocked at Paul's door to call
him, then vanished. His imagination was quick to
supply reasons for her failing to show herself : the
blows of the black hunter's fists, whose sinister
echoes he had heard in the well of the staircase, had
left marks that she was frightened to show him.
It was for him that she had suffered this : the
thought was intolerable. Or was it merely that
Viva had overslept himself, as was usual on Sunday
mornings, and was there for breakfast ?

"You'd better set about your search at once,"
Viva urged, returning as soon as his eyes were

open to the theme of the *Codex*. "It beats me that you can't remember where you bought that parchment. You artists! It seems to me that you've no eyes in your head. Imagine a man of intelligence missing a thing like that! Sheer, blindfold idiocy! By this time the other part of the volume may have vanished, and yet you sit there with that silly smile on your face! For God's sake get going, Paolo. You may still be in time."

In the evening he whirled into Paul's room like a hurricane.

"What news?" he cried. "You've found them? Tell me you've found them!"

Paul shook his head. He was sore and guilty. All day Cristina had avoided him.

"It's no good, Pietro," he said. "Why waste good time in searching for them?"

"Why waste time? The greatest archaeological and scientific discovery of the age? You'd better let me take you along with me to hospital. Your brain must be softened. At any rate you've done your best to track them down?"

He went on so persistently with his badgering, and Paul found himself tangled in such a network of palpable prevarications, that by the time they reached the dinner table he knew that he must show his hand.

"It's no use, Pietro," he said at last. "I didn't buy the damned things. I know where they came from; but if I tell you, it must be understood that I'm speaking in the strictest confidence."

"The condition's unfair," Viva grumbled. "This

is a discovery which doesn't concern us alone. It's a matter of interest to the whole scientific world. We've no right to be selfish."

"Last night you were talking of millions," Paul reminded him. "But that's by the way. Unless you can give me your word that you'll keep the secret, which isn't my own, we'll say no more about it."

For a long while, Viva tried to move him with arguments and entreaties. At last, under protest, he capitulated: "Be damned to you! Have your own way!"

"Cristina gave them to me."

He was happy to have spoken. His friend had always been so frank with him, that he hated to deceive him. Viva rose, gaping:

"Cristina? The devil!" he gasped. "She made you a present of them?" For him there could be only one interpretation of the present's meaning. "Cristina?" he cried; "Cristina? Who would have thought it?"

To himself, Paul admitted, the pages of *Codex* had been equally surprising. But that, it appeared, was not what Viva implied.

"And you, Paolo, you sly young fox!" he went on. "You, who have always pretended not to notice women! Under my very eyes ... or rather, to be exact, when I was engaged in my pious duties of alleviating human suffering, and sweating my guts out and dodging my cursed professors. Well, well, my son, I can congratulate you on your reformation, but hardly—if I may be frank—upon your taste."

He made a wry mouth as he spoke that set Paul up in arms, not so much for himself as for the slighted Cristina.

"And what the devil do you mean by that ? " he flared.

"Cristina is not . . . appetising," Viva sneered.

"Cristina's an angel of goodness and generosity," Paul cried. "You make me sick, Pietro, the way you talk about women. I'll thank you to leave her alone."

"With all the will in the world," Viva laughingly assured him. "As I've just suggested, she isn't. . . . But apparently you resent the word ? "

"I do," said Paul hotly. "On your lips I certainly resent it. You forget that I had the pleasure—no, I won't call it that—of seeing you pursue her, and seeing her turn you down. You're like the fox, Pietro, who said that the grapes were sour."

For a moment Viva flushed darkly, then quickly recovered his mocking, sly good-humour, and burst out laughing.

"Paolo, your innocence is inimitable. I think you'd mop up everything a woman told you. As for Cristina. . . . Well, we won't go into details ; but, knowing me, as you should by this time, can you really believe that I know less about the lady than you do ? If so, my boy, you're most lament- ably mistaken. You can't teach your uncle any- thing, so don't imagine it. Why, months before you came here . . ."

Paul jumped to his feet.

"You're lying, Pietro. I say that's a damnable lie ! "

Viva went white with anger ; " A lie ? I don't allow you or anyone else to speak to me like that ! By God, you shall answer for it ! "

"A lie," Paul repeated. In that moment he hated his friend more than anyone on earth. The pallid, smiling face of Viva was that of his enemy. Above the scattered dinner-table they stared at each other. It seemed that, in another instant, they must be at each other's throats. Then the door opened. Cristina entered. She looked from one to the other with a bewilderment that quickly turned to terror ; so much she knew and dreaded the violence of men.

"I thought you had finished," she began ; but neither answered her. " Paolo," she cried, " tell me, what is the matter ? "

He was too hot to answer ; but Viva quickly tumbled to the ludicrousness of the situation. The colour came back to his cheeks ; he excused himself with a laugh :

"An unimportant difference of opinion, Cristina. The question of a lady," he added maliciously. "Paolo has challenged my opinion. I withdraw. I apologise."

"If he had not apologised," Paul muttered angrily.

"Paolo ? A woman ? " Cristina spoke in a whisper. There was fear in her eyes. They stared at Paul anxiously.

"But I have apologised," Viva went on gaily. "Come come, I can't do more than that."

"He said . . ." Paul began, appealing to Cristina.

"But he withdrew it," Viva smoothly interrupted, "so there's an end of the matter. Sit down, Paolo ; don't be an ass ; sit down ! "

Gradually Paul's heat subsided. He allowed himself to be persuaded to take his seat. They finished their meal in a childish, unwonted silence. When Cristina had left them, Viva renewed his apologies.

"It's a poor thing," he said, " if old friends like ourselves can lose their tempers over our dear Cristina. Cristina's a paragon of virtue. We'll take that for granted ; we'll imagine, to save your delicate feelings, that her friend the black hunter simply doesn't exist. I wish he didn't ; his bull-neck spoils the landscape."

"He's spoiled her life," Paul answered, intensely. "Pietro, if you knew . . ."

"But I don't, my friend, and I don't even want to. Let's talk no more of Cristina. Upon my word, you sound as if you were in love with her . . ."

"Pietro, you don't understand me," Paul protested. "I haven't even . . ."

"No ? Then I'm disappointed. I still had hopes for you. We'll avoid the subject in future, and spare your tender, your too tender sentiments. What interests me is the manner in which she's shown her fancy. Those parchments. Where did she get them from ? You can tell me now."

"From our black friend," Paul admitted.

"*Dio mio !* The black hunter ? But this is

unutterably fantastic. Don't tell me that he's a connoisseur! He doesn't look like one. I confess I'm puzzled."

"So am I; it's fantastic, as you say. I can't help you. And neither can Cristina, unless it's merely that she's afraid to tell me."

"Is this just an accident, or are there more of them?"

"The attic above our heads is crammed with them: so many that he couldn't possibly miss what she's given me already."

"Inexplicable! To think of that priceless *codex* being under this very roof! I feel as if we were mad." He ran his fingers through his hair. "But, Paolo, that simplifies everything," he went on triumphantly. "Cristina will find us the rest of it."

"I shall not ask her; it isn't fair to her."

"It's every bit as fair as what you let her do before," Viva scoffed.

"That is all over. She's suffered enough frights already."

"If you're resolved to be a fool, I'll ask her myself."

Paul flushed: "I absolutely forbid you to do so Pietro."

"It was I who discovered them, under your very nose. What right have you to forbid me?"

"You've given me your word."

"Like the idiot that I was! But can't you see, as I've told you before, that this is a public concern? Have you no vestige of imagination?" He rose to his feet and walked the room, waving his arms, transported by the fervour of his own oratory.

Paul remained as stubborn as ever. " There's not a damned mule in Naples as obstinate as you are," Viva cried. "All this stupidity, for what? To protect Cristina?"

Paul agreed.

" And yet you've the face to say you're not in love with her!"

Paul laughed : " Not in the very least," he replied.

" Cold-blooded as a snake. But I've not finished with you yet. Before the week's out, I bet I'll make you see reason."

" You can try," said Paul. " For the present you're wasting breath."

Gradually Viva's excitement subsided. Now his eager imagination fastened itself on the problem of the black hunter's storeroom.

" It was always a strange house," he said ; " but this beats everything. Nobody that I've talked to seems to know who he is. The people in the *Vicolo* call him *Don Animale*—which is picturesque and accurate—but beyond that . . . nothing. What is his trade?"

" I don't think even Cristina knows. He comes and goes. He is the master ; you say that Cristina's his mistress. Or was : I fancy now she's merely a convenience. He was with her last night. I heard him. It's you who are cold. You should be sorry for her."

" With the greatest of pleasure. Let's all be sorry together! But the store of parchments! An attic full of them you say? What shall we call it? Medically, perhaps, a monomania. God knows: there are strange things in medicine! But in any case, my dear Paolo, we'll talk no more about that, or you'll start quarrelling with me again. You have quite forgiven me? You don't want me to repeat my apologies? "

They shook hands upon it. It was beyond Paul's power to quarrel for long with Viva. He even consented to join in drinking Cristina's health. "Another bottle to celebrate the occasion," Viva insisted.

"But, my God!" he exclaimed suddenly, "if I haven't forgotten to tell you the news. Cholera in Naples! Five or six deaths have been reported at the hospital this afternoon. A fulminating type! One moment you're laughing; the next you're dead."

"That sounds cheerful," Paul laughed; "But what has it got to do with us?"

"In Rome, or Paris, or London you might afford to laugh," Viva told him; "but here, no. Naples is like no other city in Europe. We have no sanitary laws. Ordinarily we get on very well without them; we're the only example of a free people in Western civilisation; but when it comes to a pest of this kind, in summer, we may have to pay for our freedom; we're as much at its mercy as any rabbit-warren in China. We've a marvellous water-supply. Old wells, of a foulness incredible. God knows how the water gets into them or where it comes from. Cholera, some authorities say, is a disease borne by water . . ."

"Thank heaven, then, *you're* safe, Pietro!" Paul interrupted.

But Viva was too professional to see the joke.

"We're none of us safe," he declared. "What do they wash our food in?"

"Damned little, as far as I can see," Paul scoffed.

"Try, for one moment to be serious. Think of the fruit and salads that are on this table. The wells in this place are as rotten as the Roman Empire that sunk them. The rats that live in them go out foraging in the *fondaci* at night. And the people who live in the *fondaci*—no mind can imagine them! I tell you, Paolo, this Naples is two cities: one on the top, the pleasant place in which we divert ourselves: another underneath, in which you and I wouldn't dare to poke our noses. Riddled like an ant-heap. Rags and rats and filth: unspeakable sub-human abominations!"

"But if cholera comes from water, what has that got to do with it?"

"Everything. You artists are incapable of logical thought. If you can't see it for yourself, I won't explain to you. But even if cholera doesn't come from water—nobody really knows, though some German (Koch's his name) has just discovered an organism—one thing's pretty clear, and that's this: if cholera once gets into the *fondaci*, why, God help Naples! Nothing but gutting by fire would clear it out, at this time of year. You mark my words! However, it may be only a scare. In any case I thought it my duty to warn you."

"A thousand thanks," Paul answered, carelessly. "How well I know you, Pietro! You doctors are never so happy as when you're freezing our blood; and on a torrid night like this . . ."

He stood at the window, watching pale lightning that washed the dense sky above the mountains behind which Pogerola lay, throwing into ominous relief black billows of cloud, that, like heralds of approaching doom, kept nightlong watch over the city's sleepless coruscations. Though the night sky was jet, the stones of Naples still radiated warmth like the lining of an oven. The air was milky warm on Paul's skin ; yet, as he stood there breathing it, he shivered.

Book Four

PARADISO

I

NEXT morning, when Paul woke, he had little time
to think of Viva's cholera-scare. Even the fate of
the Salerno *codex* shrank into insignificance. One
word that had passed almost unnoticed in the
quarrel which she had interrupted had fermented,
during the hot night, in Cristina's mind. She
swept in on him tragically, her lips tense and pallid,
her eyes hollowed by sleeplessness to dark pits in
which lurked a glimmer that was ready at any
moment to spurt into angry flame. Even before
she had let in the light Paul's waking consciousness
was aware of her volcanic imminence. With a
sleepy unwariness he asked her what was the matter.

"Is it true," she said, hotly, "what Viva said last
night?" Her passion could not even wait for his
answer. "Of course it is true! If it weren't true,
I know you'd have denied it. What woman is
this?"

"What woman?" He rubbed his eyes.
"What woman? In heaven's name, Cristina,
what are you raving about? Something that Viva
said? A private quarrel—no earthly business of
yours. But as for women . . ."

" Ah, Paolo," she laughed bitterly, " you needn't begin to lie to me. It's better that I should know. I must know ; I have a right to know," she continued with increasing passion. " Don't imagine for a moment that you can put me off like that. Must I repeat his words ? I will : ' An unimportant difference of opinion : the question of a lady.' That was what Viva said. A lady ! Who is she ? Oh, Paolo, don't smile at me like that ! This is what I've always dreaded. That Viva and his women ! Don't I know what they're like ? Can't I tell from the way in which he's behaved to me what kind of women he frequents ? And you, Paolo, as simple as a child ! What can they give you, these women of his ? It's wrong, I tell you. It's a crime ! Not for myself. . . . Will you believe that it's not of myself I'm thinking ? Paolo, my little one, I'm not jealous—not really jealous. Only as a mother's jealous for her child. That's how I love you. That's why this danger frightens me. That's why I've lain all night in hell, thinking and suffering . . ."

She put her hands to her eyes and broke into harrowing sobs through which the words that followed became lost and incoherent. " Paolo . . . for pity's sake . . . listen to me before it's too late ! "

He took the tragic figure in his arms and tried to comfort her.

" Cristina, Cristina, if only you knew how foolish you are ! You and your women ! Listen ! Will you believe me ? The lady in question happened to be yourself."

"Myself?" she gasped.   She was laughing and
crying at once.   "Myself?   Oh, Paolo!"

Gradually she controlled herself.   "I suppose I
shall have to believe you," she said;   "but that is
not enough.   Tell me more.   Why should you
quarrel about me?   I don't understand."

His loyalty to Viva checked the truth on his lips;
her quick suspicion leapt in upon his reluctance.

"I see," she said, "that means that you and he
have been discussing all that has passed between us.
I know what has happened.   I can guess what
Viva would do.   He's been trying to poison your
mind against me."

The swiftness of her intuition staggered him.
It was as swiftly interpreted.   Suddenly he seemed
to see light.   Viva had not merely been boasting
of his relations with Cristina;   Viva's apology was
nothing but a lie craftily invented to soothe a
friend's susceptibilities;   Viva and Cristina between
them had made a fool of him;   her anxiety betrayed
her guilt—first the black hunter;   then Viva;
himself the third victim of this pale woman's
hungry lust!   A flush of red anger made him
wish the lot of them to hell.   Why should he allow
their trivial sexual complications to come between
him and the one thing that mattered, to distract
him from his work?   He wrenched himself away
from her impatiently.

"I've had enough of this cursed nonsense,"
he said.   "Whom shall I believe?   I don't know
what to believe, and I don't care.   Viva and you
and your master, as you call him, had better fight it
out between yourselves.   I have work to do.

o

My life is my own.   For God's sake leave me in
peace ! "

He turned his back on her.   She pursued him to
the door.

" I knew it, I knew it ! " she cried.   " That's
Viva's revenge.   Because I wouldn't touch him he
tells you he's been my lover."   She clung to Paul
in the doorway.   " Isn't that true ? "   Her passion
in that moment, seemed to him uncouth and
grotesque.   Her vehemence offended him.   It
seemed to him ugly and alien.   The heat of the
pitiless sky shrivelled the remains of his patience.
He freed himself rudely from her hands.

" Let me go," he said.   " My God, are you too
stupid to see that I've no time for this, that I don't
want you ? "

His anger was shouting : this woman means
nothing to me ; she has deceived me, humiliated
me ; I have a right to hate her.

" Paolo ! " she entreated, and clutched again at
his arm.   His anger brightened to a blaze of
righteous resentment.   Now, at all costs, he
would make her understand :

" D'you think I care a *soldo* whether Viva's been
your lover or not ? "

He tore himself away from her.   " Paolo," she
cried, " you kill me, you crucify me.   Is that how
you treat my love ?   Listen . . . one moment !   I
swear to you. . . . There's nothing, nothing in the
world more pure, more holy.   My body, that you
despise, my heart . . ."

He slammed the door of his room behind him and
locked it.   In a tremulous fury he set himself to

work. The room was a whitehot furnace. Not
one of the watchful brooding clouds of the night
before was left. Out of a blanched sky the sun
beat down upon a sea cowed and glassy, a sea that
reflected light and heat as cruelly as the baked,
radiant stones that made all Naples like an oven.
He sat and sweated, stripped to the waist, yet
consumed by the furnace-heated air and the flaming
resentment within him. He worked and burned.
At last he threw aside his palette. There was no
virtue in him; nothing but heat and frustration.
He flung himself upon his bed in search of coolness
and composure.

Somebody was knocking at the door.

"Who is it?" he cried, rising irritably.

"Cristina," her voice answered.

"You cannot come in," he shouted. "I am
undressed."

"I must. Only for a moment. I have something here for you. Don't disturb yourself. I'll
wait."

Damning her persistence, yet moved by curiosity,
he pulled on his shirt again and flung open the door.
She stood before him meekly with a roll of parchments. "I've brought you these," she said. "I
think these are what you wanted."

He hated her meekness; even to see such
humiliation was humiliating, and made him despise
himself as well. He hardened his heart, cherishing
his own scorn. The suggestion that he could be
bribed into complaisance by such means aggravated
his anger.

"You needn't have bothered me like this," he

said roughly. "Why didn't you say what you
wanted?"

While he was speaking she had slipped into the
room. Now he was faced once more with the
unpleasantness of getting rid of her, the duty of
finally asserting his independence and his distaste.
She had brought it on her own head; he need have
no pity. He stood before her threateningly.

"Cristina," he said, with a quiet bitterness, "I
think it's time we understood each other. Frankly,
I've had enough of this. I've made a fool of
myself—remember, I don't blame you for it—I've
presumed upon your . . . kindness . . . in a way
that has made me lose my self-respect and destroyed
yours as well. If we go on like this, I shall never
get it back again as long as I live. And I can't face
that. If I can't make a living honestly, why then
I've got to confess that I've failed and go back to
Pogerola. No use complaining. I'd rather be a
peasant—which is what I am—than live here in false
pretences on your charity. That's where we stand.
And this is the end of it. Definitely. The end."

She stared at him, helplessly, like a prisoner
listening to her sentence. Then, quickly, she
recovered herself.

"But, Paolo, what have I done?" she whispered.
"How many times have I told you that nothing
will be missed?"

"As if that had anything to do with it! I've
said that before."

Her mind could only deal with one thing at a
time. "Have I no rights? Haven't I been a
slave in this house for years? What payment

have I received? Before God, Paolo, I feel that
I am innocent. I have done nothing wrong. My
conscience tells me so. And if there is any wrong,
why, as I've told you, the wrong's all mine, not
yours. It's nothing to do with you. Nothing!"

He shook his head. "No, no. Must we argue
this over again? Even if you were right, it would
make no difference. It's the rest of it, the falseness,
that shames me. I will not be indebted to you.
You put me under an obligation that I absolutely
refuse to accept."

"There is no debt, there is no obligation," she
cried fiercely. "All that I have given you I've
given from my heart. You cannot treat love as
though it were a matter of commerce."

"In our case," he answered brutally, "there is no
question of love."

"I will not believe it," she cried, "not if you tell
me so a thousand times. Can you look me in the
eyes and tell me that all that has passed between us
means nothing to you? Your lips, Paolo, your
hands, have those been lying to me?"

"I have spoken the truth this time," he answered
sullenly.

"I won't believe it," she repeated. "You do
not know yourself; you're lying because that devil
Viva has corrupted you. He's your black genius;
the one against whom I've been fighting! What
has he told you? Ah, you don't want me to know.
I can guess at his poison. You needn't even tell
me what he said. But listen, Paolo. . . . Never in
all my life—on the sacred blood of San Gennaro I
swear it—never for one moment have I loved any

man but you. And your heart has answered my
love. I have felt it. Oh, you're so simple, you
don't know what love is."

She fell at his feet; she clutched his hands and
covered them with tears and kisses. Stirred by
this pitiful abasement, he hardened himself the
more.

"It's no good, Cristina," he muttered. "You'd
better go."

He raised her to her feet, half kindly, half threatening. She could see the hard determination in his
eyes.

"Paolo," she said, "I cannot go like this. If
you send me away, my life . . . my poor life is
over."

"You must go," he repeated. "I have no more
to say."

With a single pitiful gesture of despair she left
him. When she had gone he stood powerless,
dazed beneath the heat of noon. He was so exhausted and shaken by the effort of his own determination that he could no longer think; but when
the power of thought returned to him, it brought
with it doubts and a sudden, disquieting remorse.

For weeks on end he had been fretting against the
dishonesty into which Cristina's passion had betrayed his weakness and looking for an opportunity
to assert his rebellion against it; but it was the
impulse of a moment of suspicion, in which,
despite Viva's withdrawal, he had pictured himself
as the dupe and laughing-stock of his friend and of
Cristina, that had urged him to this cruel violence.
Supposing that his suspicion of her duplicity were

groundless, as Viva, in his mocking, cynical mood
had assured him? He knew the elasticity of Viva's
conscience too well to build on that. But could he,
with equal right, refuse to believe Cristina, who had
never lied to him before, and had sworn her innocence on a relic that was sacred to her? It
seemed possible that in his anxiety not to be fooled
by others he had made a fool of himself.

Out of his folly at least one good thing had
emerged: on the score of his complicity in Cristina's
thefts he had cleared himself for ever; for by
nothing less than violence could she have been made
to understand his scruples. But in the process of
establishing his position he had wounded her more
deeply than he had any right to do, callously
discounting the sacrifices she had made, the dangers
she had faced, the blind, selfless devotion she had
squandered at his feet.

Against this background of indebtedness her
problematical innocence shone with a new, a
pitiful radiance; his own conduct accused him of a
cruelty and brutality worthy of the black hunter
himself. Ruthlessly, in a burst of careless, shameful
anger, he had hurled another stone at this creature
already crushed and battered by the assaults of life.
It was a piece of ignoble and cowardly ingratitude,
for which he could only atone by means that still
had the power to make him shudder. He could
not give her love; but kindness, tenderness, at
least, were due to her, whatever humiliation the
overture might cost him. There was no one in the
world, not even his mother, to whom he owed so
much.

The spiritual need of clearing himself was now so urgent that he almost determined to go downstairs to the basement and call her, to take back, no sooner than it was spoken, the injustice of his dismissal. Yet, when he reflected, he realised that this pre-cipitancy might only add to her distress ; for the movements of the black hunter were incalculable, and, at any moment he might surprise them together.

Sheer prudence forced him to await another opportunity. In the meantime, as far as the swelter of the day would let him, he prepared to adjust himself to the changed conditions of life, taking stock of the pigments and canvases that he had in hand, meditating a final, intensive assault upon the callous picture-market. Amid the ac-cumulated disorder of his table he found the sheaf of parchments that Cristina had brought him that morning. He smiled at the slyness with which she had left them there to tempt him. She didn't know, poor thing, the steel of his determination !

Even as he pushed them aside, shrinking from contact with the accursed thing, the fresh beauty of these last examples induced him to examine them more closely. A single glance was enough. From an ivory surface the careful script of the scribe of Salerno tempted him. Three pages more, in sequence. If only Viva knew ! Viva should never know. Viva was dangerous, even in his friendship. He put the parchments deliberately away from him, determined to prove his strength inviolable.

There, too, stood the boxes that he had finished during the week. He handled them fondly, en-

tranced by his own ingenuity. The work, at least,
was honest, however questionable its material. If
he could have stripped the rich, illuminated parchment from them and restored it, he would have
done so; but that was impossible.

"If I smashed them to bits and burned them," he
thought, "I should feel that I had done something
virtuous."

The idea was ridiculous; the mischief already
done, the crime committed; his purse so thinly
lined that it would have been fantastic to sacrifice
the fruits of so much labour. Three caskets: that
meant over a hundred francs. With care the sum
would carry him over two months. In those two
months, whether it sold or not, he could achieve his
swan-song, the first, perhaps the last elusive
masterpiece. Meanwhile the caskets faced him,
inviting destruction. He stood coquetting with the
idea of that soul-satisfying gesture. His body
vehemently rejected it, for that had already known
the ache of hunger. Cristina's wan image re-
appeared to plead with him to spare them. "At
any rate," he thought, "they will be the last. . . .
How Pietro would laugh at my scruples, damn
him, if he saw me now!"

II

IT was with a sense of mingled pride and relief
that Paul carried his last boxes to the shop in the
Toledo that evening. This journey was the symbol
of renunciation; he made it with a consciousness of

virtue comparable to that of a newly-initiated
convert, exalted and fortified by the sacraments of a
mystical religion.　He was at peace with heaven and
earth and his own soul, and when, as he left the door
of the house in the *Vicolo degli Angeli*, the beggar
who still kept his station at the mouth of the *fondaco*
whined and stretched out his hand for alms, Paul
filled it with the coppers that lay loose in his pocket,
by way of thank-offering.

"A hundred years of happiness, a hundred
sons!" the beggar wished him.　Paul laughed;
the wish was too extravagant; sufficient for that
day was its own elation.　His heart was lighter for
the gift; he wanted to open it wide to the whole
world, to embrace, in its goodwill, the listless
crowds of human beings who issued from the doors
and thronged the high balconies of the houses that
clustered round the port.　From the green cupola
of the Carmine a clangour of bells broke forth and
floated on the heavy air.　It was the *angelus*.　Down
below, in the pit of the square, the sleepy crowd
took no heed of it; but Paul, hearing, and half
ashamed, crossed himself and muttered the syllables
of the prayer which Don Ambrogio had taught
him in Pogerola, with the same spurious sense of
satisfaction as he had felt when he placed his coppers
in the beggar's hand.

In the early exaltation of that moment, Paul had
the feeling that all Naples shared with him the joy
of a new birth; but as he left the port and climbed
to the higher regions of the city, there descended on
the scene a heaviness more ponderous than that of
the low sky.　It was the hour of the *corso*, when the

café-terraces should have been crowded with black-
coated business men sipping vermouth, the streets
thick with a moving file of smart equipages and
hired carriages ; but, when he reached the city's
heart, he saw that the newsboys who cried their
papers, the urchins who scrambled for cigarette-ends
under the drinkers' feet, were lounging, in puzzled
groups, about half-empty terraces. The cabs,
unhired, stood waiting in ranks, or prowled the
deserted streets ; the drivers lolled upon their
boxes, as though they had given up hopes of finding
fares. Even in the Toledo itself, on whose narrow
pavements a man must ordinarily fight his way at
this hour of the evening, the same subduedness
showed itself. The tradesmen stood at their doors,
staring out anxiously at the street's unusual emptiness. There were no lounging shoppers to gaze
into their windows. Those who were afoot
seemed all intent on their own business. Men met,
shook hands, exchanged a hurried word, and parted,
as though they were afraid of each other or of
themselves. A newsboy, staggering under his
sheaf of unsold papers, brandished a copy pathetically in Paul's face. He would not buy it—he had
never bought a paper in his life—but as he glanced
at the sheet he saw the one word *colera*, many times
repeated.

Cholera. The sound brought back into his mind
all Viva's seriousness of the night before. He had
treated the matter as a joke, and laughed at Viva ;
but while he had been absorbed in the process of
satisfying his conscience, that little cloud had
spread into a blackness that lay like the dusk of an

eclipse on the whole city.　A shameful panic, he told himself, unworthy of reasonable men.　Yet, as the empty lengths of the Toledo received him, their silence and desolation undermined his spirit and made him feel that in his carelessness and scorn he was alone.

"This is ridiculous," he thought.　"I am happy. I am not going to let this scare get on my nerves.　I will not be afraid."

But even though he was not afraid, his individual courage began to look silly and futile in its isolation. Against the reasoned anxiety of half a million people his own unconcern had a touch of madness in it.

It was in the eyes of the shopkeeper who bought his boxes that he first encountered fear.　The man was pale as alabaster, clasping and unclasping nervous hands, irritably cursing the clumsiness of the assistants who were putting up his shutters.

"Too late," he cried, "you are too late.　I am shutting the shop.　We shall not open to-morrow. Everyone near us is doing the same.　You cannot blame them ; at a time like this we must all think for ourselves."

Paul showed him the boxes he had brought.　The shopman made a gesture of impotence, and refused to deal with them :

"What is the use of buying things now ? " he said.　"Who knows if I shall ever open this shop again ?　Why, in a week we may all of us be dead ! "

"But surely it's not as bad as that ? " Paul suggested.

The shopman lost his temper : " As bad as that ?

You talk like a fool, a fool! You know nothing
whatever about it. Have you seen the papers this
evening, or been asleep all day? As bad as that!"
he grumbled. "Isn't *this* bad enough?" He
fluttered a crumpled newspaper before Paul's eyes.
"Ten cases yesterday : all in the district of the port.
That's not too much, if it were anything but
cholera. But look; to-day! Fifty new cases.
Fifty! And forty deaths. Do you call that
nothing? If it were only among the poorer people
of the port, then, perhaps, we might laugh at it.
But it's everywhere—everywhere! Chiaia, Posillipo, Vomero. Cases appearing in the very best
quarters, let me tell you, and among the very best
people. Only this morning a senator! And now
my wife has sent down a note to say that our own
gardener collapsed at his work. Perhaps it wasn't
cholera, but the heat. God knows! They sent
him at once to the *Gesù e Maria*. After this I am
taking no risks. To-morrow morning, I'm off to
Ischia with all my family : earthquakes are fleabites
compared with cholera."

For the moment it had seemed to give him
satisfaction to express himself to Paul. Suddenly
he darted off to curse the men who still fumbled
with the shutters. He began bundling jewellery into
the safe and talking to Paul at the same time.

"Ten yesterday : fifty to-day. That's quintupled.
If it grows at the same rate! To-morrow two
hundred and fifty; twelve hundred the day after;
then six thousand! You come from the country,
if I remember rightly. If you are not a fool you'll
go back there at once while there's time."

A customer sidled in and stood waiting to be
served.   As the shopman took no notice of him, he
addressed himself to Paul.   Suddenly the shopman
became aware of the intruder's presence.   He
waved his arms and shouted at him from his
safe :

"I cannot serve you.   Can't you see that this
shop is shut ?   Ciro !   Luigi !   What in the devil's
name are you doing with those shutters ?   D'you
want to keep me in danger here all night ? "

The customer grumbled and slunk away ;   but
Paul remained.   He was obstinately determined to
leave his boxes behind him.   Tactfully, without
another word, he began to help the shopman in
stowing his valuables into the safe.   By that time
only a narrow slit of doorway remained unshuttered.
Ciro and Luigi, a pair of clumsy louts, stood grinning
sheepishly,   waiting to be paid.   The shopman
crammed the coins and notes from the till into his
pockets, then counted out the silver of their weekly
wage.   They went.   This moment, in which the
fellow's hands were full of money, seemed ripe for
action.

"My boxes. . . . I'll leave them with you ?"
Paul suggested.

"Damn you and your boxes ! " the shopman
screamed.   "I've told you already I don't want
them.   I've finished, I tell you.   Now get out of
this ! "

He urged Paul toward the slit in the shutters.
Paul stood his ground.

"But I can't carry them away," he protested.
"After all, the work was ordered."

"I tell you I don't want them. I'm in a hurry. Let me pass. I'm going to shut the door."

But Paul, standing before it, had him at his mercy and knew it. They were alone; he was determined. The shopman stared at him with helpless, hunted eyes. Capitulating, he pulled out his pocket-book, and thrust a hundred franc note into Paul's hands. It was sheer highway robbery.

"I'm afraid I've no change," Paul told him.

"No change? Is this a time to talk of change? Take it. Who knows if you will ever see me again?"

Paul laughed. "I do, for one. I'd better wish you good-bye."

"How dare you utter such an ill-omened thing?" the shopman cried. "What do you know about it?" He shuddered, overcome with superstitious awe.

"Only that I've finished decorating boxes," Paul hurriedly assured him.

"Good God! You frightened me. Why didn't you say what you meant? Even in joking you shouldn't say things like that. You never know what effect they may have."

He locked the shop door in a fever and hurried away without another word. At twenty yards' distance he hesitated, and began to run back in Paul's direction, as though he thought he'd forgotten something. Then, just as suddenly, he changed his mind, and scuttled away up the Toledo in pursuit of a retreating cab.

Paul, with the hundred franc note in his pocket, took the opposite course. By this time more than half of the shops in the street were shut. People on the pavement shrank from contact with each other; whenever friends stopped and spoke together each kept his distance. The cabmen drove furiously through streets unimpeded by traffic, as though the danger that their rashness threatened to human life had become a consideration of no importance. Everybody, afoot or awheel, seemed driven by the same haste of flight, the currents of fugitives crossing and interfusing in the panic of an up-rooted ant-hill. As desperate, this activity seemed, and as purposeless. Why should one current hasten toward the point from which another fled? A people, Paul thought, bereft of reason, stampeding blindly beneath a terror as vast and portentous as the sky.

And who, having seen that sky, could dream of escape? At sunset the cohorts of cloud, which Paul had seen the night before, had stolen back to their watchful stations. Now, as if it were obedient to some order of destruction, the hot wind from the South drove them headlong against the bastion of hills behind Naples, drove them, and left them broken, disintegrated, to fall and settle like blight on the frightened city. This sky hung so low that it seemed to touch the house-roofs: a dense impenetrable curtain of dead air, insulating the streets from the purity of the upper sky, imprisoning, hermetically, their exhalations and miasmas. And through this denseness, like a pulsating beacon of alarm, the red flame of the volcano momently glowed and faded. Beneath such a sky, Paul thought, must Pompeii and Herculaneum have waited for their doom.

In the narrow streets of the port the imminence of that sky was less apparent. Here, in the central focus of the disease, from which the upper town recoiled in horror, the panic which had infected the Toledo had not yet penetrated. The life of that crowded quarter went on as usual. Men lounged and drank among the barrels of the wine-shops. Women, like dark moths, fluttered in and out of the grocers' lighted doors. Yellow flares of naphtha hissed and flamed above the fish-stalls. The melon-vendors and hawkers of shell-fish bawled their prices; half-naked children screamed and scrambled for fruit-skins under the barrows. There, in the deeper layers of Neapolitan consciousness, the stream of life had flowed so steadily, and for so many centuries, that no portents of celestial vengeance could check its current.

The sight was reassuring. To Paul, newly come from the Toledo, its indifference was also a little sinister. The people of this quarter knew that cholera was in their midst. Why were they undisturbed? Was it no more than a token of the insensitive age-long degradation that separated them from the refined sensibilities of the modern city? Was it an inherited, Oriental fatalism? Or was it, rather, the conscious challenge of a people to whom life had given little but hardship, flung in the face of death? If it were unconscious it was pitiful; if conscious, terrible. In either case its gaiety, its vividness, were mocking and macabre. They made Paul eager for the refuge of his quiet room. He quickened his pace.

In the square of the *Mercato* the crowd grew

denser and noisier than ever. The tent of a
marionette-show had been erected in the middle of
it. Before its doors a trio of guitar and mandolines
tinkled above the hubbub of the crowd. Two
naphtha lamps illuminated an open space in which
young men and girls with white teeth and bold
eyes were laughing and shouting together. The
cantastorio, a swarthy, one-legged ruffian from
Caserta, stumped and yelled in front of the tent, to
keep his entrance clear.

In spite of his growing uneasines, Paul stopped,
fascinated by the changing colour and movement of
the scene. Like an eddy the crowd seized him.
He was drawn, in spite of himself, toward the semi-
circle of light. The showman with the wooden leg
was growing exasperated by the crowd's unruliness.
The crowd, delighted to see him lose his temper,
grew more unruly than ever. It swayed to and
fro in front of the tent, a mass compact and laughing.

" Keep clear . . . keep clear ! " the showman
shouted in his uncouth dialect. " Are you Neapolitans Christians or animals ? Do you want me
to use a knife ? Only two *soldi* admission ! Come
in, ladies and gentlemen, come in ! The finest
show in the world, just beginning ! All the bloody
battles of Orlando and Rinaldo ! Keep clear, you
devils, keep clear ! "

He waved his arm, threateningly. Paul could
see the spittle dribble as he shouted from his open
mouth. A sudden roar of laughter went up from
the crowd. A ragged man was forcing his way
through it toward the open space. " Here comes
another ! " they shouted, hustling him forward.

hurling his body on into the light. "This way, sir, this way!" the showman bawled.

Out of the edge of the crowd they flung him. He staggered onward, dazed, his hands grotesquely uplifted, until the forward impetus was spent. Then, like a moth, hurled blindly out of darkness, whose body strikes a lamp-globe and falls, stunned, he pitched forward, full length, at the feet of the bemused mandoline player. The showman caught him by the arm, attempting to raise him. He strained and pulled him to his feet. Like a stunned insect he fell again, and lay there, making inco-ordinate movements with his legs.

The crowd shrieked with delight. "He's drunk," they cried. "Master, don't you see he's drunk?"

The man lurched over on to his back; his neck extended, eyes wide open, his bearded face grey in the lamplight, beneath the tinkling mandolines. The showman lifted his arm and let it fall, then leapt away as though a scorpion had stung him.

"He's dead," he cried. "*Madonna mia* . . . he's dead!"

Suddenly, in the centre of the square, there was a dreadful silence. The mandoline player stopped in the middle of his phrase and fled. A whisper like that of wind moving in a ripe cornfield at night ran through the crowd. Cholera . . . cholera . . . cholera. The word passed through them with a shuddering sound. The crowd drew back; it scattered, disintegrated, melted like spring snow. Paul found himself standing alone, and cold with horror, in the midst of the empty square. He found himself running, running, like a scared urchin, toward the dark jaws of the *Vicolo degli Angeli*. The beggar at the mouth of the *fondaco* gave him a leer of recognition as he passed. He did not pause to take breath or think until he had reached his room.

III

IN his room a hand-borne letter from Pogerola awaited him. It wasn't often that his mother took the trouble to communicate with him, though she expected to hear every week or ten days from himself. Being deeply distrustful of posts, and convinced, through some inherited memory of Bourbon days, that every official in uniform was a potential thief and extortioner, she would wait till she heard of some stranger visiting Pogerola, and then, having hustled old Don Ambrogio into writing, stand patiently on the road, with her letter ready, in the hope of getting it carried directly from her hands to Paul's. In point of time and security, this intimate and personal method of correspondence had disadvantages. Sometimes the bearer got drunk on the way and lost Concetta's letter; as a rule he forgot all about it for a week, so that when it reached Paul it was fouled by a rich compost of dust, grease and thumbmarks. This time, however, the letter showed a speckless virginity. It had left Pogerola that very morning, and had been marked by Don Ambrogio with an unusual, thrice-underlined " *Urgente* " which filled Paul's mind with apprehension.

He opened it hurriedly. Concetta was much

perturbed. Reports of the cholera in Naples had
already reached Pogerola, magnified in the process
by accretions of rumour. She begged, she commanded Paul to return home at once, to remain in
the safety of Pogerola till the scourge had passed.
He read the letter with annoyance; her violent
solicitude seemed to him hysterical. It was impossible for her, in Pogerola, to see things in
proportion; characteristic and irritating that she
couldn't realise the importance of his work. As
long as the Institute remained open—and, so far, he
had heard no suggestion of its being closed—he
determined, whatever she might say, to stay where
he was and continue his studies. These country
people had no idea of the value of time. As a matter
of fact he had never felt in a better mood for work.
He had rid himself of the last traces of his shameful
traffic with Cristina; and now that the first horror
of the scene in the *Mercato* had passed, the imminence
of the epidemic provided an exciting background,
was, indeed, almost a source of inspiration to his
renewed labours.

It was late when Viva came home, his swarthy,
sanguine face unshaven and haggard. Into Viva's
ears Paul poured the story of what he had seen in the
Mercato.

"Cholera, undoubtedly," Viva affirmed. He
prowled about the room like a lean wolf, expounding rapidly : " That is the form which the disease is
taking. *Foudroyant* . . . fulminating, if you understand the word. It means that the poison of this
accursed *spirillum* of Koch's kills them before the
other characteristic symptoms have had time to

develop. We're helpless. Physicians here know nothing about it. As for research, at the moment that's out of the question. You might as well think of surveying the crater of Vesuvius during an eruption. Fortunately, experts are coming to help us, from Rome, Paris, Berlin. But when they get here they'll have to take their coats off and pull in with the rest of us. Why, we're actually short-handed already. The charlatans who call them-selves doctors in Naples are bolting like rats. For God's sake let's talk no more about it for the moment. I'm sick with hunger. Where the hell's Cristina ? "

He threw himself on to his bed and lay there, limp, exhausted. When, a minute later, Cristina entered the room with their supper, he didn't open his eyes. She came in timidly ; without a word she lit the candles and set her tray on the table. She seemed so youthful and gracious in the half light that Paul already overstrung with the tension of imminent drama, was troubled by the memory of his ruthlessness toward her ; the debt unpaid, the atonement uncompleted. Now that he had finished with her parchments there was no longer anything shameful in their relation. His heart softened toward her. He was now in a position to be generous without guilty obligation. Beneath her quiet, ordered movements he perceived a new occasion for compassion : this innocent creature, whom life, and he himself as fate's instrument, had used so hardly, moving about her dutiful business, utterly heedless of the vast mysterious stage already set, was like the appointed victim of a tragedy.

But for Viva's presence he would have spoken to her, making his amends, humiliating himself at the feet of her goodness, her innocence, her shadowy beauty. She would not meet his eyes; neither by word nor look could he free his heart of its new emotion. Suddenly Viva shook himself out of his dog-like doze. He jumped to his feet and rubbed his haggard eyes.

"Ready?" he cried, with all his accustomed energy. "Wait, wait, Cristina! Where the hell are you running to?" She hung in the doorway, frightened by his violence. He stalked to the table and glared at the food on it. "Salads . . ." he said. "Salads are washed with water. This is how we treat them." He picked up the plate which she had prepared and threw its contents through the window. "Water . . ." The contents of a carafe followed those of the plate. "Poison! D'you hear me? From this day forward we drink nothing but wine. I say, wine. What's the woman staring at? Are you an idiot?"

"She doesn't understand," said Paul, flying to the rescue.

"Of course she doesn't. These damned people never will. That's why they're going to die like rats in their holes."

"Then for God's sake explain. She thinks you're mad. You've frightened her."

"Explain?" cried Viva. "What have I been doing all day? Listen, Cristina! You know that the whole port is thick with cholera?"

She shook her head. She knew nothing . . . nothing about it.

" Well then, you damned well ought to," Viva
grumbled. " Cholera, I say. An epidemic. To-
morrow, pandemic. This house is in the middle
of it. Cholera comes from water. Get that into
your head to begin with. Water is poison. For
your own sake and ours keep clear of it. Fear it as
you'd fear the devil. Keep to the house, or else
you'll carry in infection. You understand? Everything you touch outside it, every person that
touches you, has the power to kill the lot of us.
And it's not a pleasant death ! I've seen it, so I
know. We're in a state of siege ; we've got to
protect ourselves. That's why I chucked your
admirable salad out of the window. Is that enough
for you ? Now do you understand ? "

There was something inspiring and characteristic
in Viva's downrightness. Whatever his faults—
and Paul had reason to know them—the man was
vivid and sincere. All the old loyalties flared up to
acclaim his strength, his ruthlessness, his realism.
In this beclouded atmosphere of threatening storm
his stature was magnified gigantically ; he rose up
like a tower, and Paul, seeing him, glowed with
admiration and confidence. This was the man, he
told himself, for an emergency. Why, even
Cristina, who hated him, must see his splendour.

Suddenly Viva stopped his tirade. He turned
and laughed in her bewildered face.

" So now that that's over and you know the
worst," he said, " we'd better eat."

He swung a chair up to the table, ravenously
clutching his knife and fork. Cristina bent over
between them, placing a dish of *maccheroni* before

him.   And, as she did so, Paul saw, in the candlelight, a thing that checked and chilled his heart :
on her white neck, as clear as if they had been
branded, the blue, bruised imprints of four fingers
and a thumb, the mark of the black hunter's mad
ferocity.   For one moment only he saw it ; but
that moment was enough.   It gathered into one
co-ordinate, overwhelming emotion, all the pity, the
gratitude, the suppressed desire which had tor-
mented his soul and body during the time that had
passed since the shock of their first embrace.   Like
the single grain which, dropped into a saturated
solution of salt, determines crystallisation, that
momentary vision striking into the turbid depths of
his consciousness precipitated the miracle called love.

  She was gone.   Outside the circle of candle-
flame she stood and waited.   Paul could not see
her there ; but all the time he was conscious of her
presence.   Viva, already tired with talk, continued
to eat with rabid intensity.   No word was spoken.
In the dim-lit silence Paul was aware, more poign-
antly than if he had seen her in the bruised flesh, of
all the sweetness, the gentleness, the devotion that
he had despised.   Out of that dusk and silence, in
the fluctuating turmoil of his heart, there was born a
new, astounding vision of Cristina, more rare and
more appealing than any that had come to him in
her moments of transfiguration.   The power of
this imagined image swept all other thought from
his mind ; it invaded, and possessed him, with the
absoluteness of religious conversion, creating a
new heaven and a new earth, consigning all memory
of what had passed before to complete oblivion.

In this strange rapture, the very existence of that familiar room, the presence of Viva, seemed no more than fantastic survivals of a forgotten life. And Naples, the doomed city cowering and shuddering beneath the sword of its dark angel, no more substantial than the fall of cloud that drooped and stole its breath : shadows of chaos, against which, like creation's blinding light, like the stupendous birth of a new sun, the love which he had denied so passionately proclaimed its solitary magnificence. From that ecstatic moment he emerged changed and trembling.   If he had seen her, he thought, he must have died of joy and strangeness.   There was no need to see her.   It was enough that she existed. She and himself together.   A new soul, miraculously, inviolably created.   A miracle as unassailable as the birth of a new star in space.   So clean, so exalted, so secure, that even if death . . ."

"What are you staring at now, Paolo ? " Viva grunted suddenly.   "Your eyes are swimming with tears.   You must have taken cold.   Coryza. Finish that bottle of wine and go to bed.   You needn't wait for me.   I promised to go back to the hospital and take my turn at nine."   He cleared his throat, pushed back his chair, lit a broken cigar and threw himself again upon his bed.   "I don't know what's the matter with you people this evening," he growled.   "You seem to be dazed, the pair of you.   Cristina, we've finished.   Why the devil don't you clear away ? "

She came to the table and removed Viva's plates. Her eyes were lowered ; she did not show him her face, but Paul shuddered at the sweetness of her

presence. Methodically she swept the crumbs
from the table. She was coming near him. His
limbs trembled, his heart fluttered wildly, faltered,
as though it must stop beating. Viva lay with
closed eyes, puffing his stale cigar. Cristina was
now so near that her arm brushed Paul's sleeve, her
pale hand stole toward him. It was over; their
hands had met. In that moment he had touched
divinity. She knew, she knew! By that brief
contact of their meeting fingers, as delicate as
moth-wings brushing nocturnal flowers, their union
had been sealed eternally, the spirit of each had
interfused the other. Indissoluble covenant, tran-
scending words! His brain reeled; his glad heart
laughed in triumph at the unconscious Viva.

Viva rolled from the bed; he rose to his feet and
pulled his hat on. Short of the doorway he found
himself face to face with the retreating Cristina.
He stared at her curiously.

"Upon my soul, Cristina, you're crying too!
The thing must be infectious."

"No, no, Pietro," she protested, smiling with a
broken voice. "It's nothing. You're mistaken.
The smoke of your cigar . . ."

She escaped his scrutiny hurriedly with her tray.

"You don't catch me with tales of that kind,"
Viva continued, addressing Paul's back. "I
suppose you've been quarrelling? What have you
been doing to her? Or has that blackguard
been torturing her again?"

Paul did not answer. "Well, well," Viva
grumbled, "I'm damned if I ever can understand
you two. Whatever it is, I wish you'd get it over."

He searched his pocket and found another stump of cigar. " I suppose I may just as well," he muttered. " They say that tobacco's an admirable disinfectant, and this stuff is strong enough to asphyxiate an elephant, let alone a *spirillum*." He hesitated, then spoke again in a graver tone. " Look here, Paolo," he said. " I want you to realise that this is no joke. In a day or two, at the present rate, your Institute is certain to be closed. Why the devil don't you get off to Pogerola until it's passed over ? There's nothing magnificent in risking your life unnecessarily. If I weren't what I am, I shouldn't remain here a second longer than I could help. *Verbum satis*, my son ! Take a hint and clear out to-morrow. Cristina and I will look after the rubbish you leave here."

Paul shook his head. Only a few hours before he had rejected the entreaties contained in his mother's letter. In the interval a new, a glorious world had been born whose flaming centre was concentrated in this house, in this very room. To leave Naples, to leave Cristina at the moment of this wonder's birth, to turn back, like a coward, from the gates of paradise !

" You can't frighten me, Pietro," he said. " I have work to be finished. I can't leave it."

" Well, go your own way," Viva answered scornfully. " I've always maintained you were born an idiot, Paolo. If you've made up your mind, let your blood be on your own head. But don't go and reproach me on your deathbed with not having warned you ! " He sighed wearily and stuck on his hat. " *Au revoir*," he said. " You

needn't wait up for me. I shan't leave the hospital
before three o'clock in the morning. And, for the
Lord's sake, tell that Cristina not to wake me
to-morrow."

He went. When he had gone Paul sat on at the
table, with tranced eyes. He stared before him,
unaware of the physical existence of Viva's room;
his body dazed, his spirit rapt in a high ethereal
ecstasy. A light flared suddenly in his eyes. One
of the candles which Cristina had lit had burnt
down to its socket. This sudden stimulus pricked
him into a mechanical reaction. He blew out the
candles. Other muscles, obedient to habit, carried his
body out on to the landing and into his own room.
The open windows admitted a tepid air; it came to
him charged with the familiar odour of oil-paint
and varnishes.

At first he could see nothing. Then, as his eyes
grew accustomed to the dark, the square of the
window defined itself as a disc, faintly illumined by
the lights of the city beneath. In an abstraction of
pure, unthinking happiness he stood, suspended.
Only one sense survived this nirvana of beatitude:
his hearing, strained, alert, like the controller of
some advanced listening-post, to catch the fall of a
footstep on the stairs.

A faint sound reached it. Immediately his brain
awoke; his heart leapt; his body's least capillaries
dilated into a flush of warmth: the singing current
lapped his brain in a rosy mist; his throat grew dry,
his limbs unnatural and tremulous. He shuddered,
like a tree caught in a squall of wind. She was
coming. At last . . . at last!

Silence. The eager sentinels had deceived him.
But even though the instant of alarm had passed
the thrill of anticipation and desire continued to
possess him; his heart still hammered its precipitate
rhythm; his limbs still glowed and trembled. The
churning of blood in his ears, the commotion of
his own shaken body, were all that he could hear.
Gradually his heart-beats slowed; his burning
limbs grew cold. He had passed from fire to ice,
in the space of one fierce moment.

And with the cold came fear, fear that she would
not come, fear for the frustration of his desire, fear
of the mocking silence. If, after all, he had been
deceiving himself? If she had neither understood
nor shared the ecstasy the promise of that mystical
contact? If, understanding and transported as she
was, she had found her terror, the black hunter,
waiting below? The mark of the beast, the stigma
of five blue bruises, burned into his brain. A pang
of jealousy, fiercer than his desire, seized him. She
was his, his, eternally. Whatever the power that
bound her, he would assert his right of possession.
"Wait, wait . . ." his reason advised him.

He had done with waiting. Hadn't he waited
month after futile month? His passion shrivelled
all prudence and reason together. Sheeted in its
flame, he passed to the door and flung it open. A
warm shadow impeded his passage. It was she,
Cristina. Like tongues of flame in the darkness
they met.

"Paolo," she whispered.

"Cristina!"

"My own, my darling!"

" Cristina . . . I love you."

" I cannot believe it. Oh, Paolo, Paolo! I cannot bear it."

" There is nobody like you, Cristina. I worship you."

" What can you worship, Paolo? I am nothing : only what you have made me."

" Yourself . . . yourself! Tell me, my love, you knew?"

" Yes, yes, I knew. You didn't love me before."

" I have loved you always. I think I must have been blind."

" No, no, you didn't love me. But you need not excuse yourself. What does it matter now? . . . Oh, Paolo, Paolo," she cried, " why am I not younger?"

" Cristina," he answered, " how can you use that word? Never again! I forbid you. Now there is no such thing as time for us. I wouldn't have you different. I want you as you are."

He drew her into the darkened room, and locked the door behind them. The sound of the key grating in its wards stabbed her with alarm. She clutched his arm.

" Oh, Paolo, what are you doing? You mustn't Suppose he came?"

" Then let him come!" he laughed. " Neither God nor devil can take you from me to-night!"

He caught her in his arms again. Her terrors melted away beneath his fire.

" It is only for you that I am afraid," she protested tenderly. " Last night, when I went for the last parchments—was it then? It seems longer

—in my hurry, my fright, I dropped something, a handkerchief, Paolo. When you went out this afternoon he came here and found it. He didn't miss anything—no, no—but he knew I'd been there in the attic. He was like a maniac, Paolo—he took me by the throat . . ."

" My darling, I know. I've seen. The sight nearly killed me. Your white throat, Cristina, my darling ! "

" No, no, that is nothing. I'm used to it. It's only for you that I'm afraid," her lips protested once more.

His own lips closed them. " There is no more fear," he told her through his kisses. He gathered her to him with strong, quivering hands. He kissed her closed eyes. They fluttered like caught birds. She was all warm, tremulous, yielding, soft as a captured nestling, in his embrace. She sighed. She was gentle, unresisting, and content.

For a long time they had spoken no word but the sweet syllables of their own murmured names. The room was solitary as a cloud; remote, becalmed, high-lifted above the sleeping city. There they lay, clasped in each other's arms, awake, and softly breathing. They had no need for words or looks. Only, at times, when Paul opened his eyes, he would see that Cristina's also were open and gazing at him. In the dusk they seemed to him of a deep, mysterious softness ; for he had never seen love in the eyes before. And her face, too, in its luminous pallor and complete repose, seemed to have lost all trace of the fears and sufferings that had left their mark upon it. It was the face of a

child, angelic in its innocence; spiritualized, made
more than human by the peace of love. So,
without words or movement, they lay and gazed
solemnly at each other, until their hearts could hold
no more of the intolerable sweetness.

The sound of a discordant clanging whose over-
tones trembled on the motionless air recalled them
simultaneously to consciousness. They listened as
its echoes died away into silence.

"Two o'clock," Cristina whispered. Her voice
was awed and childlike.

"Why should we count the strokes?" he
answered impatiently.

"Because they tell us that we are safe," she said.
"He was here this morning. I know that he won't
come to-night."

"Cristina, my sweet one, why should you think
of him? Why can't you be like me, who think of
nothing but you?"

"I can't," she told him. "When one is quiet
like this in the dark so many thoughts take hold
of one."

"I defy them to frighten you. Don't you
realise? All that is finished."

"Ah, God, if it *were* finished!" she murmured.

"I will not allow the thought of him to enter
your brain. Because you are mine, Cristina."

"Yes, I am yours," she answered dreamily.
"Nothing can alter that." She took his face in
her hands; she kissed him, long and tenderly.
"Now I must go," she said. "Good-bye, my
dear one."

He would not let her go. He needed her.

Above all he could not bear that their parting should
be marred by the mysterious uneasiness which
darkened her voice and set her spirit at a distance
from his. But his arms could no longer contain
her; she was alien, unmoved by his entreaties.

"At any moment," she said, "Viva may return."

"What does it matter?"

She shook her head. "He is bound to know.
He might even come to wake you with some urgent
news. And then . . ."

"Listen: he told me that he wouldn't be back
before three. We have another hour, at least, and
each moment is so precious. Only think what we
have wasted already!"

She smiled. "You are so eager, Paolo, and life
is only beginning. It is dangerous, I tell you,
trying to grasp too much. No, no, I must go. I
want to go; and if you love me you won't try to
prevent me."

Releasing herself from his arms she left him;
her shadow crossed the luminous square of the
window. Paul followed her. Clasped together,
they stood gazing into the starless night. All
Naples slept beneath them. Its lights were like the
smoulder of a city burnt to ashes. Quiet as death!
Above, a silence that tingled, as with vibrations of
lost starlight: beneath them, the drugged stillness
of sleep.

Suddenly that silence was lacerated by a sound of
terror, the voice of a woman, screaming and wailing
for help from the pit of the hidden street.

"Help, help!" she wailed. "My husband, my
Michele, he is dead . . . he is dead!"

The sound wavered as she ran along the street, calling and calling. Soon it was lost in that of opening windows, in the shouting of neighbours who answered her. The street was a hubbub of cries and counter-cries, confused, as in the panic of a city taken by stealth. Paul and Cristina clung together and listened. Like a black bat, fluttering out of the dark, fear flew into their hearts.

" The cholera," Paul whispered.

" Cholera," she repeated. " In the night . . ."

Monstrous, that this cold shadow should threaten their newly-won immortality ! All Paul's spirit rose in protest against it. He clasped Cristina more closely, as though, by the interposition of his own body, he could protect her.

" What can it matter to us ? " he cried. " Life and death . . . We are above both of them, so high that nothing can touch us. Yesterday, perhaps. But now we have lived, we have lived ! In this moment we're living, Cristina. To-morrow? To-morrow stretches to the end of time. We will not think of it. We're one. Nothing can part us. Death . . . let him do his worst ! I laugh, I snap my fingers at him ! "

She did not answer him. He took her silence for assent; only, in the darkness, she pressed more closely to him, moulding her body to his, as though to confirm, to accomplish that indestructible union. Then, without word or sign, her muscles relaxed. In another moment she was gone.

IV

BENEATH the black curtain of pestilence, that turned Naples into a city of night, the dark rose of their love unfolded. Its beauty was exalted, its perfume rarefied by a double danger: the shadow of the black hunter, which, even in their most abandoned moments, clouded Cristina's eyes; the imminence of that avenging angel, whose breath was destruction. Paul and Cristina were conscious of both alike, yet, in their passionate hallucination, cared for neither.

Meanwhile the epidemic developed rapidly. Two days later the Institute of Fine Arts was closed. The shopman of the Toledo had not been far out in his calculations of a geometrical progression. By the end of the week Viva's facts confirmed his estimate; two thousand cases noted, more than eight hundred deaths.

" We're right in the thick of it here," he confided to Paul. " The *Carmine's* the central focus. The filth of these streets on the edge of the port; all these old houses, riddled with *fondaci* . . . What can you expect? The cholera asks for nothing better. It flourishes here like weed on a dunghill. As for the hospitals: we've done our best, but we can't do any more. The *Pellegrini* and *Gesù e Maria* won't hold another bed. And in my opinion, it's only beginning."

He paced the room abstractedly. Paul could see that the continued strain was beginning to tell on him. All his old glossy spruceness had disappeared. His clothes hung on him, dusty and disordered. His sanguine features were drawn, grey, hungry; his cheeks unshaven.

"Why don't you clear out, you fool?" he turned upon Paul savagely. "Why, in God's name, haven't you gone already? You're doing nothing here. Your Institute's shut. You can't do any good. I've told you times on end that it's madness to stay here. Lock up this room; leave the keys with me or Cristina; get back to Pogerola and stay there snug till it's over!"

"We've thrashed all this out before, Pietro," Paul told him. "Two days ago you were raging against the people who had 'ratted.' Well, I'm not going to rat."

"Now you're blithering like a cretin. God, I've no patience with you! Ratting? I was speaking of doctors. Their position's quite different. They have a duty to their patients—to humanity and their own self-respect. With you this is merely bravado, or sheer damned ignorance. Get out of it, Paolo. Get out before it's too late!"

"Oh, yes, save my skin, carry cholera to Pogerola, and leave my friends—Cristina and you —in the lurch! Many thanks for the kind suggestion," Paul answered. "It's very polite of you."

"Polite?" Viva growled. "You can leave me out of it. Doctors carry charmed lives; it's you poor damned laymen, let me tell you, who kick the bucket. I can look after myself. And as for Cristina . . . I'm hanged if I see what Cristina has to do with it."

Paul laughed.   At times, intoxicated by the pride
of possession, he was almost tempted to enlighten
him.   Yet, for some obstinate, inexplicable reason,
he felt that its secrecy was a precious part of their
rapture, and could not abandon it.

"Cristina's in the same boat as ourselves," he
parried.

"Never mind about her! I'll look after
Cristina," said Viva.

"You'll be busy enough looking after yourself.
In any case, Pietro, I'm going to see this through."

"I suppose you think you're a hero?" Viva
sneered.

"Not in the least.   You should know me better
than that.   I'm staying because I've made up my
stupid mind, and am as stubborn as a donkey.
Leave it at that."

"You never spoke a truer word."   Viva laughed
bitterly.   Then, suddenly he turned on Paul and
gripped his hand.   "Paolo, you're the damnedest
fool in Christendom; but you're a good friend.
I don't see much of your face in these vile days,
but it's true I'd be lost without you.   The solemn
truth!   Only, for both our sakes, don't neglect the
precautions of which I've told you."

"No fear of that," Paul assured him.   "I'm
taking no risks.   I never felt less like dying in all
my days."

As soon as Viva went back to hospital Cristina
joined him, and life was sweet indeed.   They two
were as solitary as the first lovers in Eden.   That
house in the *Vicolo degli Angeli* was a world set apart.
On the day that followed their night of avowal,

the warning cloud that brooded over the city had
disappeared ; the whole sky cleared to a pure,
celestial blue. No alien step invaded their high
paradise. If ever the black hunter entered the
house, Cristina spared her lover the pain of knowing
it. The habit of furtive dissimulation which she
had learned from her dealings with her master made
her skilful to keep Paul's mind unconscious of his
existence. His name never passed her lips ; nothing
but the five black bruises on her white neck remained
to bear witness to his sinister power. For days on
end they saw no living soul but Viva.

Their life was surrounded by a strange quietness.
Under a combined tyranny of fear and heat, the
people of Naples kept their houses. That clamor-
ous town, the noisiest in Europe, suddenly became
dumb. The cabs, the hawkers' barrows disappeared, as though the plague had selected them for
early destruction. The pavements no longer grated
at dawn beneath the wheels of waggons piled high
with fodder and fruit and vegetables from the flats
below Vesuvius. The city was left to its evil
isolation. Produce might rot in the fields, and
Naples starve, for all the country-people cared.
Now the only wheels to be heard at night were
those of the long-shafted wains of the Sanitary
Authority, jolting their load of limp mortality from
stone to stone, stopping, at the muffled drivers'
commands, to pick up outcast dead or dying from
the *fondaci*, carrying them on to indiscriminate
burial in the plague-pits of Poggioreale.

Viva, or Viva's spectre, more thin, more
harassed, more irritable every day, would sprawl

on his bed and tell them how things were going.
His views were not encouraging.

"We're all at sixes and sevens," he complained.
"There's no direction. The Sanitary Authority's
like some damned old woman, throwing up her
hands and running from house to house. God,
it's fantastic! You'd think we were back in the
Middle Ages. Bonfires to be lit in the streets:
that's their latest decree. As if it weren't hot
enough as it is! Science? That counts for nothing. They won't listen to it. The only thing
that counts in these days is superstition. Portents
and relics and amulets. You can see it for yourself
in the streets. One day some wretched battered
image at a corner gets a reputation for miracles;
the next you'll see it smothered in votive offerings;
the day after that they're ready to spit on it. Upon
my soul you'd think we were savages. These
credulous fools deserve to die. I'm sick of them."

And still the tenuous microbe of cholera, which
an odd degree of heat or cold can kill, went rioting,
multiplied by quintillion on quintillion. Men
gaped at miracles, gave them their passionate faith,
and died before they could carry it back to their
homes. Quacks, hawking specifics, fell in the
streets, and were buried with gold in their pockets
that not even the scavengers would touch. Neither
faith nor science availed. In the face of their
failure the harassed city relapsed into a bored and
deadly apathy.

Out of that apathy more hideous growths arose.
Viva described them in detail. That devoted
spectre had passed beyond all reticence. "Pom-

peii . . . Pompeii ! " The word was always on
his lips. No other could suggest the enormities
that he had seen.

" To think," he told them, " that all these years
we've been fools enough to take Naples for granted,
as if it were just an ordinary civilized city ! Now
I know better. Naples is a hundred cities. A
palimpsest. You, Paolo, with your parchments,
know what that means. A palimpsest of a hundred
layers, and cholera the solvent. Up till now we've
known nothing but the modern script on the top.
The cholera's eaten away that surface like acid.
Out comes the Renaissance : fires in the streets,
amulets, religious processions ! Another layer
goes : we find ourselves staring at the dark ages.
Another : we're back in Pompeii ! But we haven't
finished yet. Oh, no ! Stratum after stratum,
down and down into geological time ! At the
present moment I reckon we're roughly ten thousand
years before Christ.

" And no wonder either ! " he cried. " I sym-
pathize. I'm a man of the stone age myself. Who
can pretend that life has any more value, any
significance ? We're being exterminated ; we've
reached a blind alley in evolution. We hate it ;
we want to survive. Not consciously. One
doesn't think about it. We're driven by something
deeper and older than thought, driven to perpetuate
ourselves, our race, humanity . . . in the usual
way. We have no shame ; such things no longer
exist. We don't care a *soldo* what anyone thinks
of us. Why the devil should we ? Our immortal
souls can take care of themselves. We still have

our bodies, thank heaven! You, Paolo, up here have no conception of what the word lust means. In the squares, in the public streets . . . All Naples, I tell you, is nothing but one gigantic brothel! As for the *fondaci* . . . your old fraud Dante would rub his eyes if he saw them. He wouldn't have the face to say he'd been in hell before. At first the sights turned me sick—though God knows my stomach's strong enough—but now they mean nothing to me. Nothing! I'm in it: I'm in it. I laugh. I glory in it. I'm like a drunken man roaring at a bad joke. You understand?"

At this he burst into peals of shrill and horrible laughter. Their ghastliness chilled Paul's heart. He saw the tight-lipped horror in Cristina's face. It seemed to him that Viva's reason was swaying on the edge of mad abysses. He caught at his arm; he held him, and tried to steady him. Then Viva stopped laughing; glared at him savagely. "What the devil's the matter with you now?"

"Pietro, this is impossible," he told him. "You can't go on indefinitely like this. You won't eat; you don't sleep. There's a breaking point, and I think you've just about reached it. You've wrecked your body already; if you go on like this you'll smash your brain as well. You can't go back to the hospital to-night."

"Can't, *can't?*" Viva cried out passionately. "And who the hell are you to talk to me like this? What right have you . . ."

"We're friends," Paul began.

"Friends?" Viva laughed harshly. "I tell you there is no more friendship. Friendship is a thing

that belonged to the age before the flood. Why
are you frightened of madness? Can't you see for
yourself that the whole world's going mad . . .
you, and I, and Cristina, and everybody in Naples?
D'you think I care for my body? You haven't
seen what I have. I know how bodies end. I
have no body left. Only one thing: pride, sense
of duty, obstinacy, idiocy—whatever you like to
call it—that tells me I've got to go on working till
I drop. And you can't stop me, Paolo; I can't
stop myself; nothing in heaven or earth can stop
me now. So you'd better leave me alone!"

His grey lips twitched as he spoke; his eyes
were dangerous and malignant; he glared at Paul
like a wild beast cut off from its den. Such
passionate determination was unanswerable. And
Viva, crouched to spring, profited by his silence:

"You think I'm crazy," he snarled. "Who are
you to teach me? My Lord, you make me sick!
What are you doing here at all? Are you afraid
to move? You talk to me about madness, and here
you hang about with your damned, dreamy artist's
inertia when you might have been safe in Pogerola
a fortnight ago! What good are you doing here,
I say? I, at any rate, can make myself useful.
You . . . you're about as useful as a child at the
breast! Whether you stay here or not makes no
odds to me. If I saw you dying of cholera to-night
I'd laugh in your face, for the cursed fool that you
are. Don't ask me for pity! If you want to die,
die, and be damned to you!"

He flung out of the room in a blind fury. Paul,
staring after him, dazed by the torrent of words,

was caught, as suddenly, in another spate. Cristina . . .

"Paolo," she was saying, her arms clasped round his neck; "Paolo, my darling, don't you see he was speaking the truth? How blind I've been! How blind, and senseless, my love! But that makes no difference to my wickedness. Now that he's opened my eyes and I can see what I've done, I could die with shame, Paolo. To think of the time that you've wasted—the danger you've faced! A fortnight ago you might have been safe in Pogerola. He's right: you can do no good here, Paolo; you must go at once! To-night . . . Not another minute!"

He took her in his arms; he tried to stop her entreaties with kisses; her purpose was hard as steel, but it could not move him.

"Do you know so little of me," he said, "as to think that I can leave you now?"

"What does it matter?" she cried. "I've had my happiness—more than I ever looked for. I thank God for it, I'm contented. If I were to die this moment, if I never saw you again, I wouldn't complain. But with you it's different, Paolo, you are so young. All your life is before you."

"My life is here in my arms. You are my life, Cristina."

"That's what you think for the moment, Paolo," she pleaded, "and I love you for thinking it. But even if I've been blind before—ah, so cruelly blind —I must see clearly now. You love me—yes, but you're too young to realise that this will not be your only love. I am much older than you, Paolo;

you've no idea how old I am. I don't deceive myself in that. This love will pass; you'll forget me; some day, when I'm forgotten, you'll love and marry a woman younger than yourself. That is certain; I know it; and I don't grudge you or her that happiness. Remember what Pietro said. There's no time to lose. Paolo, my own darling, forget me, leave me, Paolo . . ."

He would not let her go. She struggled to free herself so violently that her body was bruised by him. He tried to calm her with tender, childish words that they had invented, with kisses, with caresses. Not even these could soften her resistance. There was a force coiled in her like that of a steel spring.

" I will not listen," she repeated stubbornly; " you must go, you must go ! "

" Do you think," he cried, " that I am weaker than you; that you can force me to leave you? Even if you'd begged me to go a fortnight since I'd have refused. You never thought of such a thing till that madman Pietro put it into your head. Now it's too late."

" No, no, it isn't too late. Are you reproaching me? Oh, Paolo, that's cruel. If you can speak as cruelly as that, it's clear that you don't love me; and that is all the more reason why you should go."

" Now you are twisting my words. You know I'm not cruel. That is a lie, and you know it. You know, as well as I do, that I love you utterly, and no other living soul."

" Your mother, Paolo ? " she whispered.

" Ah, Cristina, you're clever ; but no, you don't catch me like that. I've thought of her too, and I've chosen. I love you—the words are becoming monotonous. Nothing that you say can make me leave you, so you'd better resign yourself to the inconvenience of my staying."

He laughed. She couldn't understand his laughing. His irony, which had always puzzled, now had power to wound her. He was so different from all the other men she had known, from Viva, from the black hunter. To joke, even so gently, at a moment when her whole soul was strained to accomplish its last renunciation ! She stared into his smiling eyes, hopelessly bewildered. She pulled all her forces together for a final effort.

" Then you shall stay," she said quickly. " I will not ask you to go again. You may kill yourself ; but you shall not make me a murderess. You stay for yourself, not for me. Understand that clearly. I have nothing more to do with you. I hope I shall never see you again. Now let me go. I wish it."

" Cristina," he cried, " you're joking ! "

" No, I'm not joking." She shuddered. " I leave the jokes to you. You may break as many hearts as you like with your jokes, but not mine. You cannot hurt me any more. It is finished. No, no, you need not kiss me. Once I made myself a thief for your kisses ; but that's all over. You've broken me, killed me. I can't even bear to look at you."

She put her hands to her eyes. She began to cry softly ; her voice was like a baby's wailing. She

seemed so brokenly, pitifully in his power that he
released her, hoping to woo her back to reason
when her tears had spent themselves. His own
voice wavered as he spoke to her :

"Cristina, my darling, come to me. You don't
understand. I'd rather die—you know it—than
hurt you like this."

He gathered her into his arms ; she ceased her
crying, and gazed at him with grave, stricken eyes.

"Then you will go?" she murmured.

"I cannot go."

"Ah, how you make me hate you, Paolo!" she
cried.

Her eyes were hugely black, with pupils dilated.
Paul saw in them a fixed determination which he
knew he could neither bend nor break. He spoke
solemnly :

"I will go to Pogerola," he said, "if you'll come
with me."

"Come with you? I? Oh, Paolo, what are
you saying?"

"If you'll come with me now, Cristina, I will
go this moment."

"But, Paolo, how can I come? You forget..."

He was soon to remember. He had seen that
look before ; a cloud sweeping over her face : the
shadow of fear that was cast by the black hunter.
That terror, which had darkened her life for more
than ten years, still had power, even in memory,
to turn her face ashen.

"You forget," she repeated. "He would kill
me—he would kill both of us!"

"Cristina," he cried, "how dare you frighten

yourself like this? The man's no more terrible than other men. At the worst, I can deal with him."

"You, my poor darling? Oh, Paolo, you don't know, you don't know . . ."

"At Pogerola, up in the mountains? He'd never find us there. Only be reasonable!"

"He would follow us to the ends of the earth. I daren't . . . I daren't think of it. And then, Paolo, your mother!"

"Are you frightened of women as well? We are wasting time. Cristina, I'm as strong as you are. If you will not come with me, I stay here." He passed from this threat to entreaty. "Come with me, my love. Don't you trust me?"

"Oh, Paolo . . . Trust you?"

She held out her arms to him, piteously. As he took her, he felt he had won. On that moment of hesitation he pressed in triumphantly. "Then you will come with me, Cristina? Thank God . . . thank God!" He knew, by the fear which still clouded her eyes, that his triumph was precarious; he must profit by this instant of surrender to make it certain. "There's not a second to be wasted," he said. "We must go while we've time. If we hurry, as fast as we can, to Castellamare, we may pick up some cart that's going to Pogerola to-night. You see, we have nothing to spare." He became implicit. "Go down to the basement quickly, my darling," he said, "and collect any clothes or things you want to take with you. As little as possible. We shall have to travel light. While you are there I'll pull my own stuff together—that won't take me long—and scribble a note to Pietro. Poor old devil, how happy he'll be when he gets it! Now go, my sweet one!"

He kissed her tenderly. Then without a word she left him. She went down the stairs like a woman walking in her sleep; and Paul, as soon as she was gone, set to work in a fever, sorting his scattered papers with a bewildered lack of purpose. Among them, with an effect of curious irony, his eyes fell on the folios of the Salerno *codex*. How little did they or the searchings of soul which had clung to them matter to him now! There were so many things, indeed, that he wanted to take with him, that, in the end, he found it impossible to discriminate. Cristina, by now, should be waiting for him below. He abandoned the effort of sorting, and hurriedly pencilled his note to Viva:

Dear Pietro, he wrote,
   We have gone. Now are you satisfied? God bless you!

Paul.

Then he picked up a bundle of clothes and hurried downstairs. The door of Cristina's apartment was locked from inside. He could not understand it. A sudden fear seized him that she might have tricked him after all. There was no limit to the power of the fear that might have swept back on her when once she had left him. The quietness that brooded behind that locked door carried fear to his own heart. Then a muffled sound reached his ears, like the gasps of a woman sobbing. It

R

angered him to think that her courage should have
deserted her as much as that.   He threw down his
bundle and beat on the door with his fist.

"Cristina, my love," he cried.   "I am ready.
I'm waiting.   Come quickly."

The muffled sobbing rose suddenly to a cry of
anguish or alarm.   He could not understand it.
"What is the matter?" he called.

Then, almost without warning, the key turned
in the wards, the door was thrown open.   Paul
saw, not Cristina's pitiful figure, but the monstrous
bulk of the black hunter, the dark brows lowered
for a charge above blazing eyes.   He stood there
snorting like a bull; he spoke no word.   Then,
like a maddened bull, he launched himself, his full
weight flung like a boulder from a catapult, upon
Paul's body and face.   No strength of his could
withstand the force of that animal fury.   Before
he knew what had happened he was over, crushed
to the ground.   He lay there, battered and senseless
on the marble flags.

V

RECOVERING consciousness, his dazed brain groped
in vain for any memory to which it might cling and
so regain stability.   All that surrounded him seemed
unstable, unfamiliar; above his head the high, dim
shaft of a marble stairway; below, cold flags.   He
could only use one eye, for the other was closed,
and when he dragged himself on to his elbow pain
stabbed at his side so sharply that a cry came from
his lips which woke hollow echoes in the vault

above him. It seemed as if his whole being were
wrapped in pain. It hurt him to think. Yet only
by making himself think could he escape from this
nightmare. He rubbed his closed eye—the blood
on it had clotted already—and suddenly the last
moment of sentience returned to him, flashing
across his bewildered mind the image of a body
black and monstrous launched at him, like a
thunder-bolt, through an open doorway. The vision
vanished; but now he was himself—a strangely
numb and incoordinate self, uncertainly peering,
through one undamaged eye, at the bundle of
clothes which he had abandoned when he had
called and knocked at Cristina's door.

Mastering, as best he could, the multitude of new
pains that every movement awakened, he propped
himself on to his knees, then staggered to his feet.
The thread of his broken consciousness became
continuous; the pattern of the events that had
preceded that shattering impact shook itself into
shape with the click of a figure in a kaleidoscope.
From a hazy groping after memory his mind passed
to organized thought, to purpose, to action. He
saw that the door through which the black monster
had issued was closed. He swayed to it, giddily;
then propped himself against the doorpost, and
rapped on the panels with his bruised fist.

"Cristina," his weak voice called. "Cristina
. . . are you there?"

There was no answer. As he called again, a fear
flashed through his mind that the black hunter,
having left him for dead, had carried her away
with him.

"Cristina," he called again, with all the voice that was left. "Cristina, come quickly!"

Before the echo of his calling had died away another sound reached him, a patter of quick footsteps, like the scurry of rats in a wainscot. She is there, after all, he thought, thank God! Thank God! She is coming! And he called again: "Cristina, my darling, is it you?"

Her agonized voice answered him. "Oh, Paolo, is that you? I thought he had killed you, my love, I thought you were dead."

The sound of her living voice pulled his senses together. He emerged from his nightmare at last, completely himself, so that now, when he spoke, his voice and his words were his own.

"Why don't you open the door?" he said. "Quickly! We must go at once."

"I can't open it, Paolo," she answered. "He has taken the key."

"But have you no other key? Think, think, Cristina!"

"There was only one key, and he's taken it. Oh, Paolo, did he hurt you?"

"Never mind about me," he said harshly. "There must be some window. There are windows, Cristina, I remember, opening on the street. I'll join you outside."

"But, Paolo, my dear, you forget. Those windows are barred with iron."

"Go and look," he answered her brutally. "There must be some way. And quickly! We cannot waste time!"

She obeyed him without a word. The air of the

vestibule was dense in his lungs. He felt that in another moment he must suffocate with it. It was foul, hot, tainted, like the breath of some obscene beast gorged with death. It grew thick and yellow; it smelt—was this madness?—it smelt of sulphur, as if it had leaked out of hell. He heard a patter on the flags beside him. A rat, as big as a half-grown kitten, a foul, hunched creature, loped past him into a corner and crouched, staring at him, with dazed and beady eyes. His heart went suddenly cold. Viva was right, he thought, I'm going mad. No rats are as big as that. God help me!

But he saw it . . . *he saw it!* It trembled and gazed at him out of its pitiful, narrowed eyes. All the blood in his body seemed to be rushing to his head. His head was a furnace in which his brain was melting, melting away.

The sound of a whisper recalled him. Cristina had returned to the keyhole. " It's just as I told you," she whispered. " The windows are closed, every one of them, with iron gratings. Oh, Paolo, it's you who are wasting time. He may come back again. Go—go, I beg you."

" Do you think that I'm going to leave you here at his mercy?" he cried. " There must be some way! The door . . . it is old; it may give. Stand clear, Cristina, while I try to break it in!"

He pulled all his strength together and hurled his bruised body like a ram against it. Its impact had as much effect as if it had fallen on stone. The seasoned oak held, unyielding. Again and again he flung himself against it, till his strength was spent.

" Oh, leave me, leave me, Paolo ! " again she entreated him. " You see it's no good."

" Do you want to get rid of me ? " he answered savagely. " Wait . . . I've not finished yet."

He climbed the stairs, as fast as his lost breath would let him, and dragged from the dishevelled room one of the oak trestles on which his table was supported. With this as a ram he renewed his assaults on the locked door. In vain . . . It was against such attacks as these that the builders had planned it. Gigantic stony echoes of his battering filled the stairway.

" He will hear," Cristina was crying, in a voice of terror. " He will hear. He'll come back, Paolo, he'll kill you ! "

" For God's sake, be quiet ! " he cried. Panting, he flung the trestle aside. No wood, in his feeble hands, could make an impression on that unyielding oak. What he needed was iron. A crowbar, to smash the lock in. " But I'm almost too weak to hold one," he thought. " I need someone to help me." As he stood, breathing hard, uncertain even of his legs' continued support, he passed in review all possible sources of aid. In the house there was none—no soul but himself and Cristina. And how could he call upon strangers to assist in an act of violence so obviously illegal as that which he con-templated ? There was nobody in all Naples who could help him, no friend, save Viva. And Viva, at this moment, was toiling in the foul wards of his hospital. He made a swift decision. He must go and find him.

Cristina, crouched behind the oak door, was

sobbing softly. He stooped to the keyhole.
"Cristina," he said, "for God's sake stop that
crying; that kind of thing won't help us. Listen
to me: I am going to find Pietro and get him to
help me with a crowbar or something. Be ready
to start with me as soon as I come back. I shan't
be long. Understand?"

Her broken voice answered him. "Oh, Paolo,
it's useless. If you love me at all, I beg you, I
entreat you, to leave me."

"Have you no spirit?" he cried. "Are you
such a coward?"

Her answer had filled him with a blind anger that
sent his head spinning as he tottered out into the
street. His mouth and throat were parched with
a desert's dryness.

"Water," he thought, "cold water." Water
was poison. How many times had Viva raved
about it? He could not go on burning away like
this. "The sea," he thought, "the sea. That's
what I want. Surely the sea is pure enough!"

Out of that air of suffocation he staggered into
the street. Another wave of sulphur blew into his
throat and choked him. He choked and gasped
and ran. *The Vicolo degli Angeli* was full of other
people running and crying. Naked or in rags they
poured from the mouths of the *fondaci*, and after
them, in the fume of sulphur, urged by the same
suffocating terror, came the rats, hundreds on
hundreds of them, madly darting, squealing,
crouching, in search of shelter. An aged woman,
with no cover but a dirty chemise, staggered and
fell at Paul's feet. She clutched at his thighs to

raise herself, screaming at him with her toothless mouth :

"Look how the devils have bitten me! Look at my poor legs! Why don't they let us die and be done with it?" She coughed and spluttered; the muscles of respiration dragged her mouth into a sardonic grin. "Fumigating the sewers with sulphur, driving the rats on us like this! They ought to have known. I say they ought to have known better. Rats and Christians together!" She gasped and spat. "Why don't they leave us alone? Blessed Madonna! Oh, my poor legs!"

As Paul tore himself away from her he saw them, skinny, like those of a mummy, scabbed with dirt, bloody with rat-bites.

"Water," he thought; "cold water, pure water, the sea!" But would he ever reach it? Here, in the square at least, the air was freer from sulphur than in the *Vicolo*. Huge and empty it seemed; no stalls, no barrows, not even the painted theatre of the marionettes; so vast that he doubted if he would have strength to cross it. Where was he going? Of course—Viva—the hospital!

He halted to take breath. As if that fetid air could give it him! Fine shivers, like summer lightning, flickered down his spine, his legs; he couldn't say if they were of cold or heat.

At least he had succeeded in crossing the *Mercato*. He was thankful for the achievement. Here, on this northern side of the square, lay the area, now almost deserted, in which the epidemic had started. House after house stood empty, sealed by the

official orders of the Sanitary Authority. As if
cholera mattered ! Nothing mattered now but the
burning in his brain, the suffocation of his clogged
lungs. Cold water—the hospital—Viva . . .

He floundered into a maze of narrow streets.
He fought his way through them. They were
like the *Vicolo degli Angeli* ; full of sulphur-fumes
and screaming women and squealing rats. They
screamed and shouted, these women, cursing heaven,
the rats, the Sanitary Authority. He fought his
way roughly, ruthlessly ; now it was no more
difficult to go on than to turn back. He thought :
this is strange, I must be near the sea. Wave upon
wave it seemed to be breaking, singing, in his ears.
Like the shells on Don Ambrogio's window-sill.

The streets twisted endlessly. They danced and
glimmered before his eyes. " I'm going blind,"
he thought. " I'm a painter, and I'm going blind.
I'd rather die than that." He rubbed his one eye
violently into flashes of blue light, and went lurching
on. He supposed that whether he became blind
or not he was going to die. Certainly he would
die, unless he reached the sea. He must reach it
. . . if only for Cristina. Cristina, locked in the
basement ! Viva would help him to free her. But
was this the way to the hospital ? He couldn't
remember . . .

The narrow street disgorged its fugitives into
another little square. The crowd carried him with
it and subsided, like a rapid swirling into a pool.
At last he knew where he was. There, on the
right, stood a little wine-shop that he had frequented
with Viva and his friends.

"Wine," he thought, " red wine from Gragnano, out of a cool cellar."

" It will be better than water," he thought, "perhaps it will steady me."   He dragged himself to the pavement in an agony of haste and fear lest the wine-shop should be shut.

It was open, thank God, but empty.   He shouted with all his voice that was left.   Out of a reeling background the proprietor appeared.   Paul recognized him by his prominent teeth.   Otherwise he would not have known him ; his dark hair had turned white.

" Gragnano . . . a litre," Paul gasped.

The man stared at his torn clothes, his bloody face, and shrank from him.   " You are ill ? " he asked.

" No, no . . . not ill.   The sulphur is in my throat.   Only a little faint."

He laughed, as much to assure himself as to deceive the other.

The shopkeeper brought him a jug of wine and a glass.   He stood and watched Paul drink.   " This fumigation of the sewers, it's a final stupidity," he complained.   " They tell me that down in the Port hundreds have been bitten by rats.   That's a pretty business, to be sure !   We who live in *Santa Lucia* have something to be thankful for."

" *Santa Lucia ?* " Paul thought vaguely.   " I oughtn't to be here.   Surely the hospital must be in another direction ? "

He swilled his wine, glass after glass.   The man watched him curiously.   How cool, how good it was !   He felt as if he could go on drinking it for ever. For the moment he forgot his bruises, his bruised eye, the stabbing pain in his side. Now all his consciousness seemed to be centred in that parched throat. No other thing was real. The rest of his body, the tavern-keeper who stared and smiled, the brown wine-barrels, the picture of Garibaldi on the wall opposite—all these were shifting, undulant, unsubstantial. The man's voice came to him from a great distance, like that of someone talking on a stormy beach :

" We haven't seen you and your friend lately. I didn't know whether you'd left Naples or died. You never know in these days. I suppose you've come here to meet the doctor ? He often drops in about this time. In the neighbourhood of the hospital all the taverns are shut." He was staring at Paul : " My God ! " he gasped. " I said you were ill. Why did you deny it ? Heaven help us ! "

Even as he spoke Paul felt himself sliding from his chair. The jug of wine crashed on the stone floor beside him. The wine splashed in his face with a heavenly coolness. " No, I'm not ill," he thought, " I'm only dying." He saw the tavern-keeper grotesquely taking shelter behind his butts. He shut his eyes. It was easier to surrender.

People were talking in loud voices over his head. He heard an insane jumble of words. Cholera . . . cholera . . . cholera. As if that had anything to do with it ! One voice was curiously like Viva's. It *was* Viva's. Viva had taken him by the arm and tried to pull him to his feet. His legs would not obey him. Viva's arms were round him. He

heard the panting of Viva's breath beneath the load.
He tried to speak : " Cristina—the basement . . .
the brute locked her in.   Save her ! "

He was lifted and carried out into the street.
What did that matter, as long as Viva knew ?   He
was moving ;   heavy wheels were jolting over the
uneven sets of limestone.   A new horror seized
him.   He remembered the long-shafted carts of the
Sanitary Authority that went by in the night !   The
muffled drivers had picked him up ;   they were
carrying him, living, to the pits at Poggioreale.   He
heard Viva's voice no longer.   Viva had deserted
him.   His dry throat struggled to shape words :

" I'm alive . . . alive !   Pietro, tell them it's a
mistake ;   I'm not dead yet ! "

It seemed as if he were shouting.   But nobody
heard him.   Over the limestone sets the wheels
rumbled on.

VI

FOR three weeks Paul, or the ghost of him, lay in
the hospital of *Gesù e Maria*.   Viva, finding him
collapsed in the wine-shop, had bribed a passing
carter to carry him there.   So much he knew ;   for
when, in a cloud of carbolic spray, they dragged
him through the hospital gates, a sudden clearing
of consciousness, like a window in cloud, admitted,
straight to the centre of his fuddled brain, the
familiar tones of Viva's voice, and even a momentary
vision of Viva's face.

After that, darkness.   A black tunnel of un-

PARADISO   259

measurable time through which his body passed
without sentience or volition, from which it finally
emerged exhausted, discarnate, but, miraculously,
alive, like a thin ghost in purgatory.

As soon as they saw that he had passed the climax
of the disease the doctors left him to work out his
own salvation.   Their hands were too full for them
to bother themselves with convalescents.   He lay
on a straw mattress, dozing or staring at a ceiling
painted with flying cherubim.   Around him fifty
other cholera patients of indiscriminate age and sex
fought out their lonely battles with death.   He saw
them carried into the ward, inert, as he had been
carried ; he heard them praying and blaspheming
in delirium ; sometimes he saw them carried out
again with a sheet over their faces.

For a long time he found it difficult to believe
that he had survived.   Then, suddenly, as though
a mysterious system of tourniquets had been
removed, life began to flow back into his limbs.
The nurse who brought him food, a rough peasant
woman from Caserta, smiled and joked with him
in her swift passage.   " We'll soon be seeing the
last of you," she said.   " Good-bye, and a good
riddance, that's what it will be."

" It was really cholera ? " he asked her.

" Cholera ?   *Madonna mia !*   I should think it
was cholera !   Didn't I look after you ?   I ought
to know ! "

As soon as he could arrange his thoughts, he
asked for Viva.   It seemed strange that Viva, who
had brought him to the hospital, should have
deserted him.

" Viva ? I don't know the name." The nurse shook her head.

" The doctor who brought me here."

" That doesn't help me. My memory's gone completely. There are so many doctors that I don't know half their names. But, when I find a moment to spare—which isn't often, mind you—I'll make enquiries."

That evening when she brought him his dish of soup, he asked her if she'd any news for him. She hesitated.

" Pietro Viva, that was your doctor's name."

" Pietro Viva. Yes," he answered eagerly.

" Poor fellow, he's not been here for more than a fortnight, they tell me. Probably he's gone the way of all the rest." For once the word " dead " did not come easily to her tongue ; but Paul knew what she meant.

" No, no, I won't believe it," he cried. " He was so strong, so full of life. And doctors—he told me so himself—carry charmed lives."

" Poor souls, I wish it were true," the woman murmured.

Paul would not let her go.

" It's more likely," he said, trying to persuade himself to believe what he was saying, " it's almost certain that he was too worn out to come to the hospital. If you could have seen him ! He'd been working night and day ever since the cholera began. Probably he felt he could do no more, and went back to his lodgings. I must go and find him at once. When do you think they'll allow me to go ? "

The nurse shook her head warningly. " If you

take on like this you'll lose all the ground you've
gained. You'll do no good by fretting. Lie quiet,
and get your strength, there's a good boy. Be
patient, and think no more about it."

To think no more about it! That was impossible. Day after day, night after night, he lay
there thinking of the house in the *Vicolo degli Angeli* ;
that little room, the cradle of all his dreams ; Viva,
his friend, his saviour ; Cristina, his love. It was
some consolation to remember—if memory didn't
deceive him—that, with his last words, he had told
Viva how he had left her. His body lay helpless
on the straw mattress : his spirit was always with
them, calling to them, like a ghost, unanswered,
from the other side of darkness. Of Viva he could
think with gratitude, with admiration, with passionate loyalty ; but when he thought of Cristina
it was with a tenderness that broke his heart.
Never, in reality, had she seemed to him as wholly
wonderful as now she seemed ; never so beautiful ;
never so much the consummation of all desire.
The thought of her courage, her goodness, her
beauty haunted him incessantly ; in spirit they
transported him to an ecstasy more rare than any
that he had achieved in her possession. And all the
splendour of their love, those black roses passionately flowering amid the ruins of a stricken city,
gathered defiantly and treasured under the shadow
of death, seemed nothing compared with the joys
they would attain in the new life that lay before
them when all this horror was past. The moment
of their meeting ! He lay and waited for it with
a rapturous, hushed eagerness, thrilled by delicious

tremors of returning life and hope, prolonging, almost willingly, the ecstasy of anticipation.

At the end of the third week the doctors told him, brusquely, that he could go. Although the full violence of the epidemic had spent itself, the hospital was still desperately overcrowded, the city continued to clamour for empty beds.

A grotesque, brown-bearded skeleton, Paul staggered out into the street. He stood irresolute, disorientated, as though he had been dropped from a balloon into the heart of some foreign city. The air was cool and sweet, for the drought had broken and rain fallen in the night. It seemed to him that everything about him, even the air he breathed, was unreal. He could not believe that the sombre block of buildings behind him was the hospital in which he had passed from life to death and back to life again. He could not believe that the street in which he stood had existed before, that the people who jostled him on its pavements were those whom he had met in other days. Gradually the accumulation of remembered sights and sounds and smells drove him back upon reality, until nothing remained unreal but himself. "I am I, Paul Ritchie," he told himself, "I am alive, and this is Naples!"

Regaining his sense of direction, he began to walk. Slowly, at first; for though he had given them practice, his legs seemed no longer to belong to him; it was as though he were walking on air.

With the detached intentness of a floating cloud he penetrated the centre of the city. This was the Toledo; not wholly the street he knew, for the pavements were still half empty and most of the shops shuttered. He passed the window where once his boxes had been displayed. In another life he had seen those shutters closed. He laughed to himself, remembering the shopman's agitation, wondering if the fellow and his gardener were still living. And once again, in an airy exultation, he assured himself : " I am alive . . . alive ! "

The slope of the streets falling to the Port embarrassed his wasted muscles and made his legs tremble. One after another familiar landmarks made his heart beat faster, warning him that the moment of intolerable joy was drawing near. Nothing had changed. It seemed unreasonable that nothing should have changed. Here was the Square of the *Mercato*, not empty, as he had last seen it, but scattered with the barrows of fish-hawkers, noisy with children at play. Beyond and above, the green-tiled cupola of the Carmine rose into a gentle, rain-washed sky.

Nothing was changed. A wave of passionate confidence fluttered his heart. Now it was beating so violently that he could scarcely breathe.

" It is coming," he thought, " at last ! Cristina . . . Cristina ! "

With a shiver of joy he entered the *Vicolo degli Angeli*. He knew it, every stone of the broken pavement. The houses, sombre but benevolent, rose on either side. There, on the right, crouched at the mouth of the *fondaco* as if he had never changed his station, sat the beggar who had wished him a hundred years of happiness. He stared at Paul without recognition as he passed, and Paul was too transported with eagerness to wave a salutation.

S

There stood the great arched gateway. Paul turned to enter it. He could not. The way was barred by an iron gate. The gate was fastened with a chain and a heavy padlock. To its bars, at the level of his eyes, was fixed a wooden notice-board, with a rain-spattered inscription of capitals scrawled in chalk. He stared at it; he read it over and over again. Its significance seemed powerless to penetrate his shattered brain. His brain could not accept the words that were written :

CLOSED BY ORDER OF THE SANITARY AUTHORITY.

He reeled, as though he had been smitten by a blow on the head. He put his hands to his eyes and fell on the broken pavement. He was stunned; he gave up the ghost; he ceased to exist. The beggar from the mouth of the *fondaco* limped over and regarded him dispassionately, as though he had fallen from the sky. Another dead man! Such trifles were not interesting in these days. He squatted on the ground beside Paul and began to go through his pockets methodically. Paul knew what was happening. He did not care.

Suddenly his stupor left him; he came back to life. Part of him only. A strange, unrecognizable part that detached itself from the dissolution of the rest. It freed itself from the death of the self that he knew, neither body nor soul, a pure, naked intelligence, inviolable, immune from fear or love or horror or any other emotion. It took command. It pulled his destroyed body from the ground. It

spoke with the dead tongue, with the dead lips, to
the astonished beggar.

"You know me, you have seen me before. I
used to live here. This house, how long has it
been closed?"

The beggar stared at him: "Eh, now I come to
look at you," he whined, "I seem to remember."

"Answer my question. When did they close
the house?"

"How can I mind a thing like that? A week
ago, a fortnight. Who knows? Why, they shut
them up one by one, dozens of them, because of
this cholera. Haven't you heard tell of that?"

"And the people who lived there. When did
they go? What happened to them?"

"That's a hard thing to ask! I tell you, the
cholera's been about. Oh, yes, I've had it myself."
He cackled obscenely: "but they can't kill skin
and bones; they can't kill the likes of me!"

"Listen," the obedient voice of Paul continued:
"Besides myself there were two people in the
house. A young doctor—you must remember him
—and a woman. Where have they gone?"

"God knows, young man. The house is closed.
Look at the notice. Letters mean nothing to
ignorant old people like me; but you, being young,
can read it, no doubt. I tell you, I know nothing.
No good asking me. I suppose they went, the
same as all the rest, though I never saw them
carried out."

"I must find them. How can I find them?"

"Ask me something easier," the beggar cackled.
"You can go to Poggioreale and look, or, if he is

still alive, you can ask the master of the house."

" The master of the house? You know him? His name, and where he lives?"

" How should I not know him? I've lived here fifty years. I know him as well as I know my own hands. Of course I do. He's Vincenzo Saccola, the gold-beater, a rare old bull too! Don Animale: that's the name he goes by; and if he's living you're like to find him at his shop behind the *Via Co-stantinopoli*, on the left hand side as you come from here. You go and ask him. No good asking an old man like me who hasn't filled his belly for a week."

Unthinking, still drawing strength and purpose from that mysterious survival, Paul's broken body was driven, like a derelict with set sails, across the centre of the city toward the *Via Costantinopoli*. The street of the goldbeaters? Strangers whom he accosted hurriedly showed him the way. It was a little street, with low-browed houses, shops crammed with tainted rags and crockery and rusty iron. After the cholera old clothes went cheap in Naples. The pavements on which they were heaped were thick with shabby customers routing for bargains like poultry on a midden. A stale smell of soiled clothing struggled against the puri-fication of watery sunshine.

On the left . . . Paul was pushing his way through the haggling, malodorous crowd. He went ruthlessly, without excuses, like a doomed man. Before a cavern of a shop, with wide doors thrown open, the pavement was free. Out of its darkness he heard a sound of hammering, blows falling rapidly, incessantly, one after another on a dull surface. He peered inside.

The hammerers took no notice of him. Their eyes were lowered. They went on beating with the absorbed intentness of machines, with a maddening regularity. Three workmen, standing at three tables covered with sheet lead hammering gold into leaf between two layers of parchment. The foremost table was that of the black hunter. He stood above it with his short neck bent forward, a hammer in either hand, savagely obliterating the surface of a sheet of parchment which Paul recognized, with a stab of memory, as part of the Salerno *codex*. He hammered the parchment as if he hated it, as if he were determined that no letter should survive.

When Paul spoke to him he did not break the rhythm of his work. He raised his eyes and stared, grudgingly; they were suffused, resentful, like those of some wild animal roused from a dream of lust. Evidently at first he did not recognize Paul in this spectral guise.

" You know me," Paul explained. " I was your lodger in the *Vicolo degli Angeli*. Myself and my friend Viva, the doctor."

" Yes, yes, I know you," the goldbeater growled. " I know you too well. I thought I'd finished you, you young blackguard." He smiled evilly. " It's no good coming here asking me for your rubbish. They've sealed up the house. It's empty. It'll have to be fumigated. Till then you can't enter it. Come again, in a month's time."

He lowered his bloodshot eyes and went on with

his hammering. He threw the obliterated parchment aside—it had been beaten to a thin membrane —and chose another.

"My belongings are nothing," Paul began . . .

"Then why the devil do you come here, wasting my time?" The goldbeater took a swig at a bottle of wine and wiped his mouth with the back of an enormous hand.

"Cristina and Viva. You know where they are? You can tell me?" Paul pleaded.

"Why should I know anything about them? D'you think I'm such a fool as to go risking my life down there?" the black hunter laughed brutally. "I tell you the house is empty, the doors are sealed. I suppose they're dead. If you want to find where they're buried you'd better try Poggioreale—that is, if your stomach's strong enough." He brought down his hammers together on the virgin page. His bull-neck went red with a sudden irritation. Above the thudding of the hammers he went on snarling at Paul. "Why do you stare at me like that? I don't allow strangers hanging round this shop. Come again, in a month's time, and I'll tell you if you can have your stuff. Most likely they'll burn it. I can't answer for that. If you want to take on the rooms at the same rent I dare say it'll be all right. I'm sure to have found another woman by that time. I've got my eye on one already, another red-haired one. But I warn you, you'll get more than you bargain for if you go smelling round her! Remember—the second dose will be worse than the first!"

His lips were twisted up into an evil leer. A

sudden blindness of anger fell on Paul. In that
moment he was ready for murder. If he had seen
a knife he would have used it then. But the
impulse faltered, it failed, like a flaw of wind. In
the next he was drifting, all that remained of him,
out through the noisy length of the *Via Costantinopoli*, out through the city gates and the degraded
suburbs, over roadways deep in dust, through the
flat market-gardens, into the yellowing vineyards
on the flank of Vesuvius where wine is pressed
which they call the Tears of Christ.

There, amid the songs and laughter of the grape-
harvest, the body of Paul Ritchie fell asleep ; the
soul of the boy who had loved Cristina died.

*   *   *   *

Three days later, in the streets of Pogerola, a
changeling appeared : a starved, gaunt, bearded
man, with dread in his eyes. For two years Paul
lived with his mother, in their cottage by the vineyard, sharing the peasant's life which was hers by
nature, sapping the terraces in Spring and Autumn,
training vine-shoots to trellises, cutting and binding
faggots of olive-branch for fuel.

Pogerola folk had now more cause than ever to
stare at him when he stalked through the street
with his ragged brown beard and tragic eyes. The
people would touch their heads with a significant
gesture : " The cholera in Naples," they would
say. " Paoluccio was always a bit queer, but that
business loosened a screw." The story ran that
he had been flung living into one of the plague-
pits. No wonder that the poor devil was strange !

But Paul rarely passed through the village if he could avoid it. He found no friends in Pogerola but Don Ambrogio, whose white funeral passed to the cemetery, for want of Andrea's linctus, next winter. Sometimes, during the day, business forced him to go to the piazza; but never, never at night. From the piazza of Pogerola at night one could see the lights of Naples. . . .

He forbade his mind ever to think of Naples. His " stuff," as the black goldbeater had called those ardent, early Ritchies, remained in that little cylinder of a room at the top of the house in the *Vicolo degli Angeli* until a new tenant burnt it. Paul dared not think of Naples, and, for this reason too, he dared not paint, lest the poignancy of associations should send him mad again.

In the back of his mind he was satisfied that he had once been mad. It seemed that he could only find certain immunity from a recurrence of this disaster in the stress of physical labour. Therefore, at daybreak, when his mother called him, he would rise, thankfully, and trudge to the fields with his mattock over his shoulder; and there all day, through storm and sunlight, he would toil, as though some devil drove him, closing his eyes to the beauty of the olive groves, which, on the slopes of Pogerola, are changeful as the sea—to that of the flowers which he trampled cruelly underfoot, stalking home, on the edge of darkness, to the cottage where the smoke of his mother's charcoal fire awaited him.

Concetta was a woman of few words. She knew, as well as he did, what it means to suffer in silence.

Perhaps, like the people in the village, she believed his brain had been touched. From the moment when she took him, broken as he was, into her arms, she was never moved to ask him what had happened during the black days in Naples. When they had eaten their supper they sat and looked at each other, without speaking, like animals in a shed, until their heads began to nod with sleep. Then Paul would lurch away silently into his bed-room, praying that he might be spared the torment of dreams. For, in his dreams, Cristina was still very near to him. Sometimes they almost drove him to Naples to go and search for her. He could never, in his heart, believe that she was not living . . .

In the Spring of the second year Paul's mother died. They buried her in the grave of her brother Andrea. In Pogerola people whom Paul had for-gotten stopped him, with easy tears in their eyes, and wrung his hand. He could not answer their condolences with fitting words. He had loved his mother ; yet, in his present state of annihilation, her death seemed hardly to move him. He tramped back, cold and sullen, from the cemetery to the empty house. He sat there, stunned and tearless, till, of a sudden, mercifully, tears came. Bitterly, uncontrolledly, he cried like a hurt child. All through the night he was crying to Concetta's spirit as he had never cried to her when she was alive. And when he woke next morning it seemed as if those tears had softened his heart's charred aridity, restored its power to feel. It was newly soft with tenderness and sorrow ; it suffered grievously, yet,

out of its suffering, a softer emotion was born.
For the first time since the dark days in Naples he
dared to look on beauty. Beauty unveiled her
mystery, beckoned her prodigal, her strayed wor-
shipper. He was seized with a desire to paint. . . .

VII

THE bell on the bridge of the steamer broke silence
with eight staccato beats. Like an echo, another
bell, for'ard, repeated them. Midnight . . . Paul
Ritchie, roused from his meditations, rose from his
bench, and passed, with the deliberation of a man
of sixty, out of the upper darkness which the star-lit
cupola of the *Carmine* dominated, down the companion and into the radiance of the promenade deck.
Two elderly ladies, the last surviving devotees of
Southern Romance, turned and smiled at him as he
passed : a curious, formal figure, but, in his way,
a celebrity.

Paul Ritchie bowed stiffly, acknowledging their
salutation, and entered the warm alley-way that led
to his stateroom. It struck him that this sudden
passage from the mystery of Neapolitan darkness
to the unmistakably Northern and English atmosphere of white paint and polished brass was
symbolical. It was with a cleavage as sudden and
complete that, forty years before, after his mother's
death and the sale of the mountain property, he
had left Pogerola, and passed, by way of Rome and
Paris, to the studio in St. John's Wood which he
had occupied ever since.

For forty years he had lived there, in all externals a typical Englishman, restrained, unemotional, uncommunicative, speaking English with the refined Wykehamist accent that his father had taught him. He had felt it incumbent on him to emphasize this already preponderant part of his nature, assuming an exaggerated protective colouring that shielded him from memories which possessed the unreal validity of a bad dream.

For a time, indeed, he thought and dreamed in Italian, relapsing, in moments of stress or emotion, into the dialect which he had spoken as a boy. Even in his work, at times, those memories from a dead and buried past had power to proclaim themselves : hence those strange canvases—those gloomy, vast baroque interiors, with their soaring vaults and shadowed marble stairways, in which the acute Levine had traced the influence of Ribera, called Spagnoletto. But as soon as he realised that the spirit of his work was drifting backward into these sinister and forbidden dreams, Paul Ritchie would tear himself away from London and seek relief, with an almost pathetic desperation, in the lowland fells from which his fathers had come.

Little by little the power of these resurgent influences had faded. At the age of thirty he had married—if not rapturously, happily. Had not Cristina told him that he would love again ? He had loved, and lost, and now he was alone again. Strange, obstinate courage or insensitiveness of the human soul !

With slow, deliberate steps, Paul Ritchie passed along the alley-way and entered his cabin. Now that the ordeal of memory was over, he was conscious of a curious lightening of the spirit. The experience which he had dreaded so deeply had troubled it no more than the passage of a dream. These memories were so old, so old that there was no life in them. A mirror faced him; an opaline lamp-bulb shone above it. Shrinking, instinctively, from the reflection of his own grey features, he switched off the light. He locked the cabin door, and threw himself, dressed as he was, on the narrow bunk.

There, as he lay far into the night, motionless, with closed eyes, it seemed to him, Paul Ritchie, as though he had performed in memory an act of lustration for lack of which his soul had lain in danger of torment for forty years. The thing which he feared had been faced; the sad ghost laid. The image of Cristina seemed no longer terrible, only thin, distant, pitiful. Those phantom eyes, that door forever locked, would now cease their haunting. "I am an old man," he thought, "and yet I cannot say that I'm an unhappy one." He lay there, in the darkness, as placid as a child. "If the ship had been staying here another day," he reflected. . . . Yet, on the whole, he was happier to know that she was sailing at dawn.

Anacapri.   1925
Overbury.   1929.